To Joe ...
Thank
friend and neighbor —

THE LAST DRUMBEAT

CIVIL WAR DRUMMER

Best Always

Loretta Quesinberry Pickens

LORETTA QUESINBERRY PICKENS

outskirts
press

For my granddaughters.
Haley, Katherine, Ella,
Lillian, Grace and Julia.
May you forever cherish and hold dear the
memory and contribution of those who have
gone before you.

*History tells us what people do;
historical fiction helps us imagine
how they felt.*

Guy Vanderhaeghe

*"My time is swiftly rolling on
When I must faint and die;
My body to the dust return
And there forgotten lie..."*

From an Appalachian folk tune

INTRODUCTION

News of the Civil War came to the farming areas of Southwestern Virginia in the form of threats from the wealthy slave owning tobacco farmers living in the eastern part of the state, near Richmond. "The Northerners are coming to take your land and homes!" they cried. Men in the rural, isolated, mountainous region were quick to rise up to defend their property and way of life, which their forefathers had fought so hard to acquire and pass on to future generations. Oliver, along with his brothers Isaac, Asa and Peter, and eventually their father, Andrew, joined the Confederate army, thinking most certainly the war would be a very short war, over within months. Oliver left his young wife of a year, Mahala, and infant son Lawson, (my grandfather) in the fall of 1861, joining the 54th Virginia Regiment. Early in 1862, he transferred to the 29th Virginia Regiment, becoming the drummer for the regiment for the duration of the war. Oliver joined soon after the stunning Confederate victory at the battle of Manassas, confident he would be home in time for spring planting after driving out the northern invaders.

At home, Abigail, Oliver's mother, a strong-willed, spirited woman, with six young children, and Mahala, Oliver's intuitive, resourceful wife, courageously assumed the responsibility of the farm and family, determined to hold the family together in the absence of the men they depended on.

It was war, and no one knew what the future held, or if there would be a future when it was over.

It was war.

ACKNOWLEDGMENTS

I would like to thank my family for supporting me and encouraging me to complete this story. Daughter Laura and husband Anthony-thank you. A major thank you to my brother Dennis, who shared with me a poem, written by our great-grandfather Oliver. That poem, "On the Death of My Poor Brothers" first inspired me to write this book. A special thanks to my daughter Amy and her husband John. Together we made a memorable trip to Hillsville and Dugspur, Virginia in an RV, visiting the beautiful landscape in which my ancestors chose to make their home.

In particular, I must thank my husband Tom, who patiently listened to chapter after chapter, and with his knowledge of the Civil War, encouraged me to pursue further research which brought to my attention important facts I might have overlooked. I am also grateful for his help in editing this book. If there are grammatical, spelling or punctuation errors, they are entirely his responsibility. Wink, wink.

I am also grateful to my writer's group from Sanibel and Fort Myers, Florida. They listened to, encouraged and expertly critiqued those chapters I was able to share with them. A special thanks to Wally Kain who suggested the title for the book. Thanks Wally.

I would also like to thank Yvonne and Darnell Quesinberry,

who still live, as many Quesinberry's do, in or around Hillsville and Dugspur, Virginia. My husband and I visited them several times. Yvonne saved and diligently catalogued the poem and much of the family history I used to write the story. They guided us on an inspiring visit to the site of the original family farm, the cottage by the creek, where Isaac, Asa and Oliver were born, and later the farmhouse, built by Andrew and his brothers in 1858.

Many Quesinberry's/Quesenberry's shared family stories and information with me. Thank you, Matt Guigear, Dianna Quesinberry Fulton and Fred Quesinberry for taking the time to talk at length via telephone.

I would also like to thank Douglas Cooper, who helped me organize chapters and critiqued and encouraged me in the writing of this book.

I have many friends who encouraged me along the way to get this story told, and I thank you one and all. Some flat out **badgered** me—thanks Elisabeth Smith.

Lastly, thank you to John Perry Alderman, now deceased. John Perry Alderman wrote extensive histories of Carroll County, Virginia. He chronicled the early settlements, as well as books detailing the Carroll County regiments of the Confederate Army. I learned through his work the almost daily movement of Oliver's regiment, the 54th and later the 29th Virginia Infantry. Without his work I would never have known that Oliver was indeed with Pickett's Charge at the battle of Gettysburg and with Lee at the surrender of his Army of Northern Virginia to General Grant at Appomattox.

CHAPTER ONE

OLIVER

September 12, 1861
Dugspur, Southwestern Virginia

"OLLIE, YA' SIGNIN' up today?"

I shook my head, yelling over the clamor. "No, Eli, I'm on my way home. Mahala's expecting me in an hour for supper." He threw up a hand and shouted, "Come on, Ollie, we'll likely be in the same regiment if you sign up today. You don't want to end up fighting with a bunch of strangers!"

I had dropped off food for our troops at the collection center in Hillsville and was passing through Dugspur on my way home. The small town was bustling, as it had been since the war started back in April. I stopped the wagon to take in the scene. Eli, a friend from childhood was among a large group of rambunctious men. Try as I might, it was impossible to ignore the excitement. Men shouted at one another. Horses hooves threw up clouds of dust in the air. Women gathered in circles, smiling and waving to neighbors. There was a sense of anticipation in the air, as if folks were expecting a parade.

I waved at one friend or another who called out to ask if I would sign up for the Confederate army along with them. For just a moment, I thought I saw my brothers in line, bidding me join them. I missed my brothers and I often imagined them still with the family, not off fighting the Yankees.

My brothers Isaac and Asa volunteered for the army back in April, at the very beginning of the war. We had received just a couple of letters from them. As the days went by and we heard nothing of their whereabouts, the lines of worry were etched deeper on my parents' faces. We thought the war would be over within months, as did all our neighbors. My parents' concern had grown as we heard about the deaths of our neighbors' sons from illness or wounds of battle. Still, we were certain the war would end soon, and my brothers would be home before spring.

Eli was a hard one to put off, and he ran up to the wagon with his usual determination. "Come on Oliver! Might as well sign up today with the rest of us. We'll all be together instead of waiting for conscription."

Without fully understanding my actions, I jumped off the wagon and took a place among the boisterous group. It seemed as if I had no choice, even though, in truth, I had every reason to stay out of the fighting until I was forced to join.

I married my beautiful Mahala just a year earlier, when we were eighteen. Now we had an infant son, Lawson. My parents had already given two sons to the war effort and they had pleaded with me not to volunteer.

As I joined the frenzied group, I told myself it was for my family I must join the war effort. Everyone was light-hearted and excited, full of patriotic pride. The enthusiasm was contagious and I was caught up in the exhilaration.

I asked myself how much a few weeks away from home would matter? As most of the young men in line, I had become restless and bored with the work of the farm, the day to day hard work and drudgery of farming was all we had ever known.

I could never tell my father of my feelings. He wouldn't understand. My father, Andrew, was a respected man in our town, a proud and prosperous farmer. He said two sons were enough to give to the war, that he needed my help to run the farm. But I felt we were in good shape to face the winter. It was almost the end of harvesting and my father and I had already cut enough wood to get through the cold months ahead. Mother and Mahala had canned and preserved enough vegetables and fruits to last two years. Everyone thought this would be a short-lived war, surely over by the end of winter. I would be back in plenty of time to help Father with the spring planting. I wanted to prove myself as a man, a soldier who stood up to those who would attempt to take our homes and land. Would a few months away make a difference to my family?

I was greeted by friends and we all shared a sense of elation. The thought of camping and sharing the soldier's life was like a siren's song. I wanted to carry a musket, to march and fight alongside them.

Standing in line I realized I was not fully aware of what I was doing. I had no idea of the reality of war. Most likely none of us did. My thoughts turned to Mahala and Lawson, Mother, Father, my brothers and sisters and how I would miss them. Would my wife be proud of me for joining the fight? Life would be harder for her without me. But in just one year of marriage I had witnessed Mahala's considerable resilience and strength. But if I was wounded, unable to do the work of the farm, who would care for Mahala and Lawson? What if I should die? We had heard of men who had recently died in the Battle of Manassas in northern Virginia. How could I ignore that?

I quickly dismissed my fears. There was talk of a draft law in the spring, and if it passed, I would have to join anyway.

Squaring my shoulders, I straightened my back. My loyalty was with the men around me. The obligation to save our homes for the future of our children was my first duty. That is what I told myself.

Jim Martin was just ahead of me. He turned and pounded

me on the shoulder. "Good ta see, ya', Oliver. Looks like just about every man we know is joinin' up today, don't it?"

I looked up at him. He was as tall as my brothers, almost six feet. "I reckon I am too. My father won't much like it. He was depending on my help to run the farm. It's only Peter and me at home to help him now."

"Don't worry. We'll all be back in no time after we whip them Yankee bastards. Won't be but a few weeks. Did you hear how we sent 'em runnin' back up north near Manassas? Look around! We got so many men joining up, we'll have 'em out of Virginia by spring! They think they can waltz in here and take our land? Hell no!" He snorted.

"No one's going to take Quesinberry land. I've got a wife and son now. That land is our future. We'll send them Yanks home with their tails between their legs."

Jim removed his hat and attempted to push his unruly hair under it. "Ya' reckon we'll be gettin' our uniforms and weapons today? I heard Company D took up the name Rifle Rangers. Will Hayes, ya' remember him? He's in that regiment. That's a fine name, ain't it." He said, a wide grin on his face.

"Indeed, it is a fine name, but I don't see anyone leaving with a uniform or weapon. We might have to wait on that."

Little did I know then that when weapons were finally delivered they would be altered muskets, old firearms, probably .69 caliber smoothbores, reworked from flintlock firing mechanisms to percussion caps.

Jim laughed and spat to the side. "We'll get us some Yankees for sure. I heard them boys can't hit the side of a barn ten feet in front of 'em!"

"I've heard the same. Not too good on horseback either. Our cavalry will surely send them running."

Everyone sounded optimistic, without a shred of doubt about the outcome of the war. I wondered why, in my heart I felt doubt, a niggling fear of some kind hounded me. Perhaps it was because we had heard so little from Isaac and Asa, and they had already been fighting for nearly five months. How could men be so certain the war would be over by the end of winter? Talk quickly became boastful of how we would all return heroes after we ran the northern devils away from our land. The fervor increased the closer we got to Captain Hale's desk. Men were still lining up as I went in.

When I entered the room, the captain seemed distracted. His fingers drummed impatiently on the desk. He was a heavy-set man, with a ruddy complexion. Sweat stained his uniform and he wiped his brow with a cloth which lay beside a folder. His eyes scanned the folder. He raised his head and looked me over from head to toe.

"What's your name, boy?"

"Oliver." He wrote my name in the folder and then looked up at me. "Yes?"

"Quesinberry."

"Quesinberry? Well, there's plenty of you Quesinberrys signing up. Ain't a common name. I guess they're all family?"

"Yes, my brothers Isaac and Asa enlisted back in April along with some of my cousins."

He cleared his throat and studied me. "Yes, I know. I signed them up. How old are you?"

"I'm almost nineteen, sir." I shuffled my feet waiting for the next question.

"Are you married?"

"Yes sir, I am. I got a baby too!"

He nodded and ran his finger down the paper in front of him.

"I'm going to be honest with you, son. You're a mite short for soldiering. I'm not sure you could handle a musket."

I felt my pride shrivel and heat rise to my face. I swallowed hard, and glanced behind me, fearing the other men had heard. I lowered my voice. "Are you saying that I can't fight? I'm strong and healthy. I'm as good a shot as any man here."

Captain Hale cleared his throat again. "I ain't going to turn you away. You'll be assigned to my company, Company G, 54th Virginia. Same as your brothers. You'll be leaving in a week."

"Yes sir." I couldn't help but swell with pride. As I left I nodded to the men still in line, a silent acknowledgement that I was now a soldier.

On my way home I tried to imagine my wife's and family's reaction to my impulsive decision to enlist. I knew it would be difficult to explain how I was caught up in the fervor that seemed to have taken over every man in town. I hardly understood it myself. I would tell my wife of my decision first and hope that she would understand, then my mother and father. It would be hard for my parents to say goodbye to another son. But at the moment I was full of pride. I whistled a tune as I let the horses pull the wagon home.

The trail alongside the creek that led to the cottage was cool and shaded by dense trees. Sun filtered in lazy patterns through leaves just beginning to turn a soft shade of yellow. I had always loved the path along the creek. As a boy the creek and surrounding woods were a source of endless fascination for my brothers and me. Spring brought hillsides covered in flowering shrubs and trees. In summer we fished and swam in the section that widened and deepened in front of the cottage. In winter we would skate on wooden blades our father whittled and strapped with leather onto our boots. I had only happy memories of the cottage in which Mahala and I were now raising our son.

When the cottage came into view, Mahala was sitting on the porch rocking Lawson. I took my time putting the horses in the barn, searching for the right words to explain to her what I had done.

She spoke before I placed my boot on the first step of the porch. "You joined up didn't you, Oliver?" Her dark brown hair, usually pulled into a bun, hung loosely around her shoulders. After a summer working beside me in our small garden, her skin was burnished bronze. Her amber eyes, set far apart, gazed steadily at me.

I nodded. "Yes, Mahala, I had to."

She looked away from me, toward the hills and took Lawson off her breast. Laughing, he reached for me. I took him in my arms as Mahala left the porch. She walked slowly toward the creek, not once glancing back. I didn't know what to make of her abrupt departure. She walked to the creek and sat on the bank. I waited on the porch with Lawson and rocked, hoping she would come back to me.

When it was clear she wasn't returning, I went to her and sat beside her. With Lawson in one arm I encircled her waist with the other. "Mahala, forgive me for not first discussing my decision with you. It's just that, I...well, every able-bodied man seems to be joining the war effort. I feel it is my duty. If you had been there, in town, if you could have seen...."

"What of your duty to me and your son, Oliver?" Her words were quiet and measured. She looked straight ahead. I gazed at her profile, still trying to find the words to make her understand my decision to join the army.

"It is my duty to preserve this land for our son, Mahala, and for you. It is our future. I cannot stand by and let it be taken by strangers, or let other men fight to preserve it for me. Without this land, we have nothing. Surely you can understand this."

She was quiet for a long while, looking off into the woods on the other side of the creek. I had learned not to try and interpret her quiet, intuitive nature. So, I waited. I sighed with relief when she turned to me with a bittersweet smile and placed her warm palm on my cheek.

"I know you have done what you feel you must, Oliver. But do not expect me to be happy with your decision. I hoped you would wait until you were conscripted. The war might be over by then. But it is your choice and I cannot stop you. I will miss you more than I can say, Oliver." She said softly.

I sat with Mahala and Lawson and watched the sun set behind the hills. I felt the spirit of my ancestors around us. They had settled in this quiet and fertile corner of Virginia over a hundred years ago. The ground we sat on was sacred to me. Standing Lawson between my knees, I placed a small stone in his hand. Together we tossed it into the creek where it splashed and made him burble with laughter. Lifting him above my head, I looked into his eyes. His face was a picture of pure joy. Beside me, Mahala laughed softly.

That was all I needed to hear. The laughter of my son and wife. The decision I had made was for them and I was determined to make them proud.

The morning was already warm when I climbed the hill from the cottage to help my father in the field. I was filled with apprehension at the thought of telling him I had volunteered for the army. I stopped by the well for a pail of water before I joined him.

I offered him water, which he refused, and I placed the ladle back in the pail. "Father, there's something I must tell you."

He stopped the horses and dug the tip of the plow into the newly turned soil. "You didn't enlist, did you Oliver?"

I nodded.

He removed his hat, wiped his brow with a stained cloth and stared at me. His eyes conveying both his anger and his concern.

"Oliver, what have you done? With your brothers gone, you know I need your help to run the farm. You said nothing of this. Why would you not first discuss it with your mother and me? Could you not have waited until spring to see if the conscription law passed? What were you thinking?" He shook his head irritably. "Does Mahala know? You would leave her alone to care for your son?"

I struggled to hold his eyes. I had great respect for Father, and I had tried to follow his straightforward example all my life. He set a high standard for his children. In spite of a limp caused by a fall from a hay wagon many years ago, he was strong and vigorous, never failing in his responsibilities.

"Father, I am able-bodied. How can I not join my brothers and friends to protect our homes? I do this as much for my wife and son as for myself. The talk is that the Northerners want our farms, our land. We'll be left with nothing. If I don't fight for our land, what will I give my son? Mahala understands why I need to protect our rights. Virginia was Cherokee land before it was ours. Her ancestors were forced to hide in the mountains to remain in Virginia."

Father took the ladle from the pail and hesitated before he drank. He seemed to be thinking about what I had just said, and perhaps, recalling that it was our ancestors who had settled in Virginia almost two hundred years ago, and helped drive the Indians from the land and into the mountains. Even so, we shared with them a profound connection to the land, a deep and abiding respect for all that the land provided.

Wiping his mouth with the back of his hand, he turned to speak directly to me. "Son, we are farmers. We have raised you to be a farmer. You know nothing of war. And with your small stature, you are not suited to be a soldier."

I felt the prick of his words, though I don't think he intended to hurt me. His cool blue eyes summed up what he meant-that I had not the strength nor the temperament to be a soldier.

"This will break your mother's heart. I cannot tell her."

I lifted the water ladle to my mouth and drank, knowing not what else to do with the silence between us.

"You must tell her yourself, Oliver. It has been only months since she said goodbye to your brothers."

He looked up at the sky, speaking more to it than to me.

"Go then, and you tell her."

I found my mother nursing Sara in the shade of the oak trees. Her eyes were closed as she took pleasure in a respite from her many chores.

My mother, Abigail, was forty-two years old, and the baby in her arms her tenth child. Her face looked youthful in the soft light. Her auburn hair had not a touch of gray. When open, her hazel eyes shone bright with determination. In spite of her many pregnancies, she was slim and strong. She had loved the outdoors and fresh air since childhood. Indulged by her father, who delighted in his high-spirited daughter, she retained what my father called, with a twinkle in his eye, "pluckiness."

I knew that side of her well. I remembered her telling my father, at the end of a trying day, "I won't be cooped up in this farmhouse, Andrew, no matter how many children you get me with. I will ride and walk this land as I wish. So, learn to take your medicine, Husband." I recalled the sound of her riding boots on the floor as she left the house and children in Father's care. She was gone for hours. When she returned from riding, her face was flushed with happiness and her good humor returned. Father greeted her with relief, and hastened to tell her how much he missed and appreciated her.

I studied her a bit longer, not wanting to disturb her peace. "Mother."

"Oliver, you startled me." She sat more upright and lifted Sara to her shoulder. "I was daydreaming. It is so peaceful but for that crow there." She pointed to a branch above her head. "He keeps scolding me as though I am disturbing him." She waved a hand, then laughed softly. "Pfffft, off with you. Go!" Sara fussed and Mother began to rock her. The crow continued to watch her and turned one eye toward me.

"No matter, Son. I don't believe a crow is bad luck. I prefer Mahala's belief that it captures and brings light to humans."

She smiled, and for a moment I saw the girl in her. Her cheerfulness broke my heart.

"What brings you from the field, Oliver?"

"Mother...I...." My words made a knot in my throat as I looked at her. My jaw clenched as I tried to get them out.

"What is on your mind, Son? Something is troubling you. Speak it plainly. Have I not taught you that?"

I cleared my throat. "I volunteered for the army. I leave a week from today."

Mother studied the crow for a long while. Eventually, she nodded and sighed. "So, it is bad news. You thought not to tell me, Oliver?" A hard glint came into her eyes. "Your father knew?"

"No, I told no one. Not even Mahala. I told her only last evening. I decided to volunteer when I took the wagon into Hillsville yesterday and stopped in Dugspur. There were hundreds of men signing up."

"Why didn't you tell us you were thinking of joining? Did you think to run off in the night? You know we cannot stop you." She turned her face toward the field, unwilling to show me her dismay. "I regret you thought not to ask our opinion before making such a decision. It will be hard for your father to keep the farm going with only the help of Peter. Your decision does not sit well with me."

A heaviness settled on us and stayed until the crow flew off in the direction of the field where my father turned the earth. We watched as it got smaller and until we could see it no more. Neither of us said a word.

Abruptly my mother stood, handed Sara to me and walked into the house. I was left standing next to her empty chair, holding my baby sister. I lowered my chin to the top of Sara's soft, warm head and thought of Lawson. Suddenly I was overwhelmed with the thought of leaving my wife, son and family. Everything I loved I would leave behind in a week. Doubt consumed me. I prayed that I would not live to regret the decision I had made.

September 20, 1861

When the day came to say goodbye, my family readied the wagon and rode to Hillsville to see me off. I drove separately with Mahala and Lawson in a wagon lent by her parents. She sat close to me with Lawson cradled in her arms. We were silent, and I knew she had questions and fears she didn't want to trouble me with. In town Father talked with other men sending their sons to war, and Mother stood nearby watching children at play on the hill. Mahala greeted young mothers who were also sending husbands off to battle. Neighbors smiled and greeted one another and exchanged the latest news.

When the time came to depart, some women fussed over fathers, sons, brothers and sweethearts, sniffling and wiping away tears. My mother, never one to be openly sentimental, said in a firm voice. "This war cannot last long. You and your brothers will be home soon, Son."

And as she had done for my brothers before me, she gave me three white cotton handkerchiefs embroidered with my initials. I knew it must have taken Mother all week to sew them. My fingers traced the stitched letters so carefully done. I smiled at her and placed them in my breast pocket. She took my hands and gave me a single kiss on the cheek. My father grasped my shoulders, looked me dead in the eyes, and gave me a strong shake. He had no words for me, but I felt all he wanted to say in that single gesture.

Mahala and I walked to a stand of trees some feet away to say goodbye. Her eyes glistened with tears she fought to hold back. Her lips parted in a wide smile and I was captured again by her loveliness. It was rarely spoken of, but her half-blood Cherokee grandmother had gifted Mahala with a rare beauty.

Her amber eyes were set far apart and broad cheekbones gave a striking dignity to her face.

"Mahala, I will miss you." My voice was hoarse and soft. "I would not leave you if I did not feel compelled to do so. The conscription law will be enacted in the spring. I'd be forced to join if I didn't volunteer."

"Yes, Oliver, I know you are doing what you feel you must. You will come back to us. Lawson and I will be waiting. If you do not..." She pressed her lips together, "I know you will have died bravely." Her eyes never left my face. We embraced with Lawson between us. I could feel the heartbeats of my wife and son until Lawson protested and pushed away from his mother.

"I will come home. Nothing will stop me, not even an enemy bullet. This will be over soon and then we will give Lawson some brothers and sisters."

"Yes, no doubt we will." She smiled and reached into the pocket of her dress. "I have something for you. You must always keep it with you." She withdrew a small cloth bag.

She had surprised me in our year of marriage with her knowledge and use of herbs. Her father Joseph was well known as a physician of herbal medicine, an art he learned among the Cherokee Indians and had taught Mahala.

"What have you made for me, Mahala?" I smiled tenderly at her.

"This..." She held up the bag tied with a yellow ribbon, "holds herbs that will help you ward off illness and strengthen you."

"What is in it?"

"Blackberry leaves, mint, wild rose hips and wild ginger. If you become ill or fatigued you can brew them as a tea, or if need be, chew them."

I whispered in her ear. "Thank you, Mahala. I will keep them with me always. I promise to use them."

I turned to leave, walking slowly toward the wagons which were quickly filling up with men.

"I will miss you too, Oliver. Please be safe."

I ran back to embrace her, drawing her into my arms, our kiss lingering. Breathing in the mingled scents of my wife and son, I closed my eyes, hoping I could hold on to the moment forever.

As the wagons holding the volunteers pulled away, my brothers and sisters ran alongside calling my name. My eyes filled with dust, or perhaps tears, and their images blurred as they tired and stopped chasing the wagon.

I watched until my siblings had turned back toward town and I could no longer see my parents and Mahala.

Pulling the brim of my hat low over my eyes, I took out one of my handkerchiefs. I had to swallow the lump in my throat at the sight of Mother's stitching.

One last time I looked back at Hillsville.

Pressing my lips together I turned to join in the laughter and loud talk of men who would now become my family.

CHAPTER TWO

ABIGAIL

November 1861 - Spring 1862
Quesinberry Farmhouse
Dugspur, Virginia

I HAD HOPED Oliver would wait until spring when the conscription law would have forced him to join the war effort. I thought the war might have been over by then. Now he was gone.

I ended every evening and woke each morning with a prayer on my lips for my sons. It was difficult to remain hopeful when in my heart there was a deep fear that the war would take one of them. It had been five months since Isaac and Asa left for battle. No one believed the war would last so long. Each day that passed added to my anxiety. When I told Andrew of my fears, my husband reminded me to put my faith in God, as he did. But every day I woke with a deepening sense of foreboding and I questioned my faith that God would protect our sons from harm.

We woke at 4:30, he to feed the animals, and I to start the fire in the wood stove and make breakfast. I spent the time it took for the stove to heat thinking of my boys. I sliced bacon and prepared batter for fried bread in a daze, my mind reeling with worry I could not dismiss.

When breakfast was ready I sat at the table and waited for Andrew to come from the barn. It was a long trestle table, made of pine from our own trees and fashioned by Andrew's hands. I studied it as I waited, my eyes finding the marks and stains left by each of my children. I remember asking Andrew why he made a table so long. He smiled and said, "Because we will have many children, Abigail."

"You are so sure, Mr. Quesinberry? Have I nothing to say in the matter?"

He embraced me and said, "I think we must leave that up to God, don't you, Abbie?"

We had just two little boys then, Isaac and Asa.

Looking down the length of the table I watched as my husband took his usual place at the far end. His handsome face was flushed from his work outdoors. Sensitive to my every mood, his blue eyes found mine. I wondered how I was blessed with such a kind and loving man.

The children were not yet awake. We talked in hushed tones so that they would not hear us speak of our fears for their brothers' safety.

"What is it, Abbie? You slept fitfully again last night. Is it worry for our boys that keeps you up?"

"I...I am..." I didn't want to say that I was terrified of what the future held. Wouldn't any mother be? Yet, I felt I had to hide my fears and pretend I had faith that God would protect our sons. I did it for Andrew, and repressed a surge of anger that passed through me. Why did he insist that I blindly trust in God if I had such doubt in my heart? I took a deep breath before I spoke.

"I'm just tired, Andrew. Tired of this war. Tired of constant worry. I do not think I am unlike other women who have sons or husbands off fighting. It is women who must continue working the farms and caring for their families, alone, when you all have gone to fighting."

Andrew moved from the end of the table to a chair next to me. His callused hand covered mine. "God is watching over the boys, Abbie. You must trust in His plan and be strong. Our sons are young and healthy. God is on our side. Our cause is just. We must have faith in Him."

"I wish I could believe, as you do, that our boys are safe in God's hands. But I find it hard, Andrew. I heard in town just yesterday that the Thomas boy is dead. His family doesn't know how or where he died. They're not sure if he died of fever or wounds. They don't know where his body is." I choked back a sob and rested my head on my crossed arms, hiding my face, not wanting him to see the anguish there. "I don't think, Andrew, that I could bear news of our sons' deaths. I thought the war would not last so long. I thought the boys would be home with us by now." I lifted my head and looked out the window where grey clouds were gathering above the tree line.

"We all hoped that, Abbie. But it seems this war will not be over as quickly as we thought."

To hear him voice his doubts about the war only increased my anxiety. I thought perhaps he knew more about the way the war was going than he wished to tell me.

I started to speak when Polly, holding baby Sara, burst into the kitchen, closely followed by Jane and Mary. Sara had her hair in rows of braids. Polly, overcome with giggling, presented Sara to us. "Look, Sara has enough hair for braids now." Sara looked disconcerted and pulled at one of the braids, screwing up her face as she glanced from her sisters to me.

Their laughter was contagious and I could only smile at my daughters.

"No, leave them Sara. They look pretty." Sara reached for me and I took her on my lap and kissed the top of her tightly braided head. The girls were always first to awaken in the morning, followed shortly by Peter, William and Preston, sleepy eyed and hungry.

One by one the children took their places at the table. I

was always conscious of the three empty chairs. The children knew those chairs belonged to their brothers, and never once had taken them at meals. We joined hands as Andrew bowed his head to pray.

"Dear Lord, we thank you for this day you have given us. We thank you for our health and we ask that you watch over and protect Isaac, Asa and Oliver..." He paused for a moment and cleared his throat, "who are so very far away from us. Keep them safe from harm. We thank you for the food we have before us this morning. We ask that you protect our soldiers and provide food and shelter in the cold winter to come. In your name we pray. Amen." We all repeated 'Amen' and Andrew looked down the long table with a smile I knew was meant to reassure me.

Another day began, as every other, with children laughing and teasing one another, arguing over who had the most or least chores. Seven children needed my attention. In spite of that, I felt my oldest sons' absence more than I ever thought I would. It was hard to believe that a little over a year ago all that concerned me was the birth of another baby and celebrating the marriage of Oliver and Mahala.

Shortly after their wedding, it seemed all the talk of northern aggression, states' rights, and political liberty was stirred up by wealthy tobacco farmers who lived far to the east of us, men that held slaves who picked their tobacco. They whipped up fear in the farmers in our part of Virginia that Northerners were after our land and homes. There was no talk of a war waged to keep slaves. I knew of no family who owned a slave. My fury grew when I thought my sons might be sacrificed for the benefit of rich tobacco farmers and large slave owners. How could anyone truly know how long the war would last? I had watched as hundreds of young, healthy boys, caught up in a fervor of excitement marched off to war. Even my heart raced with patriotic pride and righteous anger at the thought of Northerners attempting to take our homes. At times I imagined taking up my gun to fight alongside our soldiers. I was a better shot than most men. But I had to settle for those things considered acceptable for a woman; providing food, blankets and clothing. Andrew and I volunteered to supply as much food and goods as we could spare for our soldiers. We delivered supplies to the collection centers in Hillsville and Dugspur. Frequently, I made that trip alone. It comforted me to know I was doing something to help my boys, and for the Southern Cause.

When Isaac and Asa left for the war, Sara was just an infant. Her birth took my mind off the absence of my two oldest boys. With Oliver gone, there was a hole in my heart which grew larger every day. I missed Oliver especially. His quiet and sensitive nature was so like his father. He was the son I hoped would become a minister or a teacher. I would never tell Andrew of my dreams for Oliver. My husband thought the work of a farmer was as close to God as a man could hope to get. But Oliver was different than Isaac and Asa. His head was always buried in a book if he could find one. He was quick to learn to read from the Bible and he so perfected his penmanship I asked him to write my letters for me. I can still picture him on a stool before the fire practicing writing his letters, his head bent close to the paper. Every now and then he would shake his head in frustration and hastily cross out a line and start anew. His perseverance always made me smile.

December, 1861

We received a brief letter from Isaac last week. I studied each word he wrote. The paper was wrinkled and dirty. I thought of how he must be living. Was he warm? Did he have food and shelter? Andrew said I read too much into the appearance of the paper, but it was my way of trying to determine how my son was faring. Were the smudges from tears? No. Isaac would never cry. Perhaps it was just sweat and dirt.

I held the paper close to my nose and inhaled, as if I could capture some of his familiar scent.

Dear God, how difficult it was to be strong and have courage. I frequently felt weak and close to tears. Then I would look at my children who gathered around me, questions about their brother's letter tumbling over each other.

"Did Isaac kill some Yankees, Mama?" William's eyes were round and bright with excitement.

"Let me read his letter, Son, and then I will tell you."

"Read it out loud" Polly pleaded.

They loved their brother, and of course wanted to know all he had to say. I told them he and Asa had been with their regiment in Kentucky since early December. We had family in Kentucky, and I prayed my boys would be allowed to visit them and have some comfort. Isaac would not want to worry us, but he mentioned the poor rations and lack of equipment and supplies. I tried not to let the thought of such depravation defeat me, but it did. I wanted to bury my face in my hands and cry. I did not, for the sake of my younger children. I looked at their bright upturned faces, hopeful and innocent. They had no idea of the heartache and cost of war. It was to them all a great adventure, their big brothers off defending our homes against enemies. I could not sully their admiration with my despair.

The most recent letter was from Asa. He wrote that he and Isaac were transferred from the 54th Virginia to the 63rd Tennessee. I was quite sure they would not remain in Virginia, and my heart grew heavier at the thought they would be so far away. Asa wrote that officers were constantly being shuffled around and there was bickering among them about who should be in charge. What must our poor boys think when those in command were always in turmoil? Andrew told me it was the way of war, that there was always competition among the officers to advance in rank. All the while our boys were often left in a state of confusion. I heard there were young men called "stragglers" who left amidst all the indecision and returned home. I imagined many regretted their decision to enlist. How homesick they must have felt as Christmas approached.

January, 1862

Mahala shared a letter she received from Oliver a few days after Christmas. He said that after coming in contact with men from cities, our boys had been exposed to diseases of all kinds. He wrote that Smallpox was the most feared, but that fever was taking a toll on many soldiers who were ill-equipped and poorly fed. With the worst of winter coming on, how could it not get worse? I prayed God would let my boys survive until the war was behind us.

Mahala and Lawson seem to be content in the cottage by the creek below our house. I think of that little house with fondness, as it was Andrew's and my first home.

Mahala is independent and self-sufficient. Quiet and reserved, she is not one to gossip. She is a great help to me in the preparation of meals and caring for the children. To have a grandson living close by is a joy I never expected. Asa's children live with their mother on her family's farm and do not visit often. Lawson is very much like Oliver as a baby, content to sit for hours and play with small blocks of wood Andrew gives him.

I never gave much thought to Mahala's knowledge of herbal remedies, an art taught her by her father, but when little Preston came down with a bad cough, her brew of herbs helped him recover quickly. He was well within days. I asked her for the recipe, but she was reluctant to share, saying the measurements must be exact and prepared in a very careful manner. She kept us supplied with tonics during the winter. When I felt despondent, she never failed to bring the hopefulness of youth into my heart. Her world revolved around Lawson, and she was firm in her belief that Oliver would return home to her, and to all of us.

On many days during the winter Mahala would pull Lawson up the hill on a homemade sled. I would gather him in my arms, his cheeks rosy from the cold. I closed my eyes remembering Oliver at his age. "Look at you, young man, sitting up all by yourself on that sled! Aren't you a big boy?" He would laugh and press his cheek against mine.

"He looks the picture of health, Mahala. He's growing so fast!"

"Yes, isn't he, Mother Quesinberry. Do you think he's like Oliver at his age?"

"I do believe he is. But one forgets little details when you have so many children. He is peaceful and calm as Oliver was." I kissed his cool cheek and thought of Oliver.

Mahala touched my arm gently, sensing my sadness.

"Do not worry. Oliver will be fine. I know this in my heart."

I didn't speak of my fears with Mahala. Why should I burden her with my doubt and worry? I smiled at her and held back my tears.

"Yes, of course he will." I said.

That was what I said, but it was not at all how I felt.

CHAPTER THREE

OLIVER

January, 1862
Kentucky and Virginia

I TRANSFERRED FROM the 54th to the 29th Virginia in
early January. Given the option to take a fifty-dollar bounty
and join the regiment of my choice, or go home for a short
furlough and be drafted a month later, without choice of regiment, I decided to join the men I knew from Carrol County.
We were told we would stay in the southwestern part of
Virginia, and that settled it for me. I was not given a musket
when I joined the regiment. Instead, I was made the company
drummer. I am certain it was because of my slight stature.
At first, I felt embarrassed that I wasn't given a musket, but
having learned the importance of a drummer in battle, I have
reconciled myself to my position. But I found it difficult to accept that promises made by those in charge of the army were
rarely kept. We did not receive our wages, nor sufficient food
or supplies.

We marched in early January from Virginia to the
Cumberland Mountains in Kentucky. It was a desolate and
sparsely settled state, yet beautiful in its wildness. The valleys were blessed with rich farmland and I could see the fields

had been plowed and prepared last fall for spring planting. I had family in the state, but knew not where they lived. I wondered if I would even be welcome if I should find a few days to visit. War had torn families asunder, and now many fought against each other. I realized I might even have been battling my own relatives in the skirmishes we were engaged in with the Federals.

It rained steadily as the new year began. Deep mud made the roads nearly impassable for our wagons. Men were cold, wet and miserable. Many were ill and close to dying. I prayed that I might maintain my health as men fell ill around me.

On January 9 we fought the Union soldiers at Middle Creek in freezing rain. Our hair and clothes quickly became coated with a layer of ice. General Marshall positioned our troops and artillery on several ridges overlooking the creek valley. We skirmished for four hours before the Union withdrew. I can't say as I know who won the battle. It seemed a loss to me. Five of our men died and seven were wounded. We buried our dead and helped the wounded as best we could. Some were so physically weakened they had no chance of recovery. Two weeks after that battle we fell back to an old gristmill. We were close to starvation and resorted to shucking corn from the fields and shelling it for food. Thank God, two weeks later we were back in Tazewell, Virginia, near the Clinch River for winter camp, where rations were better. Other than the fear of being wounded or killed in battle, our greatest concern was hunger and surviving the cold. We were reduced to craving the most basic of needs, shelter and food.

We camped in Tazewell until late spring, remaining there while our officers reestablished the companies of the 29th. Our regiment had been considerably depleted over the winter months by dysentery and Typhoid fever. Deploying to southern Virginia that July, we marched west into Kentucky where we skirmished through October. We returned to Virginia in the Fall of 1862, and were finally stationed in Suffolk, near the Dismal Swamp in the state's southeastern corner. I worried about the illness that took countless men there. Fever was rampant so close to that swamp, and I prayed I would not be one of those that succumbed.

In February, my regiment came under the command of General James Longstreet and was used primarily to gather supplies and forage for anything of use nearby. We were shuffled around like cattle, never knowing from one day to the next where we would be marching. During the many months we spent in Suffolk, more men died of Typhoid fever than were lost in battle. In May, while in Suffolk with Longstreet, we learned of the battle at Chancellorsville. We were all encouraged by General Lee's victory there, and it made the march north seem less grueling.

We arrived outside the little town of Culpeper on May 20, in the aftermath of the battle. Our elation was short-lived when we learned how many of our brethren were killed. The death of Stonewall Jackson on May 10, who was accidentally shot by our own troops, dampened our spirits. General Jackson had his left arm amputated and died from pneumonia. General Lee was shattered by the death of the man he called his 'right arm'. Lee himself was suffering from rheumatism, but I would guess he was mourning the death of Jackson as well.

There was little to do while we awaited our orders. We marched, drilled and dug latrines. As we waited, rumors that we might march north grew more frequent. I dreaded the thought of marching north and leaving Virginia. I was not alone. A few men dared speak of deserting rather than leave the state. At night when all was quiet and we gathered around fires, men whispered that this was a rich man's war, fought by poor boys. We heard the Yankees felt much the same way and some were protesting the draft law in New York. Numerous Union soldiers at Chancellorsville were German immigrants who must have been sent directly into fighting from their boats. On the battlefield, the cry "Mutter" was frequently heard from wounded Union soldiers, or those in the throes of death. I could barely fathom their desperation at having traveled such a distance, only to die far from home and family.

As long as we remained in Virginia, I felt I could at any moment find my way home, which was a comfort and soothed my fears. Even so, having seen how our own dead were treated, and how little attempt was made to identify them, I knew any one of us could die and our names be unknown.

I'd had little time, and had only a few pieces of paper left, but I could not think of leaving Virginia without first writing Mahala. It would be much harder to get a letter off if we marched into northern territory. On one of my last pieces of paper I began.

My Dearest Mahala,
I pray this letter finds you and Lawson well. Please give my love to my family as I have very little paper left.

I stopped writing for a moment and looked around me. It was a heartbreaking sight. There were still wounded men moaning in agony from wounds they suffered at the battle of Chancellorsville. My instinct was to go to them and offer comfort. I thought of how I would feel if it were my brothers or myself in such agony, but I knew I could be of no help. Drugs to ease their pain were used on men with more serious wounds, those that required a limb to be severed from their bodies. My eyes wandered from one group of men to another. Some were alone writing, as I was, others played cards or dice, and some were with the 'camp women' who followed the troops.

I could never tell my dear wife of the depravity of men in camps where there was so little comfort. Men would find it where they could. I myself had thought to take solace in the company of some of those women. But when I looked in their eyes I could see desperation. Their faces blurred and I saw my own sisters, mother or Mahala. In those times when I was so tested, I prayed and reached for the herbs Mahala gave me and inhaled the clean scent. I reminded myself that there was much bravery and courage and that was what I wished to write about.

Do you remember William Mitchell? During the battle at Middle Creek he risked his life saving another man who was shot in the leg. God willing the man will survive. I am proud to be with men who show courage and kindness when in fear for their own lives. Our regiment is now under the command of a much-respected man, General James Longstreet. He is said to be always calm under fire. We marched from Suffolk just a few days ago. I thought I might find my brothers there, but I did not. Suffolk is a swampy area and the fever has taken a great many lives. I pray my brothers are not among them. We are camped outside a town called Culpeper now. I hope that General Lee's rheumatism will soon ease, and with the help of God, we can win this war in Virginia. I am doing well enough, due in large measure, I am sure, to the herbs you provided me.

I would not tell Mahala of my fear that we might soon leave Virginia and march into Maryland. To leave Virginia was a hard pill for all the men to swallow. We had felt pride in the knowledge that we were protecting our own land, homes and families. Nor would I tell her of the talk of desertion among the men if we were forced to march north.

I took a deep breath and filled my lungs with the cool evening air of mid-May. I was reminded of home as I closed my eyes and pictured the farm. It was a busy time of year. Father

LORETTA QUESINBERRY PICKENS

would have already planted corn. The cows would be calving soon. I loved being present when the newly born calves took their first wobbly steps. I shook my head as sadness threatened to overwhelm me and turned my attention back to my letter.

I may not be able to write again for a while my love. We'll be marching again soon. I think of you and Lawson every day and every night. Please pray for me as I pray for you. I love you my darling Mahala,

Oliver

I wanted to tell her how lonely I felt and how much I had grown to hate the war. I wanted to say I wished I could walk away and never look back, that the suffering I had seen had changed me. I watched nearly every day the horror and heartbreak that war inflicted on men. As we awaited our orders, disease was taking as many, if not more, than wounds of battle. That men should die of illness, moaning in agony, without at least the honor of fighting our enemy, weighed heavily on me. It was disheartening to think I might die in such a manner, hopelessly ill. If I could have disappeared and it not be noticed, or have suffered the shame, I would have done so.

At times I wondered what contribution I was making to the regiment. Was I a soldier if I carried no musket? Would I be missed if I walked away? Then I reminded myself that even without a musket, I had a duty. I was the drummer. I was in a way, the sun that rose, the cock that crowed, the sound my fellow soldiers both dreaded and awaited every morning and evening. The sound they heard as they marched into battle. My purpose was to help convey the orders of the officers. It was a position of great danger. To kill the drummer was a priority of our enemy, for without a drummer, men in the midst of battle would not know the orders of their commander. My drumbeats were what the soldiers heard above the roar of guns and artillery and the screams of wounded men.

I had less and less of my former self about me as the war dragged on. Where I used to go about my duties in a great hurry to impress my officers, I no longer did so. On endless days of drilling I often found myself in a trance. I thought of Mahala and Lawson. How I longed for the sweetness of the days I once took for granted, with my mother, father, brothers and sisters. When in battle I focused on the distant trees or hills as the fighting raged and death embraced those around me. At times when the struggle was most intense, I seemed to float above the field. I looked down on myself as I stared straight ahead. It was as if my spirit left my body and I was released from the horror of the reality around me. Then I would drum with ever increasing intensity, as if it could end the fighting.

Every day there was among the men an accounting of those who had gone missing, either in battle, or from illness since Chancellorsville. I sat outside my lean-to with a group of men escaping the fetid air inside. A soldier with a patch over his eye asked, "Have ya' seen John Shepard about?" A soldier across from us answered, "I think he fell alongside Jim Bowman. They were fighting together last I saw them."

It went on like this day after day. Questions filled the air in a sea of hope and longing. My voice joined the others. "Have you seen my brothers, Isaac and Asa. Tall men, with beards. They would have been together. At least, I believe that is so." No voice responded, and I didn't know whether to feel relieved or distressed.

The search to find a friend, a mate, a brother, was never ending. Only God knew who lived or who died and I prayed my brothers still lived.

The news of the death of my brothers was delivered as would be the news of lost horses or saddles.

"Your brothers did not return for duty, Oliver. They are

among the missing." Officer Moore said, without emotion, his eyes gazing somewhere above my head. I felt a strong sensation in my chest and the tent seemed to close around me. I felt the rapid beating of my heart, but more palpable was a pain I had never known before, a squeezing and twisting in my stomach.

"When, Sir?" I asked, hardly moving my lips. I studied him closely, looking for any hint or clue about my brothers' fate, but I could find none. "Where have they fallen? I helped bury many who fell on the field at Chancellorsville. My brothers were not among them. I was told they might have been transferred to the 63rd Tennessee."

"I know not when or where they died. They are gone, Oliver. They are on my list of missing soldiers." Officer Moore pointed to a paper on his field desk. The thud of his finger against the wood produced the same sensation in my chest and I struggled to catch my breath.

"Do you know, Sir, where I might find their graves. I would go there and say a prayer. I would like to say goodbye to my brothers. It would give some comfort to my parents that I know where they are buried and that I said a prayer for them."

"It's of no use. Thousands of boys are gone and buried, your brothers among them." I again studied him. This time I saw the tiredness in his eyes, like a light that was dimmed. Death seemed to be of little consequence to him. I imagined he could have received news of his own brother's death and his reaction would be no different. "Will you write your parents, Son?" He asked.

"Yes. Sir. I will." I managed to say. The words pushed out of my gut and past the pain to my lips.

My dear family. I missed them so. Death had entered nearly every home in Carroll County, but it had yet to darken my parents' door. Now I had to tell them of the death of my beloved brothers. I had to shake my head to erase the image of Isaac and Asa left for dead on the field, or buried in a trench as those I had helped bury, having never been identified. I knew all too well the fate of dead soldiers. I had been called upon to dispose of the men who died while fighting at Chancellorsville, or was as likely these days, men who drew their last breath before succumbing to illness. Burying our fallen was a gruesome and somber affair. There was silence as we dug the trenches, thinking it could be our own fate to be so buried. We often had not the use of shovels or carts. We used whatever was at hand to dig into the hard earth. All men had died in agony and it was seen on their faces as we put them into the ground.

How many did we bury? One lost all sense of connection to the cold bodies we handled. In an attempt to be known, soldiers would put their names to paper and then in a pocket. I hadn't the heart nor stomach to search for a piece of paper to identify a corpse which was putrid. When handling the bodies, I had to cover my face with a handkerchief. Still the stench was nearly unbearable.

Would I be as disposable as those men if I should be killed? As disposable as my brothers? The realization that I must tell my family my brothers were gone jolted me back to the heartbreaking task at hand.

Before the day ended I had to write my family. I tried, but I found it ever so hard. My heart would not allow my pencil to write plainly of the death of my brothers. My hand seemed constrained by the pain in my heart. My thoughts were scrambled, my handwriting barely legible. If I were with my family I would embrace them and pray with them. But I seemed unable to write words so devastating on smudged and wrinkled paper. I closed my eyes and remembered my brothers on the day they left for war. I felt proud of them. They looked hard and ready for battle. I thought they would surely come home. I saw my brothers as invincible and they could suffer no harm. I realized it was on that day the desire was born in me to join the war.

I struggled to find words to comfort my parents.

Dearest Mother and Father,
It is with aching heart I must tell you of the death of Isaac
and Asa. They have fallen…

I stopped and scratched the words out. It was not right. I started anew.

Dearest Family,
Isaac and Asa died on or around May 3. I have just been
informed.…

I crumpled the paper. I could not go on. I knew not how to write of my brothers' deaths in a plain way. The thought entered my head that they might have deserted. Many a brave soldier had been overcome with fear amidst the indescribable horror of battle. My heart lifted a bit at the thought. I would not condemn my brothers if it were so. Indeed, I did not condemn those poor men who turned and ran as I beat the drum and the carnage raged around us.

I searched among my things for more paper. Paper and ink were hard to come by. I had only a pencil and I'd carelessly used all the paper I had. It was late afternoon and close to supper when I left my tent in search of paper.

I first went to the tents and lean-tos of men I knew.

"No, I have no paper for ya', Oliver. I doubt you'll be finding extra. I'll be holding on to what little I have to write my wife." Said Henry Long. Others stared blankly and did not respond when I asked. I feared I would not find more.

I ventured nearer to the officers' tents, in hopes that one of them might help. It was strange that I knew so little of them. I knew just a few of their names. But surely there was among them one who would have compassion and offer me a few pieces of paper.

As I drew closer to their tents, I saw a Negro man tending a fire. I was aware that wealthy officers often brought a slave to the battlefield with them, to care for all their needs. I watched quietly as the man tended the fire. I was captured by his presence and knew not how I should approach him. Even though his hair was white, he was tall and muscular. His skin glistened in the firelight and he hummed a tune softly as he worked. I gathered my courage and coughed to make him aware of my presence.

"Good evening." I said softly.

"Good evenin'" he responded, with a slight nod in my direction. Then he turned his attention back to the fire.

"That smells just like my mama's chicken. I can't remember when last I had a decent dinner. How do you come by chicken? Men have scavenged all day for food, with little success. Seems the Union soldiers have taken almost everything from the farms around here."

"This be reg'lar dinner for Massa. His mama an' daddy send a wagon load of food ever couple weeks from Richmond. We get chicken, beef, pork, vegetables too." His voice was soft, as if not wanting to offend me.

I swallowed hard. It was almost more than I could bear. Thousands of near starving men behind me and a feast in front of me. The unfairness of officers having such an abundance of food, as soldiers starved, angered me. My jaw clenched and I felt suddenly dizzy and steadied myself by leaning against a tree.

"You feelin' alright, mister? You might best get back down there with the rest of them soldiers. Maybe they find somethin' to eat up in them hills. What you doin' wanderin' around these officers' tents?"

"Yes. I should. I will go back. But I'm searching for paper to write my family of bad news. I need...." I forced myself to hold his unflinching gaze. "My brothers have been killed. I'm in search of paper to write my family. To give them the news..." I felt my heart sink speaking of their deaths, and I struggled to hold back tears, "...of the death of my brothers. I used the last of my paper. I'm looking for more. Do you think you...what is your name?"

"Jacob."

"Jacob, do you think your mas...your...I'm sorry, what do you call him?"

"I call him Massa. I sent here by his family to take care of him. I do cookin', washin', cleanin'. This here be easier than workin' that big house, or out in the tabacca fields. Just one person to wait on. He ain't a bad sort. His mama an' daddy decent to their people."

I studied the man before me, a slave to a rich white officer. He was kind, with a spirit that was not broken despite his servitude. I'd never before spoken to a slave, nor had I known a man who owned one. I believed now the war was as much, if not more, about rich men keeping their slaves as it was about farmers holding on to their land. There was a terrible rage building inside me and I felt dizzy from hunger. I staggered and Jacob came to my side, taking my elbow.

"You feelin' sick? You in that fightin' up in Chanslerville?"

"No. I'm a drummer. My regiment arrived after the battle. I helped bury the dead at Chancellorsville. My brothers are dead, but I don't know where or how they died. But they're gone. I must write to my family, but I have no paper."

Jacob glanced toward the officer's tents. "Mister. I know where Massa keep his paper. I get you a little. Then you get outta' here. Get back with them men down there. Don't tell no one 'bout it. They all be coming up here and get me in trouble."

"I will tell no one. But you won't be punished if you give me paper, will you, Jacob? I wouldn't want that."

Jacob nodded. "It alright. I know where Massa keep the paper. I write a little myself. Missis' taught me. You stay here, I be right back."

Standing alone, the world seemed to shrink around me. It was more than hunger and grief over my brothers' death I despaired of. The enormity and absurdity of war overwhelmed me. It felt as though all the troubles of mankind were concentrated in this one spot. The men below, hungry, alone, longing for their families, my brothers, dead...knowing not what they really died for. The Union soldiers we slaughtered, many newly arrived German and Irish immigrants, no more certain of what they fought for than my brothers. Jacob, serving a man who would keep him a slave. Me, fighting a battle to keep him a slave as he showed me kindness. None of us quite knowing how or why we were in this moment of hell on earth. My knees buckled and I fell to the ground and looked to the heavens, trying to contain my sobs. I wept for my brothers, my family, for Mahala and Lawson, my home. And for the kindness Jacob was showing me, which was how I had been taught men should treat one another.

I hastily wiped my eyes and stood as I heard Jacob approach. He carried a few sheets of paper in one hand and a wooden bowl in the other. I took the paper and tried not to stare at the bowl of food.

He gave the bowl to me. "This for you. You look mighty hungry."

I was overwhelmed at the smell and sight of the roasted chicken he was sharing with me. "Jacob, how can I thank you? I'm so grateful...I'm..."

Jacob interrupted me as I struggled to express myself.

"Mister. What they call you?"

"Oliver. Oliver Quesinberry."

"Oliver, you go now. It alright. God be knowin' what's to be. Look here. You missin' your mama and daddy ain't you? You wantin' your family. It hard. But maybe all this be over soon."

"Thank you, Jacob. Thank you for this. I pray it is all over soon."

He smiled, then put his finger to his lips, "Shhhh."

I nodded my head and set off for camp. Half way back, I

stopped and carefully folded the paper and put it in my pocket. I ate the chicken slowly, savoring every last bite.

I arrived at camp as the men were finishing off supper.

"Where you been?" Asked George Tate, who shared my lean-to. "You missed supper. Leastways, that's what they called it." He made a face. "Some kind of mash. I swear, our hogs wouldn't eat it at home."

I rubbed my stomach and grimaced, indicating I didn't feel well.

"You got quickstep? You sleep close to the door so you can get out fast. I ain't wanting to get fever or nothin'."

I nodded. "It's a clear night, I won't mind sleeping outside." I gathered my pallet and candle and stepped out. If the weather permitted I preferred sleeping in the fresh air. Perhaps it would help clear my mind to face the painful letter I had to write my family.

The letter I wrote that night was not a letter at all. It was not written simply and plainly, as my mother had taught me. The words were wrenched from the pit of my stomach, from an ache lodged in my heart that I was unable to describe. A cry from my soul. A poem. A last tribute to my brothers. It was all that I could write. With plain words I could not express my sorrow. My mother would understand a poem. And oh, how she would grieve.

I awoke the next morning, as usual, at 5 to sound reveille, morning roll call and breakfast call. Then I awaited the letter carrier. My hand trembled as I handed off the envelope. It was clean and white, with a message cruel and devastating. The letter carrier reached down, his hand black with dirt. His clothes and horse were covered with mud and grime. Stench filled my nostrils. Filthy saddlebags bulged. It was hard to watch as he stuffed my envelope amongst letters soiled with dirt and perhaps blood. An envelope that contained a message which would bring unbearable sorrow to my family. But it was done. I turned away quickly. It was time to beat my drum for the drill.

CHAPTER FOUR

ABIGAIL

Dugspur, Virginia
May, 1863

I OFTEN WATCHED Andrew from the kitchen window as he was finishing his chores. The tall, rugged man I married still made my heart skip a beat. As he led the horses into the barn he brushed the dirt from his clothes. A gentle soul, he loved the land and everything that was born of it. Earth and animals were things he knew best, and they yielded easily to him. He smiled as one of the dogs ran to greet him. His smile, rare these days, still reached something deep inside me. The sun was setting behind the barn as he finished his work. The work of the farm was harder for him now, with only Peter to help. Jane, Polly and I did what we could to lend a hand, but we could not replace Isaac, Asa and Oliver. Three grown sons off fighting in a cursed war when we so needed their help at home. It was a heartache for me.

I had a special place in my heart for my first three children. I was young when they were babies. Mothering brave and adventurous boys reminded me of my own fearlessness as a child. My father, a strong, stocky man with no hint of romance or female understanding, delighted in my independent nature. "Abigail is no one's fool," he would say, when my older brothers tried to hoodwink me and I put them in their place. Much to my older brothers' dismay, no one rode a horse as fearlessly as I did. It became second nature to jump on a horse's back, sometimes with saddle and sometimes not. I was by far the best female rider in the county. Father saw me, somehow, beyond my gender and to the heart of me. A heart that loved freedom and adventure and would not shrink when afraid or bow when humbled, a heart that mirrored his own.

Mother was not fond of my high spiritedness and seemed to want to tamp it down. After riding one afternoon, Mother caught sight of me sliding off my horse like a boy, my skirt bunched up around my waist. I still remember her face as she strode up, took my arm and marched me to the kitchen. "Abigail, you act too coarse for a girl. It is your father who has encouraged this behavior. You will never get a husband if you do not curb your common ways. I must speak with him again." She pushed me into a chair and thrust a bowl of vegetables onto my lap to prepare for our dinner. With a red face, I chopped every vegetable into fine pieces, all the while thinking of how different I was from what my mother clearly wanted-ed in a daughter.

Thank goodness I found a husband who loved me as my father did. I didn't have many suitors when I reached courting age. My pride, and father's love, made me self-reliant which seemed to discourage boys who wanted a compliant mate. I regularly beat the boys in horsemanship and many could not reconcile it. Andrew was unlike the others. He had a way with horses which was different from my own. While I enjoyed the feeling of bending a horse to my will and taking it as far and fast as it would go, Andrew's quietness won a horse over. He seemed to persuade the horse to agree with him by appealing to its heart. I dare say he did the same with me. His easy and kind nature was soothing to my wildness and I found myself drawn to him. I felt he fancied my strong-willed nature and I

LORETTA QUESINBERRY PICKENS

loved him for that. I also loved that he wouldn't give in to my will when I pushed him too far. Although gentle and patient by nature, Andrew could turn hard quicker than lightning. Once he put his mind to resolving a problem, he didn't stop until it was resolved. That hardness didn't show often, but there was no breaking him when it did.

As I finished preparing supper, I took pleasure in the glow of the soft evening light outside the kitchen window. Walking from the barn Andrew paused, his eyes fixed on a horse and rider rapidly approaching the house. I heard the horse's hooves thudding on the hard earth that led to our home. My heart leapt with joy when I saw it was the letter-carrier. A letter! From one of our boys? We had received just two letters each from Asa and Isaac, and that was not long after they left. Oliver had written more often, but his last letter came months ago. Since that early mail, the war effort had picked up and our troops had it harder than ever. Supplies of all sorts were not available, and even if they wanted to write, there was a shortage of both ink and paper. If it was a letter from one of them, I would think it was from Oliver. He had a soft heart and would know how desperate we were for news of how he was and how the war was going.

The rider talked briefly with Andrew and handed him an envelope. A letter could bring joy or despair and I prayed that this one brought joy. Every day we heard of another family in the county who had lost a son or husband. Miraculously, we had been spared. I feared the longer the war dragged on, the less would be our good fortune. Dread constricted my heart until I saw Andrew's face light up as he looked at the envelope and his appearance calmed my fear.

I held my breath and watched as Andrew walked to the barn, letter in hand, and disappeared to take care of the last chores before coming in for supper. I was restless with anticipation, but had to tend to the children and to our supper.

When Andrew opened the front door, the children ran to

him, talking excitedly. I hurried to put supper out as he walked past the children and sat at the table. That was unusual for him as he typically engaged them in news of their day before sitting down to eat. His behavior troubled me and I studied his face. My heart skipped a beat. He was ashen and strangely looked much older. His mournful air hit me like a hammer and panic filled my breast. My heart pounded as the fear I had lost a boy overcame me. Devastating coldness rocked me back and I almost fell over.

"The letter," I said, and sat beside him at the table. "Andrew, where is the letter?" Without realizing it, I had raised my voice and my children stared at me in alarm. Preston started to cry and I hushed him much more sternly than was usual, but he did not so much as make a sound after that.

Andrew spread the creased paper on the table and smoothed it with his rough hands.

"Abigail, it's from Oliver. It's a poem. A poem." His voice trailed off and he pushed it toward me.

"A poem? Isn't that just like Oliver. He has such a way with words. He would make as fine a minister as your father." I responded lightheartedly, as if I could ward off bad news with chatter. I knew I was grinning as I prattled on. My children gaped at me. I stopped myself and looked at Andrew who was silent, his face stricken. His hands were clasped, his knuckles white. I felt weak and suddenly exhausted. I saw tears falling on his rough work shirt and his hands trembled.

I touched Andrew's hand and locked eyes with him. "Please, read it for me. I won't be able to do it." Andrew softened his eyes and nodded. Lowering my head to my arms on the table, I closed my eyes. Some of the children started to whimper.

Then Andrew took a ragged breath and read Oliver's words.

On the Death of My Two Brothers May 1863
My life is like a drooping flower

that once was fresh and gay
now smote by grief's heart crushing power
is fading fast away
My brothers now since thou art gone
oh what is life to me
My aching heart now sad and lone
must constant weep for thee
led by their patriotic hearts
while in their twenty-fourth and sixth year
from kindred home and friends to part
a soldiers fate to share
tis for my country's weal said they
that we obey her call
dear sisters do not grieve for us
if in her cause we fall
but when the dying hour drew nigh
to bid them quickly go
they heaved a sad lugubrious sigh
and tears began to flow
with quivering lips and tearful eye
and grief never felt before
they sadly bade us each good bye
alas forever more
Then with electric speed they sped
unto Virginian soil
but ere a year away had fled
was freed from life's turmoil

where prostrate on their dying bed
with none but strangers nigh
They raised their languid eyes and said
a take us or we die
unto our home far far away
to that blest spot we'll fly
where Father, Mother and dear Sisters may
be near us when we die
take us to where the loved ones are
ere life with us is over
we fain would breathe the blessed air
that's breathed by them once more
They raised their dying eyes in pain
kind angels they espied
they closed them then for ever again
and faintly smiled and died
We would a tender parents voice
had breathed into their ear
and bid their troubled heart rejoice
when death was drawing near
we would a loving Mother there
had stood beside their bed
and watched them with a mother's care
and tears of sorrow shed
We would an only brothers when
they felt deaths awful power
had tenderly bent over them then

and soothed their dying hour
Far away my brothers sleep
and over their lonely graves
no kindred bends and sadly weeps
no flowers over them wave
My brothers now since thou art gone
oh, what is life to me
my aching heart now sad and lone
must constant weep for thee
We weep to think it was thy lot
to die thus far away
to grieve for friends and see them not
when life was waning away
and there unmourned, unpitied too
by strangers hands be carried
unto their graves where but the dew
did weep when thou wert buried

By the time Andrew finished, I was sobbing. I doubled over, with a pain so searing it left me gasping. "No! Not my boys, Andrew!" I pressed my fist against my lips. "No, no, no!" The children started to cry to see me so distraught.

"Abbie." Andrew put his arms around me. I was rocking myself and Andrew as well. He murmured softly, "Abbie, Abbie, please stop. Please. The children."

I cannot remember the next hours. The supper went cold and uneaten. Somehow, Andrew got our children to bed, as I remained by the fire, rocking and crying. When he returned, he sat with me in complete silence.

Eventually, a need to see Oliver's words, to make sure they

were real, burned inside me.

"I want to read the letter for myself, Andrew. I need to see how his hand has written those words. I need to see his words."

Andrew looked solemnly at me and placed the letter on the table beside my chair. I stopped rocking and stared at him, barely breathing. The chair I sat in had rocked Isaac, Asa and Oliver. I had comforted all my children in the rocker. Would it now hold me as I read about their leaving this earth?

My hand shook as I reached for the paper. I could not stop the howl that escaped my lips when I had read but a few lines. I doubled over, as I moved back and forth, the letter pressed to my bosom.

"Isaac, Asa, my boys!" I caught my breath and wailed, "My beautiful boys! Why Andrew? Why? For what?"

Andrew fell to his knees and took my hands in his. Bringing his face close to mine, he said, very low and softly. "Oh, Abbie, I know not why. It is war. I have yet to figure the reason for all the death and destruction. We are not alone. Boys are dying everywhere, nearly every family in these parts has been changed by this war."

I was unable to stop my agonized cry. "Changed, Andrew? You mean destroyed by this war? As we will be? I always believed deep inside me, that my boys would come home again. When they left, I told myself they could very well be hurt or killed. Really though, truly, at the bottom of my heart, I didn't believe it. I was certain they would come home! I was certain!"

"Abbie, the little ones, you will wake them." His hands tightened on mine.

"Oliver wrote this," I waved the letter in front of Andrew's face, "but how would he know? He couldn't have seen his brothers dead with his own eyes. He is a drummer and would not have been in the same place or time with Isaac and Asa. They could be wounded, or have fever and be in the hospital."

Andrew slowly moved his face away from mine and his

expression changed to one of confusion and doubt. That made me even more determined, as that sort of reaction usually did.

"I will find them, Andrew. My boys will not be buried where I cannot find them. Fall to dust without my tears shed on their graves?"

"Abigail, they are buried. Did you not just read Oliver's letter? They are gone." Andrew dropped my hands and stood before me. His lips tightened and he closed his eyes. He walked closer to the fire, his back to me. "We still have Oliver. He is a drummer, Abbie. He'll be safe and return to us."

I started rocking again, a hard, fast rock that sounded like a march. "Will he? Will he, Andrew? You know nothing! No more than I know! How can we be sure Isaac and Asa did not join the Home Guard? How many of your brother's sons are in the Guard? Who can tell me they're not hiding out in the hills with the Guard? Perhaps they are wounded or ill and recovering among them. They might have deserted. Many soldiers have done so."

Andrew spun around and grabbed the back of my chair to stop my rocking. "That is not what they wished to be, Abbie. Nor did we. You would have them spy on their own? Our neighbors' sons? You would have them be deserters?" His voice was stern and hard.

I looked up at him and spat out the words, "I would have them alive!"

Andrew let go of my chair and made his way to the door. Before he opened it, he said, "Abbie, we did not raise our sons to desert anything. You, of all people know that." He reached for the handle, then dropped his hand and turned to face me. "You must grieve as you will, and so shall I. If you must believe they still breathe, I cannot stop you. But do not tell yourself, nor me, that they are something other than who they are. My sons are not cowards or deserters, Abigail."

With that, Andrew opened the door and stepped into the moonlit night and I was left alone with my thoughts and anguish.

I stared at the fire and recalled with bitterness the words about northern aggression, tariffs, state's rights and exploitation which whipped up a frenzy in farmers that could not be calmed. All the talk made us fearful of losing our land and homes and created a fierce desire to fight in order to keep what we cherished. I didn't believe it anymore. It was my sons, sons of farmers, poor boys, who were starving and dying of illness, not the sons of rich men, not the sons of slave holders. Their sons were officers with plenty of food and clothing. I heard they took their slaves as body servants with them to the battlefield. I had even heard Negro servants of rich men received thirty dollars a month, while our poor boys, dying on the fields were paid eleven. The sons of rich men were often sent to Europe, or could use their money to buy a man to fight for them. There was boiling inside me anger unlike any I had ever known.

Oliver's letter had brought to me an unbearable ache and an uncontrollable feeling that my sons needed to be found. Oliver could not know for certain they were dead. Isaac and Asa were in Tennessee with a different regiment, not with Oliver. How could he know they were dead? My head ached from my doubt and grief. My heart was shattered into a million pieces and I feared I could not carry on.

At last, Andrew quietly opened the door. He went straight to our bedroom without saying a word to me. I followed him a short while later, hoping we might take comfort from each other in our grief. But Andrew slept soundly. The endless hours passed and I did not sleep, nor did I close my eyes.

When the hazy light of early morning filtered through the windows, I was still awake. The ache in my heart had grown heavier and my eyes burned from tears I had shed for hours. I felt my grief turn to ice in my veins and a wild fury possessed me.

I knew that I would never rest until I knew how and where my sons perished. I made a silent vow to my sons. I will find you.

CHAPTER FIVE

OLIVER

June 7, 1863
Culpeper, Virginia

GENERAL LEE CALLED a review of the entire cavalry corps on a plain near Brandy Station near Culpeper. Although there was hardly a man in the infantry with a full set of clothes, we cleaned and mended as best we could what we had. Our weapons were polished and we all waited in anticipation of the cavalry.

I waved to Henry Atkins and noticed his left arm was still bandaged. I recalled when he had been wounded. We were stationed in Suffolk back in April, when the city was taken by the Union forces. General Lee had sent Longstreet to check the Union's advances there. His orders were also to obtain badly needed supplies. It was there, for the first time, our regiment was given a division commander, Major General George Pickett. When we left Suffolk and were marching north, we were unaware that we were headed to Chancellorsville, where a major battle was raging.

I moved to Henry's side. "How are you, Henry?"

"Good as anyone, I reckon. This here arm been pesterin' me a bit. Ain't nothin'. I killed the damn Yankee who shot me.

Ain't no bullet in it, just grazed me." He grinned, showing several missing teeth.

I nodded and again marveled at what men endured every day.

"Have you been to the field hospital? Has a doctor looked at it?"

"Nah. I poured me some whiskey on it. Don't trust them doctors. They'll take my arm off quick as anything." He snickered.

I knew there was no point in argument. Doctors were so overwhelmed caring for the severely wounded at Chancellorsville, they hadn't time to waste checking a soldier's arm or leg for infection or gangrene. It was often easier to cut it off.

Henry poked me in the side. "Here they come! It's a grand day ain't it, Oliver? Look at them horses! They ain't no way them Yanks gonna' beat our cal'vry." A grin spread across his face and he straightened his back.

"They do look mighty fine." Together we jostled for a better view.

Indeed, it was a grand event. Perhaps as many as eight thousand mounted men passed by General Lee in a walk, then a trot. They looked in fine form and I felt the pride that swelled in the men surrounding me. We smiled and stood taller. The excitement was contagious and before long men were shouting and waving hats in the air. The horses' hooves kicked up dust as they paraded in front of us.

In truth, among the infantry our cavalry was thought to be all but useless. The cavalry often failed in their duty of monitoring the movements of the Union and had not yet engaged in battle. Instead, they conducted raids behind enemy lines to distract and confuse them. We, in the infantry, were often left without knowledge of what to expect from the enemy. Those of us without horses did most of the fighting and dying on the ground. We put our skepticism of the cavalry behind us on that day. Impressed with the pageantry, we were all united in our pride for the Southern Cause as we watched the parade.

One more battle, I thought, as I watched the cavalry proudly parade by. One more, and we would be done with the war and could return home to our loved ones. It was this hope that sustained the infantry, that the next battle would be the last and the enemy would be defeated.

Henry punched my shoulder, "Well, ain't it somethin'! I've never seen so many fine lookin' horses!" Henry coughed and bent over to catch his breath. I wondered if he might have the fever. Men weakened from wounds and dysentery easily fell ill with other diseases. I took a pinch of my herbs and chewed them slowly. I'd grown accustomed to the bitter and tart combination and I found the taste pleasing now. I couldn't attribute my health to anything else. I had remained unaffected while countless men from rural areas had succumbed to disease.

Two days after the review, the enemy crossed the Rappahannock River and attacked our cavalry in their camps near Brandy Station. There were heavy losses in the charges and countercharges on both sides. We thought our cavalry was much stronger than the Union's, which was mostly comprised of men raised in towns and cities, with little knowledge of horses. General Stuart held the field and inflicted twice as many casualties as we suffered. During the battle General Lee's son William was wounded. Lee did not shrink from duty because of that, and I thought that was what made him so beloved by the troops. He grieved over the harm inflicted on a loved one, as we did, and bravely continued the fight.

The Union suffered a heavy loss and re-crossed the river, but it was evident they were much improved in their skill on horseback. That was one more concern for us, as they also had

superior weapons, food and supplies. As of late we had nothing to eat but fritters and rancid bacon.

Yesterday, I received a letter from my sister Jane. She
wrote that Mother would not accept the deaths of Isaac and
Asa.

Dear Oliver,

*"I hope this letter finds you well. We received your let-
ter and are all heartbroken. Mother cannot accept that
Isaac and Asa are dead. We all find it hard to believe
that they are gone, but Father fears grief has so consumed Mother that she is not in her right mind. She
would even have them be deserters or wounded and
hiding out with the Home Guard rather than accept
their deaths."*

I knew my mother would not be at peace unless she tried to
learn more about the fate of my brothers. I could understand
her doubt about the news of their deaths. It was not unheard of
for men to leave the army with wounds, or as deserters, to be
presumed dead, and in fact, have taken refuge with the Home
Guard. Many had done so. I felt in my heart that my brothers
were dead, but still, I felt sympathy for my mother. I thought
of all the hundreds of unknown men I had helped bury, and
of their families who would never learn what had happened to
their loved ones' bodies. How it must haunt families to think
it possible that their loved ones still lived. It comforted me to
know Mother would not accept my own death so easily. I had
witnessed the return to battle of men thought to be dead, who
had in fact, left in desperation to visit their families.

"Father works from dawn till dusk. We try to help as

much as possible, but we are no substitute for you, Isaac and Asa."

No doubt the work of the farm required all Father's time and attention. Three of his grown sons were not there to help him.

"Thus far, there have been no raids from the Union on our farm. For that we are grateful."

I thought the reason the Union forces had yet to plunder our farm must surely be because our farm was so isolated in the southwestern part of Virginia near the border with North Carolina.

"Mahala and Lawson are well indeed. Her brother is a captain in the army now. It is good to have her and Lawson close by. Mahala is a great help to Mother and Lawson is a delight to all of us. Please write if it is possible. Your letters are a comfort to all of us. We miss you and pray for your safe return.

Your loving sister,

Jane"

At night as I prayed for sleep I thought of Mahala. I wondered if I could take a quick "French leave" and go home to visit. Once we headed north there wouldn't be an opportunity for a leave of any sort. As the war continued, the former tolerance for soldiers who deserted, straggled, or took French leaves was met with harsh punishment by officers. But men still took that chance as the talk grew of leaving Virginia and marching north into Pennsylvania. I mourned the thought of leaving Virginia. I feared that should I die in battle on northern soil, I would not even be buried on the land I had fought to protect.

I awoke on a clear June morning before 5 and watched as the sun rose in a pink glow over the distant hills. It made me long for the mountains of southwest Virginia. I turned my face to the west, toward my home.

For a moment I was there and could taste the breakfast of bacon, eggs and biscuits prepared by Mahala and Mother. Father would be already about the work of the farm. I closed my eyes and could smell the newly turned soil and feel in my hand the weight and shape of corn seeds, each seed a small kernel of nourishment and hope. I imagined gently rubbing them together in my palm while I dropped them one by one a few inches apart into a planting furrow Father made with the edge of his hoe. The furrow, made straight by a string attached to sticks at either end, was filled in quickly by Isaac and Asa, who covered each seed with an inch and a half of rich soil. How easily we worked together. Later we would sit in the shade of an apple tree and share a mid-day meal brought to the field by one of my sisters, surveying with pride the work we had accomplished. I now dreamt of, and missed so very much, those hours spent with my family, and the gratifying work of farming.

I was jolted back to reality when I thought of my brothers. I'd had little time to mourn their deaths, but at night before I fell asleep, my tears flowed freely and I ached with sadness. A pain staked my heart as I thought of my brothers. They were gone, but I was still here and had a duty. It was time for me to sound reveille. I raised up on my elbows and surveyed my surroundings. Men slept huddled together in makeshift tents, or sprawled on the ground. The morning was cool and fresh and I breathed deeply before I stood.

Sam Wilson emerged from his lean-to and together we

gazed toward home. He enlisted the same day as I did in Dugspur. Together we said goodbye to our wives and family. We had both lost a considerable amount of weight, but he looked like a skeleton. His clothes hung from his body. I wondered if he might have 'camp fever'. He groaned and rushed toward the latrine in the woods. "Be right back, Ollie."

When he returned I was still gazing west toward our home. He joined me and together we watched as the mountains were brushed by the first golden morning light. "I heard Lee's marching us up into Pennsylvania. I don't want to do that. Do you, Ollie?"

I thought of my father, grandfather and great grandfather, who for over a hundred years had farmed our land in Virginia. We worked hard, often from morning till night, and had always been grateful and felt God had blessed us.

Though I scarcely believed it, I had become bored and tired of the hoe and plow and eager for the adventure of war, excited to join the fight to save our homes from Northern invaders. I left the farm with grand hopes of returning a hero. But there was little glory in the life I led and I wished I could again feel the weight of a hoe in my hand. I longed for the godly work of farming that brought forth life.

Sam nudged my shoulder. "Did you hear me, Ollie?"

"No, I don't want to leave Virginia either, Sam. I've got a wife and baby I haven't seen for almost two years. I never thought to be away from them so long." I lowered my voice and swallowed hard. "I expect that's why so many are deserting and straggling these days. We were told we'd stay close to home."

"Well, I don't see the sense in it. We can stay right where we are and let the Yanks come and fight us here, on our own land."

I gave him a wry smile and shouldered my drum. "We don't have a choice now, do we? I better get to sounding reveille."

Sam waved a hand and rushed back to the latrine.

I called after him. "Better see a doctor, Sam. You're look-ing mighty skinny."

He threw up a hand as he broke into a run. Fevers and dis-eases were killing men off in great numbers and I hoped Sam was not one of them.

Rubbing my hands together briskly, I took up my drum. My hands were callused from the endless use of drum sticks. Although the wooden shafts were covered with leather over cotton balls, the covering had nearly worn out. My bass drum was blue for the infantry, with eleven stars of the Confederate states painted on it. When I joined the 29th regiment, I was taught a series of drumbeats that soldiers must hear above the noise and confusion of battle. My drum beats conveyed the orders of the officer who commanded me. I sounded a pat-tern which told men where to meet, when to commence firing, when to advance or retreat, and the "long roll," which was the signal to attack.

I began the drumming of reveille. Haggard and hollow-eyed men emerged slowly from their tents and lean-tos, or wearily off the bare ground.

Emmanuel Martin staggered toward me. "God, Oliver, is it really five? Seems like I just laid down on that damn ground and closed my eyes." He yawned and pulled a suspender over his shoulder. Rubbing a hand across his scruffy face, he asked, "What gruel are they feeding us this morning?"

I shrugged my shoulders. Would we even have breakfast? I looked away and then at the ground. "Only God knows. But I have to sound breakfast call either way." I hoisted my drum to my other shoulder. It was tattered and beaten up. I would soon be needing a new one if the war lasted much lon-ger. Many thought drummers were safer amidst battle. Truth be told, we were often the first target for the Union soldier. Without my loud beats, officers would have only their voices to convey their orders which could not be heard over the roar of battle. I never imagined the other duties and responsibilities my position would require. I had been called on to serve as an assistant in the field hospital. The most loathsome thing required of me was to hold down a man in the throes of agony as a limb was severed from his body. It was made worse if I knew the man and had to look in his eyes and then carry away his limb and bury it. Would he recall me as the person who took a part of his body from him without a word spoken? I thought about the reaction of their families when they returned home without a leg or arm.

I had not a musket, but on the battlefield in the heat of the fight, I had often put aside my drum and used the weapon of a man who had fallen beside me and commenced to firing. I had saved myself more than once. But not once had I been able to do so without thinking about the man who fell in battle by my hand. I wondered if other men felt the same sense of regret that I did when I watched the light go from their eyes and they fell to the ground.

It was hard to remember the time before this war started, when our country seemed as one. I thought of all the men on both sides of the war who would never go home, or return with parts of them left behind. I wondered if our country would ever be united again? It saddened me to think that the war might forever divide us.

I had received no news of my family since the letter from my sister, Jane, almost four weeks ago. Letters were often intercepted by the Union. The few letters that got through spoke of the struggle our families endured to keep from starving. Some men had gone missing after learning of the desperation of their families. I have had many thoughts of doing so myself after hearing of the suffering. I worried so for Mahala and Lawson, and I wondered how I could have left them with so little thought. Often, I regretted that I did not listen to my father who was so opposed to my joining the war.

As we marched north, men were sent out each day to search for deserters, or men who might be conscripted into the army. Although men spoke quietly of their feelings, a good number thought Lee had sacrificed too many men to win the battle at Chancellorsville. Our infantry was diminished and there was a desperate attempt to find any man of conscription age. I noticed that often fewer men returned from these expeditions than were sent out. That made the job of those of us who remained with the regiment more difficult, and I felt a mixture of resentment and envy when I imagined them back with their families. I stayed because I had such a fear of not being respected by my family, and not living up to my oath. How could I run away from a war that had taken my brothers? I had put myself in the war, and with God's help, I would get home when it was over.

I didn't need a letter from my sister to know the death of my brothers was a terrible blow to my family. A first-born son and brother, gone. Isaac was tall and strong, very much like Father. Being the oldest in the family, he was loved by all of us. Isaac, mother would say, meant "he will laugh." My favorite memory of him was from a time when I was still young enough to explore and play. Isaac, as the oldest, spent most of his days helping Father. One day, I was in the woods just off our fields busy making a fort of sticks and rocks. Isaac caught sight of me as he worked and sneaked off to join me. Although just three years older than me, and my age being only six, he was past the age of indulging in such play. However, on that rare day, he joined me and became a boy again. It seemed like a long while that we played soldier, fighting an invisible enemy in the shade of the trees, though it was probably not much more than a half hour. Father's loud and stern voice called Isaac's name and stopped the game, but not before Isaac placed his last stick on our fort, and with a broad grin said, "I've been hit, Ollie. Keep the family safe." I watched him go, the sun hitting his dark hair as he joined Father in the field. How could one so vibrant be gone?

Unlike Isaac, Asa never seemed a boy, and went right from cradle to field. He was always trying to outdo Isaac and seemed to be in a great hurry to be older. Rarely a smile crossed his face. Asa meant "healer," although that was not a good description of him. He was a very good farmer and, except for Isaac and Father, he had little interest in other people. His connection was to the land. A name that meant "fearless" would have fit him best. He was always first to try something new and take the lead.

Mother told me my name meant I would be peaceful, and that I, most of all, followed my name. She would often catch me off in the barn seeking solitude from the busy, crowded house. I was grateful she allowed me that time to myself. When Isaac and Asa fought, I could sometimes come between them and persuade them to reconcile. Mother hoped I would follow my grandfather into the ministry. But over the last two years I had begun to doubt my faith in God because of what I had watched men endure. Grandfather would weep now if he knew how diminished my faith in Him was. I did not see God's benevolent hand in the war. I saw the work of evil, the work of man. God had left the land and watched as we mortals made a mess of it. Good man against good man, knowing not where or how it would all end.

To keep restless soldiers busy, when we were not marching or fighting, the officers made us practice skills of soldiering, loading and firing muskets, marching in formation and digging ditches and latrines. We rebuilt bridges that had been destroyed by the Yankees. When there was free time, we did our best to forget why we were there. There was always gambling of some kind, cards and horseshoes, cockroach races, even louse races. A letter or book from home was read over and over to ease the loneliness. But men were anxious and uneasy, quick to rise to a fist fight.

Amidst all this drudgery, there remained a glimmer of hope. Hope the Union would give up the battle before we marched north into their territory. We had heard talk that Northerners were also weary of the toll war was taking on their families, and some had turned against Lincoln.

There was so little humor or contentment in camp that I often sought the company of Jacob. He reminded me of my grandfather. He seemed not to hold bitterness in his heart toward me, even though I fought with an army that would keep him enslaved. There was an undeniable bond between us and I cherished my time with him. A peaceful soul, he was ever tranquil amidst all the turmoil. Frequently, I found him fishing in the rivers and streams near the camps. Again, when in search of him, I found him there. He nodded a greeting as I settled alongside him.

"Morning, Jacob."

"Mornin'." His smile restored some hope to my heart. If he could be so cheerful with his lot in life, I had to try. We sat in silent companionship for a while listening to the soothing sound of water gently running over rocks.

"How does it go? Are the fish biting?" I watched the end of his line, waiting for a fish to bite.

"Ain't bad. Couple of trout." He gestured toward an old pail.

"Do you have much time for fishing?" Picking up a warm river stone, I rolled its smooth surface in the palm of my hand.

"I get time to myself. Massa like fish fried up the way I do 'em."

"I'm sure he does. I think we all would. We've not had a decent meal of meat or vegetables in some time now. We soldiers are damn near starving to death!" I threw the stone in the river angrily and Jacob looked at me with surprise.

"Sorry, Jacob, but I'm getting tired of the officers having food without seeming to care if we soldiers starve to death. I've been scrounging around looking for wild greens, now that it's getting warmer. My mother used to find them and make a meal of them before the garden vegetables were in. We don't have supplies coming in like the officers do, and I reckon we always depended on our mothers or wives to cook for us. I'm not sure I'd even know how to clean and fry a fish."

Jacob glanced at me and said, "I show you how to clean and fry up a fish if you want, Oliver. It ain't hard."

"I'd like that, if we have time. No one knows how long we'll be here and where we're going next."

"This been a long stretch a time with no fightin'. I hear them officer's talking 'bout where you goin' next."

I sighed, keeping my eyes on his line. "Yes. It has been a long time. But they keep us busy with one thing or another. And we're still burying men who are dying from disease and wounds every day. I wish there was something the doctors could do to prevent all the illness. The fever is taking more men than wounds these days. I feel pity for those who are so weak and suffering."

Jacob nodded, and his tone became somber. "You hear where your brothers was killed?"

"No. I've heard nothing. My family received my letter. I wish I could have told them in person, rather than send such sad news in a letter."

"Was they in this regiment, your brothers?"

"I don't believe so, Jacob. They enlisted half a year before me. I thought they were in my first regiment, the 54th Virginia. But I've heard talk that some men from the 54th were transferred to the 63rd Tennessee. The word is Tennessee men fight battles nearly every day. If they were transferred, it's possible my brothers were not at Chancellorsville at all."

"You think yer brothers fightin' there? In Tennessee?"

"I don't know. That's the truth of it. I joined the 54th, the unit my brothers signed up for. But here I am now in the 29th."

I pondered again the possibility that my brothers might not have been killed. There were at least thirty members of my family enlisted in the army. Many of our surnames and given names the same, names usually taken from the bible. Could the Isaac and Asa listed as killed be from another family, and not my own? I dared not entertain such hope, but I could not stop myself.

"Do you have family, Jacob?"

"I never did marry. Didn't want to bring children into a life of slavery." I looked at him and took in what he was saying. I was unable to imagine the hardships of a slave. Thinking of how much I loved and missed Mahala and Lawson, I could not imagine not wanting a family.

"What will you do when the war is over, Jacob? If the North wins, will you go to a city? Find work there? If we win, will you remain with your...your master?"

"I don't know. It ain't never been up to me. If I honest, I ain't give it much thought. What would I do up north? Where I work? Where I live? I'm too old for all of that." I hadn't before seen sadness cross Jacob's face. Seeing it tugged at my heart.

"I ask myself the same question, Jacob. Where will my home be when this war is over? My family has lived in Virginia more than a hundred years. It is where my wife Mahala and I hope to raise our family. But so many families have been destroyed and farms abandoned. I'm not sure my family and our farm will survive this war. I'm not even sure I want to live in Virginia anymore." It struck me that I had never had such a thought before. How could I think of not wanting to live in Virginia?

"We of the same mind there, Oliver. I don't know where my home be." He turned to face me, "But you got a choice in that. You have a home and land, and you have your boy to take care of. I ain't never had that choice."

We were quiet for a while as I considered Jacob's life. I had never before thought about it. My freedom was like the air I breathed, invisible, but very real. It occurred to me that I had not had such an honest talk with anyone who was not family. Not with a fellow soldier. I doubted I would even have had it with my brothers were they with me, for fear it might have been perceived as weak. I stood to leave, and Jacob lifted his head.

"We might be leavin' this place right soon. Them officers talkin' about gettin' up north quick. I don't know what it like up there."

"I don't know either, Jacob. I've never been outside of Virginia until this war took me into Kentucky. I've not been further than Carroll County, where I was born, until now."

The thought of leaving Virginia was suddenly real and left me longing to be home.

"Perhaps it won't come to pass, Jacob. I pray not, I don't want to leave Virginia."

I stood to leave. "Well, I better get back before dinner call. Good luck with the fishing, Jacob."

"I pray we stay here too, Oliver. I pray so too." His eyes found mine and I nodded.

We were different and yet so much the same. Connected in spirit by the only home we knew. Both unsure of where we would call home if we survived the war.

CHAPTER SIX

ABIGAIL

Quesinberry Farmhouse
Dugspur, Carroll County, Virginia
MAY, 1863

NIGHT AFTER NIGHT, Andrew slept while I sat alone in front of the fireplace. I had not slept soundly for weeks. I rocked most of the night, smoking my pipe. My mind raced with questions that tormented me. Where were my boys? Could they be alive? If not, where were their bodies? I had only the words of Oliver, written in anguished poetry, speaking of their death. No official word had come from the army. Would it not come if their deaths were certain? I knew Oliver was not on the battlefield with his brothers, nor had he seen their bodies. Only an officer would have told him of their deaths. Did that officer walk among the dead boys and attach a name to a corpse? Oliver was grieving the loss of his brothers, but how could he without question, accept the word of an officer as truth? I could not. I was tortured by the thought my boys might still be alive and need my help. Endless days of sorrow and sleepless nights had completely worn me down.

Andrew watched my every move, as if he thought I had lost my mind. I might have. I could only think of finding my boys. It felt as though a piece of my heart was missing, and the sadness I felt made me feel desperate. In the rare moments when I was lucid enough to examine my thoughts, even I was bewildered by my steadfast belief that my sons were still alive. I had spent my life raising them to be strong in the face of adversity and to be dutiful and see things they started to the end. I could not imagine them gone from the earth. Wishing them deserters so that they might still be living was not who I thought I was. I took pride in raising strong independent children. But the war had changed me. How could I live with the helplessness I felt? Two children gone from the earth. It was a sorrow I knew not how to express. In my suffering, the health and laughter of my other children offended me in some unfathomable way. My grief was such that I couldn't bear the expression of cheerfulness around me.

My first baby, Isaac, was gone? We named him well, for he always had a smile on his face. A smile which never failed to bring me cheer. His brothers and sisters adored him. Asa, my second child—gone? He was always serious and diligent. I recalled how proud he was when he planted my treasured white roses which climbed around our front door. Those roses mocked me now with their beauty and vigor, while he is lost at war.

This I know, they were born to be farmers, as their father and grandfather before them. They loved this land. My boys were not meant for soldiering, even though Andrew would disagree with me. He said that no man was born to be a soldier, but became soldiers when they were called on to protect their families and land. But my boys were destined to live and work on our farm...to bring up their families as we did, as our ancestors did. Their flesh and bones were formed from what we grew on our land, and they fought in this cursed war to protect it. I could not believe that God would take them from me and from their home.

When I went to Hillsville, I saw the mothers of sons who

had died in battle. Anna Carson and Margaret Phillips, among many others. Their eyes were hollow, no light inside them... no joy. Their hair turned gray overnight and sorrow bent their backs. Not yet fifty years old and they walked the earth as ghosts of the women I knew. Anna had been my closest girl-hood friend, and I remembered her carefree spirit. She was almost as good a rider as I. When we could escape our chores, we would race each other on horseback to the river. In sum-mer we'd plunge into the rushing water in just our petticoats, laughing and splashing.

When I last saw her in town she looked like an old woman. I asked about her family. I saw in her eyes such sadness that I had to restrain myself from taking her into my arms as I would a child.

She shook her head and murmured, "I don't know, Abigail. I hardly see a reason for living these days. You know my Thomas joined up too? I'm not sure I can keep up with all the work now that he's gone. The baby is only six months old." Her baby peeked at me as he rested his head on his mother's shoulder.

She had five children, all under the age of fourteen. Her little boys weren't old enough to help her with the endless work of farming, and now her husband had gone to fight too? I looked down and noticed her hands were red and rough from hard work. My heart ached for her.

"Maybe Peter could lend you a hand, Anna. He's strong for a sixteen-year-old. I'll ask him."

"No. Thank you, Abbie. That's very kind, but I've been talk-ing with Mary Abbot. We're thinking of packing up and mov-ing to Richmond till this war fighting is over. I hear there's work there for women with so many of the men gone." She struggled to compose herself. "I've got to feed my young'uns. I've got five mouths to feed." Tears shimmered in her eyes.

"I know, Anna. I'm sorry. If there is anything we can do to help...."

She wearily shook her head. "God bless and thank you, Abigail."

I couldn't dispel the image of how frail and defenseless Anna seemed to me. I refused to become one of those passive women, compliant and accepting of whatever heartache war brought. I wanted to shout my anger and frustration. My boys must come home, and if God had thought it best to take their souls while protecting our land, their bodies would lie at home in our rich earth. An icy fury was building inside me unlike any I had ever known, and it overwhelmed me. I felt as though I might shatter into a million pieces.

Shortly after I spoke with Anna, I asked Peter to sit by the fire with me, after the family had gone to bed. No one knew I had decided to search for my boys. To speak of it would only confirm what Andrew thought, that I was mad. Mad with grief and despair.

I couldn't explain the sorrow and torment that had led to the plan I was about to share with my son. I could only hope that he would listen and understand. I touched his arm and searched his face. "I have decided to look for your brothers, Peter. I have to try to find out how they died, where they are buried, or if they might be wounded and need help. Maybe they deserted?"

He listened with his head bowed as I told him I thought Isaac and Asa might still be alive. Peter was solemn, and resembled Asa in his severe dark looks. He raised his head slowly and I saw pity in his eyes.

"Don't feel pity for me, Son. Indeed, I hope they have deserted the army...gone into the hills to join the Home Guard. I would wish them alive and traitors, rather than dead for a cause they never knew or understood!"

Peter looked away, stared into the fire, and murmured, "But, Mother, they are fighting to save our land." I studied his profile, so like his brother. His skin was bronze from months of work in the fields. He was beginning to grow a full copper-colored beard, which was surprising given his black hair. His shoulders were broad, his back and arms muscled from farm work.

"I am not so sure of that anymore, Son. I fear that your brothers are fighting to protect the wealth of tobacco farmers. I think this war is about rich men keeping their slaves. Please hear me out, Peter," I whispered. "We will leave two weeks from tomorrow. Your sister Jane is almost fifteen and Mary twelve. They know how to run this house and care for the younger ones. They may not like it, but I'm confident they can handle the responsibility for a few weeks. I would like your help, Son. Will you go with me?" He was silent. "Are you afraid, Peter?"

"Afraid? No. But this war is not yet over, Mother. I could be forced to join. You know what we hear about the condition of our army. Our soldiers starve and freeze, while northern troops plunder our homes and food. I know you are grief-stricken, we all are. But how can you think we could go unmolested into the heart of this war?"

"You're not yet seventeen, Peter. You must be eighteen to be conscripted. I have given three sons to this war. They would not dare take you—unless you volunteer."

I saw a flash of defiance in his eyes. A trait I knew he had inherited from me. "And if I do volunteer, Mother?"

"Don't speak of it, Peter. You mustn't. Your father and I need you. Think of your sisters and little brothers. How will we feed our family? We cannot manage this farm alone."

"I have no doubt, Mother, that you could manage anything on your own."

I wasn't sure if my son's words were meant as a compliment or not, but I took them as such. I needed Peter to have confidence in me. I quietly removed a map I had hidden earlier under a loose stone on the fireplace hearth. I spread and smoothed it between us. "Look, Peter, we will follow a route cousin Elizabeth has sent. It takes us through the mountains.

Here, let me show you."

Cousin Elizabeth Quesinberry, a distant relative, lived on the Potomac River in Northern Virginia. I wasn't sure if she was part of the "Secret Line" which passed information on Union troop activity to Confederate officers, or a Unionist, helping Southern deserters escape to Northern states. She could be both. It mattered not. She was family and I would use whatever information I could get from her to find my sons.

"See, Peter. Elizabeth has circled the areas where the Home Guard is most likely to camp in the mountains. We will be safe if we stay with them while searching for your brothers." I gazed at Peter's face as his eyes moved over the map. I was looking for hesitation or fear. I saw neither.

"There are many Quesinberry men in the Home Guard. They will know if Isaac and Asa are among them or…" I hesitated. "…or if they are deserters."

Peter did not raise his head to look at me. His voice was low and hard. "You would have my brothers be deserters or part of the Home Guard? It would not shame you, Mother? Isn't the purpose of the Home Guard to capture deserters and return them to the army? For money?"

I rested my hand on his until his eyes found mine. He was right to question me. I was not the mother I was just two years ago. My boys' character was more important to me then and feeling shame was a luxury, but the burning desire to believe they still lived, at any cost, had overwhelmed me and brought me to my knees.

"I know I am not myself, Son. But I cannot accept that your brothers do not still breathe. There is so much confusion about men who have died or are in the hospital—or those who have deserted. If there is a chance they're still alive, deserters or with the Home Guard, I must try to find them." I cast my eyes down, refusing to let Peter see the pain on my face. We remained in silence for a while. Peter had never seen me so fragile and I struggled to break the tension between us.

I finally managed to say, "Son, you must know that the first purpose of the Guard is to protect innocent Southern families against the Union forces. They do report on deserters and those who are sympathetic to the Union, but many soldiers seek the safety of the Guard to heal from illness or wounds received in battle. Your brothers could be among them. Isaac and Asa could be alive, Peter!"

"Do you really think that Mother? Oliver wrote that they are dead. Why would he think that? What if we find out that they are dead? Will you accept it?" His eyes darted from my face to the fire.

"I—I don't know. But I know I have to try to find them. My sorrow is breaking my heart. I won't be much good as a mother and wife grieving as I am, and my doubt about the deaths of your brothers is real. How could Oliver know for certain they are gone? Isaac and Asa were transferred to the Tennessee regiment last year in the early days of May. Oliver was never in battle with them. They were near the Great Dismal Swamp. The talk is that there are battles nearly every day. Thousands of soldiers were killed or got the fever. Your brothers could have the fever and be in the hospital. How could officers identify every man? Isaac and Asa may have escaped into the mountains. There were thousands of boys..." my voice broke as I stifled a sob, "...thousands."

In my mind's eye, I saw a field covered with the bodies of young men. I wondered who could walk among them and identify each one. I had heard that when buried, they were thrown into a common grave. Trenches were dug hastily where the soldiers fell and then quickly abandoned. Anything of use other men grabbed before their brethren were entombed forever in unmarked graves. That could not be the fate of my boys. I could not stand it. I breathed deeply and gathered courage.

"Peter, if I spoke of you now...if you were presumed dead in battle, one among thousands, and I had not a lock of your hair to be certain, would you have me think you dead, without question?" I lowered my voice and placed a hand on his shoulder. "Truly, Son. They may have deserted or be wounded and trying to reach home. The Phillips boy found his way home to recover from his wounds. His family thought he had died."

Peter swallowed hard and lifted his eyes to mine. "No, Mother, I would not want you to forget about me. I would want someone to search for me, my body, my grave. But what of Father? You know he will not agree to this."

"Peter, he has no choice. He knows me as I am. He will not try to stop me, for he knows he cannot."

We were silent for a few minutes, the only sound the soft crackle of the fire. I knew Peter was thinking of his father. He was the most rebellious of my sons and had many conflicts with my husband.

"Don't think harshly of your father, Peter. He's the son of a minister, taught to be patient, and accept God's plan for us. He is a good and clever man, but he knew the girl he married would never act as chattel and obey his every word. Indeed, that is why he married me."

With that, I saw a smile tease the corners of his mouth as he nodded his head in agreement. His finger followed a path I had traced on the map.

I took my pipe from the fireplace mantle and lit it.

"So, Mother, how and where shall we begin this journey?"

I had only a week left to prepare. My tongue grew sharp, driving Andrew to spend longer hours in the fields and barn. I gave orders and directions without time allowed for questions or argument from my children. Jane and Mary were cautious around me. They sensed a change, but dared not question me. They worked efficiently, as if they knew they would soon be on their own. In many ways they already were, as my mind was no longer on the farm. I was grateful the younger children were oblivious to the chaos. Even baby Sara had easily accepted milk from the cow in a bottle.

Andrew questioned me only once about my frequent trips into town to gather information about regiments and the location of the Home Guard. My answer confirmed what he already knew. "I'm going to find my boys, Andrew. Perhaps someone in town may know the whereabouts of their regiment, or the location of the Home Guard. Alive or dead, I will find them and bring them home."

He stared long into my eyes. But said not a word.

I searched for information among the people in town. It was the women who whispered answers to my questions. Yes, they said, their boys, or those they knew, were in the local Home Guard. There were even women among the Guard, they confided in hushed conversations. Their men turned their backs and walked away. They feared their wives would somehow catch my madness.

Ha! I thought to myself. I was not the first Quesinberry woman to be called mad. They forgot, however, that I was a Banks. In my mother's words, I acted too 'coarse for a girl'. She thought I was too stubborn and headstrong, and needed to learn to control my independent ways. It was not for lack of trying that I could never sew a straight seam. My mind would not settle to such a task. I wished to be outdoors, in all weather. I learned to shoot and fish, and to Mother's dismay, smoke a pipe. She would shake her head and lament. "Abigail will never find a husband. What man would want such a girl, unable to properly cook or sew? You have ruined your daughter with your indulgence, William. She is undisciplined and runs wild with her brothers."

"Oh, let her be." My father would smile to reassure her. "She'll make a fine wife for the right man."

Andrew was the one. I knew it when first my eyes fell on him at his grandfather's church. I would lower my head, my bonnet shielding my face, but my eyes would not leave Andrew. He felt it and his piercing blue eyes found mine. I blush, even now, for the look that passed between us was not one of a chaste nature. It was electric and it made me catch my breath. No one was more astonished than my mother when Minister Quesinberry's grandson Andrew came calling.

My dear husband, Andrew. Was it only three weeks ago I held my breath and watched as you walked from the barn with Oliver's letter in your hand?

I long for life before that letter. No, before the war. If my boys were gone, I feared I would be forever changed. I would never again be the wife and mother I was.

I might never be myself again.

CHAPTER SEVEN

OLIVER

Late June, 1863
Northern Virginia

THERE WAS DAILY as we marched north, a desperate search to find men to fill the ranks of those lost to disease and at the battle of Chancellorsville. It seemed to me just as many men deserted as were being conscripted.

I had somehow avoided the duty of searching the country-side for deserters and able-bodied men of conscription age. And if I had a choice, I would not follow my captain's orders to go in search of them. I would find it hard to force any man to join the army.

Reluctantly, I joined a group of men assigned this duty. We were given orders to shoot deserters who refused to re-turn to battle, and to force any man of conscription age to join the regiment. My heart was with those that desired to stay at home in Virginia. I saw in every man myself, my deceased brothers, my companions. Every wretched soul fighting this war was my brother and I would not willingly take his life. The shame that would come from deserting would be punishment enough. I dreaded even witnessing the act if one of my group should carry out the order to shoot a deserter or a man who refused conscription. As our weary group departed, we were told to search barns and every outbuilding around farms.

I observed the men with me. I was familiar with most, and waved to John Bowers who enlisted with me. He appeared to have lost thirty pounds. We nodded a greeting and set out into the hills. Everyone made the effort to appear orderly until the camp was out of sight. Then we separated into smaller groups.

I fell in alongside John, and we walked in silence for some time until I asked, "How are you doing, John? Have you heard news of your family and how folks are faring at home?" I noticed his shoes were held together with strips of leather. Many of the supplies and goods we received were of shoddy quality and often fell apart within weeks. John walked with a limp and his hand was bandaged. The wound beneath oozed a dark spot and I tried to keep my eyes away from the stained cloth.

"Yes. I received a letter from my sister two weeks ago. It was dated April 2, more than a month ago. Mother is very ill. My sister fears she won't make it through the summer." He stumbled, but recovered without my help.

"Is it only your sister there on the farm with your mother? Is your brother Paul still with his regiment?" I slowed my pace to match his.

"Paul was transferred. I'm not sure where he is now." He stopped to catch his breath. "Yes, it is only my sister at home with Mother. Minnie is only sixteen. I worry about how she can care for Mother and run the farm. She said that some of the neighbors have helped with planting this spring, your father among them." He stopped again and bent over, his hands on his knees. "What of your brothers? Are they still in the 54th?"

A sharp pain passed through me when I realized that I had yet to speak of their deaths with anyone who knew them. I paused before I spoke. "They are both gone, among the dead." John and I walked in silence while the words took effect. "I got word in early May, just after Chancellorsville, that they were missing. At some point, I believe they may have been transferred to the 63rd Tennessee. I've heard that regiment was sent south, down around Suffolk. They died in battle with that regiment, or from the fever. I'm not sure."

John shook his head and sighed, "I'm sorry to hear that. I know it is a heartache for you and your family. So many are gone from our hometown." He stopped and leaned against a tree for support. "Do you ever regret volunteering for the army, Oliver?"

I studied John, allowing him time to rest. I hardly recognized my old friend, he was so wasted. I feared he had a disease or that his arm had become infected. I remembered him working the field along with his brother next to the old county road. He was young and healthy, with a full life ahead of him. A life with a wife and children. He volunteered with me in Dugspur. We were among a large group of men from Carroll and Floyd counties. Those who joined at the same time now kept a certain distance from one another. If we recognized one another at all, we were overcome with sadness at what we had become. Once healthy and fearless young men, we were all now close to death and could be gone overnight. It made me heartsick to see how the war had made strangers of old friends, but that separation made it easier if a friend or neighbor should be killed.

I gazed into the woods next to the path on which we were walking. The quiet of the woods calmed my spirit. I had always been drawn to it. I remembered walks around the outskirts of Dugspur in early spring with Mahala. She knew the woods like no one else and showed me plants, berries and herbs which contained healing properties her father had shown her. It was a lifetime ago. If I survived the war I vowed I would never leave her side again.

Beside me John was silent, but for a frequent cough which he stifled in the crook of his arm. As I waited for him to recover, my mind wandered back to a summer day six years ago. It was the wedding day of John's older brother Paul and Virginia Thompson. Weddings were happy occasions, a time for celebration and kinship. Nearly every family from Hillsville and Dugspur were in attendance. I was a boy of fourteen. I recalled my brothers, Isaac and Asa, teasing the young groom. Girls wearing their best summer dresses surrounded the bride, admiring her homemade gown. Women covered long tables made from sawhorses and planks of wood with white cloths. The tables were laden with a mouthwatering abundance of food. Roasted ham and chicken, potato salad and coleslaw, heaped high in wooden bowls, pies and cakes of so many kinds you could not name all of them. Fiddlers played as people clapped and swayed. That was the first time I saw Mahala. She wore a pale blue dress. Her shy smile and amber colored eyes captured my imagination. She looked unlike most girls I knew. Her face was both soft and strong. I felt at peace when my gaze met hers and I knew not why. When the groom grabbed his bride around the waist and started to dance, I wanted to do the same with Mahala, but I was shy, and she was the first girl to have captured my fancy. At sixteen I began to court her and only two years later we were married. What a beautiful vision my Mahala was on our wedding day. I closed my eyes and thought of her on that day.

John abruptly pushed off the tree and started walking again. I turned from my thoughts and the serenity of the woods and matched my stride to his.

John looked at me quizzically. "Do you, Oliver, regret volunteering?"

"Oh, I'm sorry, John." I said, with a wave of my hand. "I was thinking of your brother's wedding. This day reminds me of that day. A lovely sunny day...so bright and...." I stopped myself from saying more. Would it distress John to recall that day? Perhaps it was best not to speak of fanciful memories. I cleared my throat.

"At times, I do regret volunteering for this war. Were you led to believe, as I was, that our homes and farms were threatened? That Northerners were envious of our land and farms?"

John nodded in agreement. "I thought that was why they were coming here. To take our farms and make themselves rich. I was sure of it."

I shook my head angrily and kicked the dirt. "Would you have fought this war if you had known the reason for it wasn't at all clear? I still can't understand what it is we are doing. What will we win? I'm afraid the truth is we are fighting for wealthy men to protect their riches and keep their slaves."

"I don't know." John stopped to tighten the strips of leather on his shoes. "I think I was tired of farming. I watched my father work the land until the day he died. I thought only of the adventure of war, the excitement, and leaving the drudgery of the farm." He closed his eyes, his head drooping.

"Are you feeling alright, John?" I placed a hand on his shoulder and felt a tremor go through his body. There was a sheen of sweat on his pale face. I watched as he struggled to control his breathing. He walked to the side of the path and reclined on the grass, closing his eyes. Having served in the field hospital, I knew the signs of disease, smallpox, scarlet fever, measles, 'the fever' and others with names I couldn't remember. They were all rampant. Countless men died before they ever saw a battle. They became ill and died soon after they enlisted.

I squatted next to John and tried to give him a sip of water. "Go on without me, Oliver. I feel so very tired. I've had these spells lately and haven't been able to keep anything down the last few weeks. I'll just rest here for a few minutes. I'll catch up with you."

I looked around for someone who might help me get John back to the camp. The other men had disappeared into the woods. "I'll stay with you. Perhaps all you need is a rest. How long have you had a fever?"

"It's a while now. I can't seem to shake it. I wish I had

Mother's cure for such. I do miss her." His body tremored again. "Dammit! Had you any idea this war would be so long and so damn bloody? We've not been paid a salary for months. My mother and sister need that money. I worry about them." He turned away and coughed into a rag.

John was in very bad shape. Possibly having both camp fever and an infected arm. Working with the field doctors I had learned the symptoms well. I felt fortunate to have escaped the fever so far. John could also have dysentery. It was very common among the men, and with their weakened physical condition, many became fatally ill. I hoped that John would not be one of them, and that he would live to make it home.

I offered him water again, finding no resemblance to the young, healthy boy I knew in Dugspur.

"Are you feeling better? Do you think you can walk back to camp with me? You should have told the captain how sick you felt. He would have put you in the field hospital." I eased back on my heels, away from him. As much as I felt for John, I didn't want the fever.

"No, no, no! Not that cursed place. Men go there to die. Some say the curatives doctors give do more harm than good." John stared at me. "You help there. What have you seen?"

"I can't deny it. The doctors say that the hand to hand combat at the battle of Chancellorsville is still killing soldiers. They blame it on the blood and sputum that—well, that was everywhere. It spread disease."

John's eyelids slowly closed. He looked as if he was sleeping. I watched his chest rise and fall, his breathing labored. He was gaunt, his skin stretched tight over hollow cheeks. I closed my eyes and started a silent prayer, but before I finished, shots rang out in the distance.

"John," I shook him gently. "John, are you able to walk?"

"No. Let me rest here for a while and I'll feel better. Come back this way, and I'll be up and about. It is just a rest I need."

I observed him carefully. I believed he truly could not

walk. "Rest then. I'll come and help you get back to camp. Try to drink some water. It might help."

"Yes. Yes."

I walked toward the sound of the gun shots and shouts. Was it a deserter they'd found, or a man being forced to join the army? I braced myself for the sight of a brutal confrontation.

When I found the rest of the men, a young man in filthy clothes was being shoved at gunpoint ahead of them.

"We found us a deserter, Oliver. Yes sir, we did!" George Springer shouted, as he poked the poor soul with the point of his musket. My heart pounded with what my eyes beheld. I had the strongest desire to free the man.

I looked away toward the place I'd left John Bowers. I could not bring myself to be a part of such brutality.

"I'll go back this way. I left my water there when I heard the shots." No one heard, as they were laughing at, and tormenting, the man they had captured.

When I returned to the place I had left John Bowers, he was gone. I felt certain I wouldn't see him again. I prayed he would make it home.

CHAPTER EIGHT

ABIGAIL

June, 1863
Dugspur, Virginia

"ANDREW, LET GO of the reins." Astride my horse I looked down on my husband. Beside me, Peter looked straight ahead into the distance.

"Abigail, must you? We are not the first family to lose sons in this war. Who among them have gone searching in the mountains for their sons? I'm afraid your grief has consumed you, that you are not thinking clearly. I fear you won't be safe, that you might not return." Andrew placed a hand on my leg and pressed, urging me to respond. He glanced behind him where the children stood. The look on their faces was one of disbelief.

I pressed my lips together and took a deep breath. "Look after each other, children. I promise to be home soon." The baby reached for me, calling, "Mama, Mama." Jane shushed her and held Sara closer. Jane's eyes found mine and I read the anger and resentment on her face.

I lowered my voice so that only Andrew could hear. "We have had enough words on this matter, Andrew. I care not what others think of my actions. I will not grieve forever and be haunted by the thought our sons might still be alive. I must know or I will never again know peace. Surely you can understand?"

"I know I cannot stop you, Abbie. It is just that...I don't understand why you must leave us. We need you, you know that. You can't tell me how long you will be away. Do you know? I will worry so for your safety. The mountains are full of deserters from both sides of this war. Even some of our kinsmen have become nothing more than a band of thieves."

"We will be careful Andrew. We'll stay in the mountains and look for the Guard camps. I won't be foolish." I gazed at Andrew's face, his concern and worry clearly evident there. I knew a part of me was selfish and cruel to leave him and my children. He was the kindest of men, accepting of God's plan. I was likely taking advantage of that. He had never demanded that I obey his will, as most men did.

Perhaps I was losing my mind. I couldn't explain the logic of what I was doing. I only knew I could not rest. My mind was forever in turmoil. My younger children must have thought I cared less for them than Isaac and Asa. It wasn't so—and yet, I didn't know why I was unable to accept the burden of my sons' deaths as other women had done, as even Andrew had done. I felt such anger about the inequity of the war. I felt it most intensely when I heard of wealthy men who were allowed to pay a fee to avoid conscription, and slave holders who were exempt from conscription if they held twenty or more slaves. Exempt— because they held slaves, while my sons died! How could Andrew not understand my anger? I wondered that he did not share it.

"I must do this, Andrew. If I do not, then I will surely lose my mind. I will be of no use to you or our children. I ask your forgiveness for my weakness."

"Abbie, please."

"Andrew, be at peace. I know I am doing what I must. If I can't find them, I might at least find out how and where they died. Peter will be with me. We have kinsmen among the Home Guard. We'll be safe. I promise you." I brushed the top of his head with a kiss. "I love you. Watch over the children."

Turning to Peter, I said firmly, "Let's go, Son. Have you the map?"

"Yes, Mother." He placed his hand on his jacket where I had sewn a large pocket.

It wasn't easy to ride away from my husband and children, and I glanced back toward the farm. Andrew stood with his head bowed. The younger children ran behind our horses for a while, until I turned and told them they must go back. Tears sprang to my eyes and I looked away so Peter wouldn't see them.

I had not been entirely truthful with Andrew, or Peter for that matter. I had only a general idea of where the Home Guard might be in the mountains. They moved around from place to place. I had traveled the mountains and woods most of my life and always felt safe there. I knew them well. They were a place of peace and beauty for me, but no longer. I knew there were strangers hiding in them now. I was on edge as Peter and I rode deeper into the wilderness. My pistol was hidden inside the pocket of my skirt. Peter was armed as well. I was mindful that there could be Union deserters hiding in the mountains, as well as runaway slaves and common thieves. I doubted there was much we had that they would want, a little food, perhaps the horses. Yes, I thought, most likely the horses. I was a good shot and was willing to take that chance. I was glad Peter had thought to bring one of the dogs. My father used to say, "a good dog will save many a night's sleep." One of our hounds ran alongside Peter's horse, sniffing the air and running off into the brush now and then.

At mid-day we stopped alongside a stream to rest and water the horses. I spread a blanket and Peter and I shared our first meal of biscuits and bacon. Peter seemed shy around me. I realized we had never before had time alone. I knew very little about this silent, handsome boy of mine. It surprised me that I felt awkward talking to him.

"I'm glad you're with me, Peter. Did you come because you felt you had to protect me, or do you believe as I do that your brothers might still be alive?"

I handed him a slice of apple, one of the last from the root cellar. There were still many root vegetables left, carrots, potatoes and such. And the early spring greens were coming in. Mahala and I canned and dried enough fruits and vegetables last fall to see us through until spring. I had seen to it that my family would not starve, and I took pride in that.

"Both, Mother. I wouldn't have you travel these mountains alone. And I know you would have done so."

"How do you know I would have done this alone?"

"You really think your children know so little of you? Do you not remember I watched you plunge into Big Reed Island Creek to get to Hillsville with food for our soldiers? The creek was a raging torrent, filled with logs and debris. You would not allow me to cross with you and no one else followed. We thought you would drown. They said you acted as if you were taking food to your own starving children. Some said you had lost your mind."

"But I didn't drown, did I?" I recalled now though, how frightened I was. I was regarded as reckless by those who remained on the other side of the creek.

"The truth is, Peter, I was afraid. That is why I insisted you not cross the creek with me. I wasn't sure I would make it. But all I could think of was those boys and men fighting and starving for food. I often feel as if those fighting this war are all my boys, my sons."

Peter threw a stone into the water, and then another. I touched his arm lightly. "You know, Peter, women are fighting this war too. We are left without husbands and sons to help us with the work of a farm, left alone to provide for our children. All we can do is watch, helplessly, as our sons and husbands die, or are wounded for a cause we don't understand or fully support. At first, we all thought it was a war to protect our homes and land. But now we know it is slavery, tobacco and cotton. That is what this war is about. In the end it is to protect men who became wealthy from the sale of cotton and tobacco. Men who own slaves who pick those crops."

"What are we to do, Mother? Our family has farmed our land for a hundred years. Are we to leave? Where would we go? West Virginia seceded. Kentucky is divided. Where would we call home if we do not fight for Virginia? We have nothing else. We have only our land, our farms and our families, or what is left of them."

"We will do what we have always done. We will persevere, farm our land, and raise our families on that land. Do not lose sight of who you are, Peter. You are the son of one of the oldest families to settle in Virginia. This too will pass, Son. We will stay on the land your ancestors gave their lives for. Now perhaps your brothers."

He stared at me and said. "I hope you are right, Mother. There is so little to sustain hope when everything we have taken for granted is no longer certain."

"But here we are, Peter. We will have courage and we will survive." For the first time since his childhood, I embraced my son.

He pulled away slightly, embarrassed, and cleared his throat.

"Well, Mother. I think we should move on. We have been an hour resting here."

I smiled at him. But beneath the smile I felt my stomach twist. I was not truly certain we would survive the war. We knew many families whose farms and land were already destroyed.

"We will survive this war, Peter. We have to."

CHAPTER NINE

OLIVER

Late June, 1863
Shenandoah Valley

I WAS CAPTIVATED by the splendor of the Shenandoah Valley, bounded by the Blue Ridge Mountains to the East and the Appalachian Mountains to the West. My great-grandfather spoke of how the region impressed him when first he saw it. Mahala said in her grandmother's language Shenandoah means "Daughter of the Stars." It was so striking in its beauty that I almost forgot we were marching north.

Lee was wise to send General Ewell ahead to clear out the Union forces and make way for our infantry. I hoped that Ewell was able to cross the Potomac into Maryland and draw the Yankees out of Virginia altogether. I found comfort in knowing our army might have better food supplies in Maryland, and not depend for food solely on the farmers of Virginia, who struggled to feed their own families.

The Blue Ridge Mountains to the east kept our movements hidden from the Union army while we marched ahead into Maryland. I guessed we were near the area of Sharpsburg. I knew men were, as was I, thinking of the battle of Sharpsburg last year. McClellan's men fought a fierce battle against us, and we lost countless men there.

General Lee issued a warning to officers and troops to avoid destroying private property when we reached Maryland. The order stated we were to pay in Confederate money for anything we confiscated. But our money was worth only a fraction of northern currency and I doubted farmers or merchants would willingly sell goods to us. If they refused we were commanded to leave a receipt listing what we took. Most of us felt we had to uphold the honor of the South and follow Lee's orders. It was a fact, in spite of orders, some would not hesitate to plunder, the need for food was so great.

Lee's admonishment concerning the respect of private property did not apply to Negroes. They were to be rounded up and sent South to be sold back into slavery. It made no difference if they were freemen or runaway slaves.

I saw a few the other day, shackled together. I couldn't turn my eyes away from the sight. Knowing Jacob as I did, I was sickened. It seemed a sin to me that wealthy men were using their money to buy slaves, or commanding their return to slavery, while soldiers were without food. Why did they not use their money to supply food for the army? It reaffirmed my belief that rich men cared more for their wealth and retaining their slaves than for those of us fighting on their behalf.

I thought of Jacob when I saw the group of shackled men, and I wondered what he would think if he should see them. I hadn't seen him for some time and I missed his kind and thoughtful company.

It wasn't difficult to find Jacob, although I took some risk in doing so, venturing near the officers' tents. It was the scent of food he was preparing that drew me to him. He lifted a hand in greeting as I approached.

"Oliver. It good to see you."

"And you, Jacob. Are you well?"

"Good as I reckon any man these days."

He gestured toward a stump and I sat beside him.

"I swear, Jacob, you are as good a cook as my mother. But I said that before, didn't I? What is that you are making?"

"Just beef an onions. Some general been raidin' up in Maryland already. They's livestock an foodstuff been finding its way to the officers. I got plenty extra." He said with a wink.

My mouth watered at the thought Jacob would share with me the meal he was preparing for the officers.

It was good to be around Jacob. He reminded me of Grandfather. He was a decent man, honest, with good humor that came only with age.

I hesitated to broach the subject of the captured Negroes, but I wanted to know if he had seen the shackled men and how he felt about it. Even more, I wanted to understand how I felt.

"Jacob, did you see those men being sent back into slavery the other day?"

He shook his head, indicating that he had not.

"When we cross into Pennsylvania you could be a free man. Would you take that chance, Jacob?"

He studied the back of his hands which grasped his knees. His hands were gnarled with blue veins that stood out. He slowly lifted his eyes to mine. I saw in his eyes an ancient history. It was all there, from his childhood in Africa to the elderly man before me. A man without a home or a country.

"What good it do me to be a free man now? I'm an old man. There ain't work for such as me up there. A young man...well, that different, I reckon."

"What do you mean, 'you reckon'? Wouldn't every slave want to be free?"

"You free, Oliver? You a free man?"

"Well, I am not free now. I'm a soldier. I have to follow the orders of my officers. If not, well, I could be punished. Even hung."

"We ain't much different right now then, are we? We both have a Massa. That friend of yours, that James Bowers? Home Guard done killed him. The officer's talk. I listen. Home Guard took him right outta his home. He try to escape and they shoot him. He a free man now ain't he?"

I wanted to shout a curse, to curse the army and the war. I was horrified anew at the way war turned men into animals. On the field we were brothers and yet became creatures who brutalized and murdered one another if commanded to do so.

"But after the war, Jacob? You and your people could be free. You could live as you please. Is that not what you want?"

"I want what you want. I want peace. I want to be treated with respect. I want food and a roof over my head."

"Will you not have that if the North wins this war and you are free to make a different life?"

"Some think it. I'm not so sure. I think it's gonna be a long time afore slaves be free. This here war ain't gonna change men's hearts so fast. I be dead and gone long afore ever that happen."

There was truth in what Jacob said. I knew it as well as he. It was difficult to accept and we silently shared sadness over the realization that the war was unlikely to improve the lives of slaves for years to come.

I broke the silence. "Tomorrow or the next day we'll be leaving Virginia altogether and crossing over the Potomac river into Maryland. I'll be up at five to wake the men. I guess I'd better get some rest."

"I reckon so, Oliver."

There were no guarantees for any among us. We might live or die. We may be free or not. It was not the first time the tragedy of war stupefied me.

"Well then. Goodnight, Jacob."

"Hold up there. You ain't leaving without some a this here stew."

He filled a wooden bowl with food. My mouth watered as my eyes filled. I knew I might not see Jacob again. I struggled to express myself but I couldn't find the words.

"That's mighty kind, Jacob. Thank you." My words seemed

empty to me because my heart was so full of gratitude for the goodness in Jacob and I knew not how to express it.

"You welcome, Oliver. You be careful now."

"Yes, I will be. And you too, Jacob. Sleep well. Tomorrow will be another long day of marching."

It rained steadily for several days. We trudged through mud so thick it often sucked our shoes from our feet. Horses and wagons became mired in the deep ruts. We were wet even in our sleep. The mountains of Virginia were shrouded in fog behind us, and melancholy settled on men who mourned the thought of leaving our beloved state.

When we camped I pulled my damp blanket around me and prayed for my family. I prayed I might survive the war and live to see my wife and child, Mother, Father, brothers and sisters again. I could think of little else to raise my spirit as the days passed. It was impossible to ignore how many men I had known who were now dead or had diseases that would surely kill them. I was a fool to think that I might survive the war while so many others were gone. Why would God spare me? I had lost nearly all faith in Him. Yet, I still prayed. I prayed to God. It was all that any of us had hope in.

CHAPTER TEN

ABIGAIL

Late May, 1863
Southwestern Virginia

TWO DAYS PETER and I had traveled in the mountains. We had seen evidence of camps, though had yet to encounter another human being. In the evening we stopped and set up the tent. Our meals were simple, beans with salt pork, biscuits, a slice or two of dried beef. We were lucky to have an abundance of wild greens to supplement our diet. Peter told me he preferred to sleep outside in order to give me privacy, but I think it was as much to stand guard against intruders. Our dog Sam was always at his side. I slept well at night, more peacefully in the open air than I had at home. I felt I had a purpose, although in my heart, I knew it might bring me the truth of what had happened to my sons, that they were dead.

I was learning more about Peter's temperament. He was more like me than any of my children. There was a stubbornness about him that Andrew attributed to me, a certain disdain for his own safety. He showed no fear of what we might find ahead. We had talked about how we would approach whomever we might come upon in the hills, Home Guard, Unionists, deserters from both the Union and Confederacy.

My biggest fear was encountering common thieves who were taking advantage of the war to plunder without fear of reprisal. Our story was that we were traveling to visit my ailing mother. I hoped we would have nothing to fear from the Home Guard. We might sympathize with Unionists, fellow Southerners who were against the cursed war. I might even have wished the swift delivery North and freedom for a Confederate deserter, or a runaway slave, so little loyalty I now felt for the Southern Cause. Support for the war was no longer as strong among our friends and neighbors as it once had been. Two years ago, many proudly watched as fathers, sons and brothers joined the army. My mind had changed greatly as the war progressed. Once there had been solidarity among our friends and neighbors. We all wanted to protect our homes and land. Our pride was strong in what our grandfathers and fathers had sacrificed to achieve. But as war dragged on, and our boys died in such great numbers, what good was our land if there was no one left to farm it?

On the third day of travel Sam rushed ahead, barking and circling back to us. I was certain he sensed strangers and was trying to warn us. Peter and I slowed our pace and I spoke earnestly with him.

"Son, if there are men ahead, we must approach cautiously. We don't know if they are our own men or Union."

He nodded and called the dog to his side. Slowly we moved toward a campsite partially hidden in the woods. A tall man warily stepped forward, a musket cradled in his arms. Behind him were a group of men who stared at us. He raised a hand in a gesture that could only mean we should venture no further. He nodded in my direction and I acknowledged him with a slight dip of my head. He was clearly shocked to see a woman. Peter lifted a hand in greeting.

"Ma'am. Are you from around these parts?" His eyes were piercing and darted from Peter to me.

I took a moment to consider his question and what

information he was trying to gain from my response.

"Yes, from Dugspur. My son and I are traveling to visit my mother who is in poor health." He studied my face as I continued speaking. "I see there are soldiers in your group. My sons serve in the 54th Virginia." I stopped talking and watched for recognition. The man stepped away to rejoin the other men, neither indicating we should join the group nor move on.

Peter and I exchanged an uncertain glance, knowing not if we should stay or leave. A barefoot man with his leg wrapped in bandages stepped forward.

"The 54th Virginia? All those men are under the command of General Lee. I was there at Chancellorsville when Lee divided the troops. Men were slaughtered as animals would be. Did your sons survive?"

He leaned on a crutch which was merely a Y shaped branch.

"I don't know. What little information we receive of this war is through infrequent letters. My son Oliver has written that they are among the missing. But I don't know how he can be sure. It seems regiments are moved around and transferred on a moment's notice. Did you find it so?"

He shuffled on his crutch and stared at the ground. He lifted his head slowly and looked into my eyes. "Ma'am, at times it seems we were simply cannon fodder. General Lee had no concern for how many men he put at risk by dividing us. We fought hard. I was proud to be counted among those brave soldiers. It was a shame Stonewall Jackson was shot by our own men after we chased those damn Yankees through the woods at night. Many of our men lay for hours on the field moaning in pain. Even before that battle we had neither proper food nor shelter, and rarely received our pay. Now men are beginning to desert in great numbers. Not only because we are leaving Virginia, but because only poor boys are being conscripted and our families are becoming desperate at home." He gestured toward the men behind him. "We are all either wounded or deserters here." It was stated as simple fact, without embarrassment

"Oh, I see." I was shocked by the bitterness in his voice and the extent of his anger toward the Confederacy. "I see that you are wounded. Will you stay here or return to battle when you are healed?"

"I will go home, Ma'am. At least I hope to, if I can escape those who would put a price on my head and return me to battle. I want no more of this war. I want to be with my family."

"Where is your home?"

"South Carolina. I joined the 15th South Carolina in 1861. I fought at the Battle of Port Royal Sound. Then I was transferred to the Army of Northern Virginia." He grimaced and transferred his crutch to his other arm.

"Where is your home, Ma'am?"

"We're from Carroll County, Virginia. My sons, Isaac and Asa joined the war in 1861. In truth I am looking for them. I would thank God if they are still alive, even wounded, or as deserters."

I saw compassion on his face as he responded. "You say they joined the 54th? Some of that regiment broke off to join the 63rd Tennessee. What are your sons' names?"

"Isaac and Asa Quesinberry. My son Oliver is a drummer for the regiment unless he has been transferred as well. How do they fare, the men in that regiment?" I was aware of the tears that stung my eyes. I wiped them away briskly, annoyed that I cried so easily. This was no time for weakness. "Of course, it is a large group of men. You might not know them. You say you were at Chancellorsville?"

"Yes, Ma'am. I left that battle as many others did, wounded and angry, grieving how many of our friends had died. We weren't prepared for such slaughter. Some men turned and ran in the midst of battle. I dragged myself off the field with a bullet in my leg. With the help of God I managed to work the bullet out. I don't believe my leg is infected. I've tried to keep it clean, and used some whiskey on it. I didn't know where

I would end up. I just tried to find my way home, and here I am. No one could have known what was expected of us. We were not ready for it...." His voice cracked and he turned away briefly, before asking, "This is your boy? He looks nearly of conscription age."

Peter would not look at me.

"But he is not! He's only seventeen." I turned to Peter in alarm. "We're searching for his brothers, in hopes we might find out how they died, or if they might still be alive. He would not have me travel alone and I wanted his company."

"I see. We can only hope this cursed war is over before he is forced to join. I pray you find your mother well. But have a care, Ma'am, there are those who would force your son into battle against your wishes."

"They would first have to kill me. I have three sons fighting, I will not let another go that way!" I had raised my voice and the other men gawked at me.

I felt Peter's hand on mine. "Mother, we should go. Perhaps this man...Sir, what is your name?"

"Phillip. Phillip Brewster."

"Perhaps you can give us an idea of where we might find the Home Guard. We are hoping to find those who would be from southwest Virginia, from Floyd or Carroll County. Many of our kinsmen are among them."

"You have only to ride ahead. There are men who would call themselves Home Guard, so take care, for there are many more who are stragglers, deserters or mercenaries. Good luck to you."

Peter took hold of my reins and we turned to leave. I pulled them from him and turned back to Phillip Brewster.

"And God Bless you, sir. I will pray for your safe return home."

He lifted his eyes to mine. "Thank you, Ma'am. God Bless you and keep you safe in your journey."

I rode slowly behind Peter. I glanced back once more.

Phillip Brewster still watched. It was all that I could do to keep from turning back and taking him into my arms.

I was not at all sure he would ever feel his mother's arms around him again. As I was not sure I would ever again embrace Isaac, Asa or Oliver.

CHAPTER ELEVEN

OLIVER

June, 1863
Shenandoah Valley

WE WERE TOLD by our officers, that our regiment, the 29th Virginia, would not march into Maryland as expected. On direct orders from President Jefferson Davis, we were to be sent back to Richmond. Preparations were underway to turn around and head back to southern Virginia. My whole regiment was overjoyed and celebrating the turn of events. Not one of us wanted to leave Virginia and cross into northern territory. General Lee issued the orders to break up Corse and Giles regiments under General Pickett, and send some back towards Richmond as a defense against the Union. The other regiments were to continue the march north under Pickett. Pickett's Brigade they were called.

I prayed for the sake of the men marching north that Lee had made the right decision in dividing us and giving Pickett his head. We watched in silence as those headed north wearily prepared to leave.

The weather had changed. It was hot and men were sluggish. I waved to Jacob, who was among those going ahead. I would miss him as much, if not more, than any of my friends from Carroll County. Jacob returned my wave as he pulled himself onto an officer's wagon.

As I began to gather my few belongings and drum, an officer I didn't recognize approached. He pointed at me and signaled I should follow him.

Why was I being singled out? I feared it was because I knew several men who were among the stragglers missing in the last few days. Men from Carroll County. What questions would I be asked? How would I answer honestly, when in truth, I felt sympathy for them? We stepped to the side and he removed his cap, wiping sweat from his brow. He was around my age, with deep set gray eyes and thick red hair.

"Are you the drummer for your regiment?" His voice sounded tired and hollow.

"Yes sir. I am."

"You'll be needed as we go north. There's a shortage of musicians and drummers. Get your things and prepare to march into Maryland."

I stared in disbelief. I was confused and certain he had made a mistake. I had just been rejoicing at the thought of being closer to my loved ones, elated at the thought of going back to Richmond with my regiment. I knew I dared not refuse my duty, although I would think to give up my drum and follow my heart towards home. I thought surely, he was mistaken.

"Sir, I am with the 29th Virginia. I am under the command of General Corse. I was told just this morning we were going back to Richmond to defend the city."

"Look man, I am as weary and confused as you. This war is not a puzzle we can easily fit together. I am only following orders, as you must. The order has been given. Get your things together, drummer. You are marching with us."

I turned away in a state of rage. I wanted to strike the man. I had no control over my life or future. But why should I have been surprised? The infantry was shuffled around in fits and starts. We'd been marched for days and then boarded onto trains and sent back to where we started.

Get my things together? I had only a ragged jacket; boots, which were falling apart, a pallet, handkerchiefs, Mahala's herbs and my drum. I examined the drum. It was still damp from days of rain. I needed a new one, but I knew that I wouldn't be able to get one before we marched into Maryland. I would have to make do.

Whistling a tune, Thomas Shepard from Hillsville, slapped me on the back with a great guffaw.

"Oliver! We're going home! Praise the Lord! We don't have to cross into northern territory!" He lowered his voice, "I think there would have been more stragglers and deserters if we had been ordered to do so. I've even heard General Corse might give us all a furlough to visit our families. I am so anxious to see my Emily and the children." He stopped speaking and punched me on the shoulder. "Man, do you hear me? We're going home!"

A furlough. I could have seen Mahala and Lawson, and the rest of my family. I longed to walk away from the army and this brutal war. I had a sense of foreboding about moving ahead with Pickett's Brigade. I knew nothing of the man, but still, I was afraid for my life.

"Oliver! What is wrong with you? Did you not hear me?"

"Yes, I did. I'm not going with you. They need drummers. I'm going north."

"Man, I am sorry to hear that. How can that be? Our regiment was ordered to Richmond." He put a hand on my shoulder. "Damn, Oliver, that is sorry news."

"I know." I kicked my drum aside in anger. "This drum is a curse now. I have no choice but to follow my orders."

He lowered his voice and leaned toward me. "You do have a choice. You know what that is. How many men do we know who have made that decision, especially at the thought of leaving Virginia while their families are so desperate at home? I might have deserted myself if forced to go into northern territory. What's the sense in it? The only reason I joined this war was to keep the damn Northerners off my land."

"I cannot desert. I'm bound by my duty, my oath. My brothers were killed fighting for Virginia. They would never have given up. I have to go on, if only to fight in their honor."

I said those words with conviction, but my eyes lingered on the mountains to the south. I knew them well. I could get lost in those mountains for months. I could survive for years if need be. It wouldn't be difficult to fall behind. Better men than I had done so.

"Tom, if you get a furlough, will you go to see my family? Tell them I am going north with Lee and will be unable to write to them for a while. Give them my love and tell them I pray for them every day." He nodded. "And tell them I am well. That I am healthy and...and that I miss them...." I stopped when I saw the pity in his eyes.

"I will, Oliver. I'm sorry about your brothers. Take care of yourself. Seems like we have no say at all in what happens. This God damned war is a curse. I never in a million years thought we'd be so long away from home, or so poorly equipped. How many good men are gone? It breaks my heart to think of how they died. I don't even know where my best friend is buried. I know his family will ask. I don't think I can tell them the truth, that I have no idea what happened to his body. I tried to get to him after that battle at Chancellorsville, but I couldn't find him. There were too many bodies on the field. Piled on top of each other. Half of them with their heads blown off."

I put a hand on his arm and gave a squeeze. He sighed deeply, his eyes darting to mine and then away.

"Jesus Christ, I'm sorry Oliver. I'm just so weary and tired."

"I know, Tom. Every time I think I can't stand anymore, or that my regiment has had enough, some invisible power seems to take over and we all rise up to take care of each other. Somehow, we band together and go on, even if we don't know why."

"Well, God be with you, Oliver. God be with you."

As I watched Tom walk away the sun illuminated the distant mountain tops in golden light and seemed to beckon to me. I wanted to walk home. The desire to see my family before leaving Virginia was so strong, the need made me feel physically ill. I stood immobile, unable to move in one direction or the other. My heart drew me home and duty pulled me ahead. And as if God heard me, an eagle soared toward the waning light. My spirit and heart followed.

CHAPTER TWELVE

ABIGAIL

June, 1863
Southwestern Virginia

WE RODE FOR hours through the woods in silence. Even
the horses' hooves were quiet on the soft forest floor. Peter ut-
tered not a word. I knew his mind was on the group of men we
had left a few miles back.

White Dogwood trees near the end of their blooming
cycle appeared as clouds in the midst of lush green foliage.
Mountain Laurel was bursting forth in frothy white balls.
It had been a very long time since I rode through mountain
woods. I hesitated to break the spell cast by the peacefulness
surrounding us. I could easily imagine there was not a war
raging, that I was simply out for a pleasurable ride with my
son. It was jarring to remember we were searching for Isaac
and Asa, missing, perhaps dead.

I glanced at Peter. His hat was pulled low over his face.
We were in the shade of trees and I wondered why he wore it
so. But I understood him well enough to know he was deep in
thought. Like Isaac and Asa, he shared little with me. Oliver
was always the son who spoke freely of his feelings.

Reluctantly, I broke the silence. "What did you make of

those men back there, Peter?"

"I thought they were a sad lot. All of them deserters or wounded. Do you think they represent our army, Mother? How can we win a war with such men?" He quickly glanced at me. "I think I should volunteer."

Fear twisted my stomach. I peered at my son. Only seventeen and more fearless than any of his brothers. I recognized in him my own headstrong stubbornness that so often led to heartache and regret. Stubbornness, which had led to this journey. I knew I had to tread lightly and not challenge him.

"Please don't volunteer, Peter. We need you at home. Your father needs you. We know so little of this war. It seems to me that our men are mistreated. That last man we spoke to, what was his name?" I wished to remind Peter of the sad state of the men we had encountered.

"Brewster. Phillip Brewster."

"Yes, that was it. He seemed a decent man. A brave man. Yet he won't go back to fight this battle. Why should he? I don't see the point of this war anymore. Soldiers are starving and we are starving at home. It no longer feels like we are fighting to protect our home and land. So many of our neighbors have given up trying to keep their farms going with the men gone. Only poor boys are fighting, not the rich men who stirred up the fear that our land was being taken in the first place. Does it seem that way to you?"

Peter slowly shook his head. He took off his hat and wiped his brow. His dark hair lifted in the slight breeze. He held the hat in his hands and stared down at it, then turned to me.

"It's not rich men that hold slaves I would fight for. I am beginning to hate those who would have my brothers' dead rather than free men they own, their slaves. No, I would not fight for them! I would fight for those soldiers we just left. They are worn out from this war. I reckon I would even fight for those who have deserted. I can only think men in such a low state have lost faith in their fellow men and in God. How can I not fight with them and for my brothers? Should they think we no longer care if they live or die?"

"Peter, you mustn't think that way," I said firmly. "Your father believes that God is on our side, that God will always be on our side."

"Is He, Mother? Is He on our side? You think the Yankees do not believe God is on their side, the side that would free the slaves? You think that man Lincoln does not think God is on his side?" He spat the words out.

"We are simple people, Son, and we have always put our faith in God. Your father is a good man, a man of faith. Our neighbors are all God-fearing people." Peter was staring at me and I hesitated. I was not what many would consider a woman of faith. I had doubted my faith and was now testing the love and trust of my husband and children. Even my own mother would say I was not doing God's work, that I was being selfish and neglecting my duties as a wife and mother.

"Peter, two of your brothers might have already died. I pray God that Oliver is still alive. Our family has given enough blood for this war. We hold no slaves. Why should my sons die to keep men enslaved? Do you care about the condition of slaves? What do you know of how they live?"

"Nothing more than you. I know many are mistreated by their owners. We have all heard that. I don't understand how men of God can treat other men worse than their animals. So, how can we believe God is on our side in this war?"

I had no answer to Peter's question. I had my own doubts about whether God took sides in this cruel war.

"I don't know Peter, if God is watching over any of these men in battle. But those men we just saw, they look like they have been treated as animals would be, worse yet, unfed and unclothed."

There was a knot in my stomach. A knot of fear and sadness. Asa, Isaac, Oliver, I had sent them all off to war, strong and healthy. Now I couldn't let myself imagine my boys in such a state as the men behind us. A tendril of doubt tightened around my heart. Why would my sons be spared? My boys were no better than the men we had just left. Those men, with their appearance and words, made evident the reality of the war. All men were the same in battle. All simply disposable.

I felt at that moment I might be mad to think somehow I, or my family, would be spared the hurt and heartache that many of our neighbors had already endured. How could I have left my husband, children, and all I knew and loved to search for sons who were reported dead? Other women accepted such a burden as they mourned for their husbands and sons. Their hair turned white and the light went out of their eyes. Their sorrow bent their backs and etched deep lines in their faces. But they carried on. They didn't feel the need to go off into the mountains in search of their loved ones. They took care of their families as best they could, and wept silently in church.

Why could I not accept what other women had endured?

Andrew asked me that question over and over. I had not a clear answer. I was driven by a force I could not explain. It was as though I had misplaced my heart.

"Son, do you think as your father? Do you think grief has driven me mad?"

Peter pushed his hair from his eyes and cleared his throat. He wouldn't look at me. I knew he was trying to find the right words to respond. I swallowed hard at the thought he might think I was indeed mad, not "right in my head" as his father had said.

"I don't know, Mother. This war has driven strong men insane. You saw the men back there. Some simply sat and rocked back and forth, in a stupor. They are not fit for battle anymore." He lowered his voice. "They are not fit for their families either."

"We will be fine, Peter. I'll be fine, I promise you. I will take care of my family. We will search a few more days for your brothers. If we find or hear nothing, we'll go home." I saw relief wash over my son's face.

Ahead we saw smoke coming from the woods. Peter and I exchanged a glance. I stiffened my back and sat straighter in my saddle. Sam ran ahead, barking and circling back to us.

I dared not think of what we might find. More wounded men? Deserters? The Home Guard? Thieves and desperate men? My heart thumped with fear. My hand instantly felt for my pistol.

What was I doing? I was putting not only myself in danger, but Peter as well. The realization was like a bolt of lightning. It was no wonder that my husband thought I had been driven mad by grief, to have left my home, my children. I could still picture the expressions on their faces, looks of disbelief and bewilderment. I had so rarely thought of them the days I'd been gone. How could they not think I had abandoned them? My head spun with regret and confusion.

The dog ran ahead, stopped and lowered to the ground, growling. He didn't return to us. I knew he was warning us.

Peter halted his horse and murmured in a low, husky voice, "Maybe we shouldn't go on. Sam is acting strange. Should we turn around? Take another route?"

But it was too late. Emerging as ghosts from the woods, appeared a group of men. Several had their weapons drawn, aimed at us.

God help us. We could only proceed. I gulped air, nearly choking, my fear was so great. I tightened my grip on my pistol. Spirit sensed my fear and threw his head back, snorting. From the corner of my eye I watched Peter slowly let his hand fall to his gun.

Again, the look on Andrew's and my children's faces as I left them flashed before my eyes.

This was no place for a sane woman. What would my consuming grief and willfulness cost me?

CHAPTER THIRTEEN

ABIGAIL

June, 1863
Southwestern Virginia

THE GROUP OF men sprouted like poison mushrooms amidst the heaviest of woods. We approached them slowly.

My heart raced and a deafening sound filled my ears. The horses sensed fear and sidled backwards, tossing their heads. The dog stood with hackles raised between our horses. I dared not look at Peter. He mustn't know how frightened I was.

No one stepped forward. Unmoving, they stood before us like menacing scarecrows. Most were half clothed and shoeless. Behind them I could make out other men. A few lay upon mats inside rough lean-to's. They pushed up on their elbows to peer at us.

This was a harder looking lot than we had encountered earlier. I searched their faces for a glimmer of welcome or recognition. I saw none. My hand tightened on my pistol within the folds of my skirt. I'd never shot a man, a deer, yes, a fox that killed my laying hens, a rattlesnake, but if my hand was forced I knew I could kill a man. I narrowed my eyes and waited to see who would make the first move.

A familiar and uncontrollable force took over my senses

and I urged my horse forward. I knew the sensation well. It was the same reaction I had when I plunged on horseback into flooded Reed Island Creek with food for our soldiers. It made me feel invincible. No doubt that impulse was what Andrew thought of as madness. But I had found that it had served me well. He may call it what he wished, but that 'madness' had saved my life and benefited my family in many ways.

Peter moved alongside me and I could sense his tension. His knuckles were white on his reins.

"Good evening." That was all I said, and waited.

A tall man stepped forward. He walked with a limp and I wondered if there would be a man without a limp left in Virginia when the war ended. He wore mended trousers and a clean white shirt. I marveled at that, the white shirt. His beard was full and looked neatly trimmed. He removed his hat slowly, revealing an abundance of straw-colored hair. His steely gray eyes never left my face. He wasn't much older than the sons I searched for. I was shocked when a woman, dressed as a man, stepped from a tent and stood, motionless by his side. I had heard of women who followed their men into the war, usually young women in love. No doubt I would have followed Andrew into battle when we were young and so much in love. I would have fought by his side if need be.

"Ma'am?" His eyes fell on Peter, taking his measure, perhaps thinking he might be of conscription age. There was no peace for a mother of sons. I lived in fear Peter would ignore my pleas and join the army, even before conscription age. Peter was restless and eager to support his fellow Virginians on the battlefield. I took comfort in knowing Peter was now aware of what war could do to men. Perhaps now he wouldn't be so eager to enlist.

I no longer felt the need to pretend we were traveling to visit my mother. The men we encountered in the mountains didn't care about our reason for traveling. If not Home Guard, they were desperate, either escaping or deserting the army.

I'd heard there were even southern men who were turning against the Southern Cause and joining the Union.

"I am looking for my sons. They are listed as dead or missing, but no one has given me proof that they are dead. I am in search of Isaac and Asa Quesinberry. I think perhaps they might be injured or ill and hiding in these mountains. I am looking for them and...I...." I stumbled on my words, unable to fully express myself. What was I doing here? Would I want my sons to be among these walking skeletons? It was in these woods that I understood the brutal reality of war. What I saw before me were not men. They were the shells of men. I couldn't know their stories, if they were deserters, or if so, why. The truth was I had no less respect for these men than those men who continued to fight. I understood the heart of both, and if my sons were somewhere in the mountains hiding out as deserters, I would love them no less.

Peter cleared his throat and spoke over me.

"My mother is looking for my brothers. They were in Company B, 54th Virginia. She..." He turned to look at me, "cannot accept their deaths and..."

"Peter, I am here, beside you! I can speak for myself!" I did not much like his manner. How dare he interrupt me!

"It is true. I am unable to accept they are gone." I eased off my saddle and stood erect. "I am Abigail Banks Quesinberry. I was born in Floyd County. I am searching for my sons, Isaac and Asa. Yes, I grieve for them, and pray they might still be alive and have taken shelter after being wounded or falling ill." I glared at Peter who would presume to speak for me. "I will find them if I can, or their bodies, or some proof that they are gone from this earth. If any of you can help me I would be grateful."

The woman approached me. I saw pity in her eyes. She turned to the man beside her and spoke to him in a low voice. I couldn't hear her words, but the man slipped back into the group.

"Abigail, was it?" Her voice was husky, with a hard edge. Under her coarse exterior I could see she was a pretty, delicate young woman. Her brown eyes were bright, but dark smudges of fatigue encircled her eyes. She looked to be only eighteen or nineteen years old.

"Yes. Abigail Quesinberry. And what is your name?"

"Elizabeth Turner. Elizabeth Wright now." She smiled and I noticed the thin band of gold on her ring finger.

"These men are mostly deserters, Ma'am. My husband," she swallowed hard and lowered her voice, "...is a deserter. He would not have left the army had I not pleaded with him. I've seen enough of this war. This isn't our home anymore, or what's left of it." Her hands cradled her stomach. I knew well the signs of pregnancy, although the bulge under her shirt was barely visible.

"Are you from Floyd County, Elizabeth? Is your family from these parts?"

"No. No longer. They moved to West Virginia when the war started. James wouldn't go. He joined up along with his brother. I couldn't bear to be separated from him. I signed up with him. I did the cooking and laundry for his regiment. But I'm...I'm expecting a child. I want to have my baby where I have family."

"Of course, I understand. Will you go to West Virginia then?"

She nodded. "Yes, we'll leave in the next day or two."

"Elizabeth, do you think there could be anyone here who might have knowledge of the men from my sons' regiment?"

She put a hand on mine and looked into my eyes. "These men are so defeated from this war. Many have no idea which regiment they were a part of. Men are constantly shuffled around at the whim of officers. If there is a need to fill the ranks of a regiment where too many men have died...well...it is as if they are simply bodies, not men. As you can see, most are injured. They're just trying to make it home to their families.

I'm afraid some won't make it. I tend to their wounds as best I can, but James and I will move on soon."

I covered her hand with my own. It was good to talk with another woman. It seemed the men were first caught up in the glory and excitement of war, and then were either killed or wounded in body or spirit. Women were left to pick up the pieces and carry on.

"It is safe to stay here with us tonight if you want." She whispered. "You and your son will not be in danger. These men will not harm you. We all fear the Home Guard, but they aren't near us now. They've moved north to protect supplies for Lee. They won't be rounding up men to take back to the army for a while. But you must be careful if you travel further. It is becoming harder to escape the bands of thieves scavenging the countryside. I'll ask the men if they know anything of your sons. Quesinberry is not a common name. Most were in the same regiments. Which regiment were your sons in? Perhaps one of the men will know something."

"I'm not sure. They enlisted with the 54th Virginia, but I have heard many from their regiment were transferred to the 63rd Tennessee."

"I'll talk with them. It's all I can do."

"Thank you." I watched her walk back to her husband, marveling at her strength. She could have been my daughter. I smiled to myself and wondered if any of my girls would have her courage.

Peter, who had been crouching beside his horse, peered up at me when I approached and jumped to his feet. "Are we moving on then?"

"We'll spend the night here, Peter, and leave in the morning. One of these men might have news of your brothers." I said this with conviction, but in truth, I was losing heart.

"I would prefer to move on, Mother. We needn't spend the night with this group. Some appear to be suffering from disease and fever. I don't want to become ill, or for you to catch a fever. We are finding nothing of interest about Isaac or Asa. It is time we go home." He said this as a challenge, staring directly in my eyes.

"Nothing of interest? What an odd choice of words, Peter. And yet you wish to enlist in the very war they are trying to escape?" I turned to unsaddle my horse. "You set up the tent. I'll find something we might share for supper with these men, and woman."

He turned away abruptly, muttering words I couldn't make out. There was no doubt in my mind his words were meant to insult me. He had lost patience with my mission, which had clearly become only an irritating obligation to him.

He was tired of my company, and I with his. We were now in a struggle of wills and I was unsure which of us was stronger.

CHAPTER FOURTEEN

ABIGAIL

June, 1863
Southwestern Virginia

"MOTHER."

My eyes flew open. Bolting upright from my pallet, I instinctively reached for my gun.

"Mother, it's Peter."

Oh. It was Peter. I closed my eyes and breathed deeply to
calm the blood that had rushed to my head.

"What? What is it?"

"It's that woman. Elizabeth. She's leaving with her husband and wants to talk to you. She said it's important."

Outside the tent opening, I could see a hazy pink-purple
glow at the horizon. The sun had not yet risen.

"Where is she?" There was a chill in the air and I pulled
my shawl around my shoulders. Mornings were cool in the
mountains. Dense trees held the night air close to the earth
and released it in what seemed a single breath mid-day.

Peter helped me to my feet and gestured with his chin toward the tent opening.

"She's just outside. Her husband is waiting to leave."

I hastily ran fingers through my hair and wrapped the

waist length tangle into a bun atop my head.

"Roll up the pallets, Son, and saddle the horses. We'll get an early start today."

He nodded and ducked out before me. I heard him mutter. "She's coming. I hope this won't take long."

Elizabeth was barely visible. My eyes adjusted to the dim light and I saw she was still dressed as a man. She nervously twisted a hat in her hands.

"Good morning, Elizabeth. You are leaving then?"

"Yes. I hope John and I will be with my family tonight. Let's sit for a moment, Abigail. I need to talk to you."

Her manner was somber and I feared bad news. My instinct was to reject it outright, as if in doing so, I might control the outcome.

"Is it about my sons? Is it about Asa or Isaac?"

"I don't know. It might be. John spoke with the men last night. There is one among them who said he wished to speak with you. His name is James Kirby. It may be nothing, Abigail, but these men don't share their stories with ease. Most don't want to speak about the war. They want to talk of other things, family, home and farming. But I wanted to let you know before we left. It's up to you if you want to speak with him." Her cool, callused hand covered mine, as if trying to protect me. "You don't have to speak to him, Abigail."

I placed my other hand over hers. "Thank you, Elizabeth. If he wants to speak with me, then I must listen. That is why I am here, isn't it, to learn of any news of my sons? Please, tell me his name again."

"James Kirby. He'll find you Abigail."

She walked toward her husband, stopped, and then quickly walked back to me. "We must leave now, Abigail. I pray you find peace in your journey."

We embraced and I could feel the taut swelling of her stomach, a new life. I felt a tug at my womb. Elizabeth had yet to know the sudden and profoundly strong bond a new mother felt for her newborn.

"Good luck to you and John, and your baby. I wish you well." Unwanted tears came to my eyes and I dashed them away. "God speed, Elizabeth."

Her sweet smile and kind eyes shimmered in front of me for a moment. Then she turned and mounted her horse beside her husband. I smiled and waved a hand.

I found Peter prepared to move on, the tent and pallets rolled neatly, the horses saddled. I knew I would disappoint him when I told him we must wait a while longer.

"We have to stay until the men are up and about, Peter. One of them wishes to speak with me."

His shoulders slumped and irritation contorted his face. "Oh, Mother. What is it you really want to hear? Will you accept it if someone tells you they know for certain Isaac and Asa are dead?" He lowered his head but I heard him mumble. "I think not. I think you will never accept their deaths. But I will, and I will not go on searching. It's foolish."

I was determined not to lose my temper with him and tried to remain calm.

"I must speak to him, Son. Surely you understand." I reached for his hand, but he abruptly turned away.

"I'll make a fire then. Make breakfast. If we have any food left. You are so quick to share what we have with everyone." There was bitterness in his voice. His attitude annoyed me, and my anger flared. I forgot his youth and spoke harshly.

"Yes, Peter. We have enough to share, and you should be grateful. Whatever we have, it is more than these men have eaten in weeks."

His look of disdain cut to my core. We had been too long together. Peter acted now as if he were my guardian. It was not a feeling I was accustomed to. Nor did I like it.

With the smell of our fire and salt pork, men begin to stir. I guessed sleep must be a luxury for them, as well as an escape from reality.

A man approached me cautiously. He was painfully thin. His left arm was in a sling of some type. No, he had no arm, it ended at his elbow. I swallowed hard and prepared for what was to come.

"Ma'am? Mrs. Quesinberry?"

"Yes. I am Mrs. Quesinberry."

He nodded and sat down beside me where I sat on a rough log.

We were silent for what seemed a very long time. His thin, worn boots jiggled nervously.

I knew I must drag from him words I might not wish to hear.

"Did you know my sons? Did you know Asa or Isaac?"

He stared at his right hand which dangled between his knees.

Slowly, he lifted his eyes to mine. They were shadowed with sorrow and pity. "Yes, Ma'am."

The heaviness of his spirit was such that I steeled myself for his words.

He reached into his pocket and pulled out a stained cloth. At first, I thought he meant to blow his nose or wipe his mouth. Then I saw that it was folded flat on his palm. He handed it to me.

I opened it slowly, spreading it across my lap. There were the letters, 'ARQ'. Asa Richard Quesinberry. Letters I embroidered on that handkerchief. My hands trembled. My heart thumped in my chest as I struggled to catch my breath.

"Where did you find this?"

"It was given to me. By your son, Asa."

A pain throbbed in my temple. I took several deep breaths. Waves of terror were building in me. The stain? Was it blood?

Out of nowhere a senseless thought filled my head. How would I get the stain out? Perhaps vinegar and salt rubbed into the cloth...left in the sun for hours? I swayed, and he put his hand on my back.

"Ma'am. Are you all right?"

"Yes. I'm sorry. Are these blood stains?" I stared at the handkerchief still open on my lap.

"Yes, Ma'am."

"Is it Asa's blood?" My chest heaved...my heart felt too large for my chest. My arms hung limply at my sides. I was afraid to touch the handkerchief, it was like a coiled snake, ready to strike.

"No. It is my own."

Relief flooded through me, but I was suddenly exhausted and weak.

"How did you get his handkerchief?"

"I was on the train that carried wounded and ill men from Suffolk to the hospital in Petersburg. Asa and I were together, and became friends, if such a thing is possible among men in pain and agony. The trip took several days. My left arm was infected. Your son gave me one of his handkerchiefs to bind it."

"Then he is alive? He's still in the hospital at Petersburg?"

"No, Ma'am. He is not."

"But how do you know. You are here." I was unable to stop trembling.

"My arm was amputated. There was no choice. When I was well enough, I was released to come home and recover. I went to see Asa before I left, to see how he fared and to thank him. He was no longer in his cot. There was another...."

"Then, where is he? Was he released, his wounds healed?"

My questions came like snatches of empty air. As though I was trying to hold on to vapor.

"He had no wounds Ma'am. When we were transferred to the 63rd Tennessee, we were sent down around Suffolk. He died of the fever that was so bad. There were many, many hundreds..."

"Stop! Please, stop!" He recoiled, and I realized I was screaming.

"I'm sorry, Ma'am. I thought you would rather know. I am so very sorry." He struggled to his feet.

"No. I'm sorry. Please. Sit. I do want to know. Tell me all you know of my son."

Wearily, he sat down.

"How do you know all this?"

"I was in the same regiment as Asa. We were dispatched together to Suffolk. Asa was in a scouting party sent into the Great Swamp. There were many who got the fever and died. Your son...." He looked stricken and I knew in my heart what was to come. "Asa died. I survived, the fever and my wound. Thank God."

"You mean my son died of a fever? He had no wounds?"

"No, Ma'am, he had no wounds. He died of the fever. He was one of many."

"Were you there with him, when he died? Did he mention his brother, Isaac?"

"No, Ma'am, he never mentioned him by name. He spoke only of his family while we were on the train, and how much he missed all of you and his home. His fever was bad. Some of what he said I couldn't understand. I never saw him again after we got to the hospital. Those with fever were separated from the rest of us."

"Then how can you be sure he died if you were not with him?"

"I wanted to thank him for giving me, well, that handkerchief there. To return it." He gestured with his chin toward my lap. "When I went to say goodbye, the doctor told me he had died. I'm sorry, Ma'am."

It was unimaginable to me that my strong young son died, not of wounds from battle, but of a fever. I recalled the nights

I had spent when he was a child, nursing him from fever. He was always quick to recover. Oh, my Asa. If only I could have helped you. You would not have died. I would not have let you die. I wrapped my arms around my stomach and rocked. It was painful and so hard to bear the thought of Asa suffering so.

"Ma'am? Should I call your son?"

"No. Thank you, James. I will be fine. It is such a shock."

"Yes, Ma'am. I am sorry to bring you such bad news." He stood to leave.

"James. I thank you. Have you any idea where my son was buried?"

"No, Ma'am."

I smiled and nodded. My eyes closed in prayer. I knew, my Asa was no longer upon this earth. The knowledge of his death came as a terrible tragedy and a terrible relief.

I folded the handkerchief with care. With love. Perhaps one day his children might want it.

My thoughts turned to Isaac. Oh, God, why could I not be at peace? How could I go on searching? I was tired and so burdened with sadness. My heart was broken and my spirit shattered.

I sat for some time with my eyes closed. Memories of Asa as a baby and a little boy flashed through my mind. That was all I had left of him. There was nothing else. I shook my head and reminded myself that Asa had a wife and children. We had yet to tell them of his death. I would not let Andrew tell them, because I couldn't accept it. Asa's blood flowed in those babies. I took some comfort in that thought. I'd found out how Asa died, and even though I didn't know where he was buried, it had brought me some consolation.

If Asa had fever, might Isaac have become ill with it also? Perhaps I could find Isaac, or some word of him. He might still be in hospital, or recovering. I knew in my heart, I was grasping at straw. But I would not give up. If there was any chance I might find word of Isaac's fate I knew I would seek it.

Peter would demand we return home now that we had proof of Asa's death. I was certain I would have a battle with him. But I felt already a surge of fierce determination rising. With or without Peter. I would search for Isaac.

CHAPTER FIFTEEN

ABIGAIL

June, 1863
Southwestern Virginia

I FEARED THE confrontation I would have with Peter when I told him the story of how Asa died. I was afraid he would insist, no demand, that we return home. He may have been right to question me for what probably seemed to him a lack of concern for Oliver and the rest of my children. I love Oliver, as I love all my children, but I could understand how they must think I cared less for them than Isaac and Asa. It wasn't true, yet I couldn't let go of the slightest chance that Isaac might be alive, and return home. No matter that I had evidence of Asa's death...I was not willing to give up on Isaac. I felt as though Isaac and Asa were watching and judging me.

For some reason I felt more at peace while I searched for my sons. Perhaps it was the tranquility I had always felt in the woods. As a child I always ran off into the mountains when I needed solace. My mother would say that I was aloof and callous. In truth, I felt things so deeply that I could only find peace when I was alone. Alone, as I was now, as I might be again. Did I need to escape Andrew and my children to properly grieve for my sons?

Peter had grown more and more impatient with me. His manner verged on disrespect. I recalled how I had felt exasperation with my own mother. Her passive and compliant nature annoyed me. That was most likely why I tried so hard to be different from her. How I must have hurt her. It was my son now who looked upon me in such a manner. It was my obstinate nature that irritated him. Thinking of my mother, who passed long ago, I regretted that I had treated her so heartlessly.

Peter stood alert by the horses he saddled earlier. When he saw me approach there was no expression on his face. Only a challenge in his eyes.

"I have to talk to you, Son."

He quickly mounted his horse and stared down at me. "We can talk as we ride. If we leave soon we can be home tomorrow."

"Peter, I can't leave yet. Please. Let us sit for a moment and talk. I have news of Asa."

I could see it in his eyes. He knew the truth already. He sighed deeply and slid off his horse to the ground. "He is dead, isn't he, Mother. Isaac is dead too. You must accept it." He extended his hand as if to touch mine, then quickly withdrew it.

For the first time in a long while I saw compassion on his face. He spread a blanket on the ground and sat with his head bowed. He slowly removed his hat and raised his head; his eyes searched my face.

At that moment I knew I must choose to return home with Peter or continue to search for news of Isaac on my own.

"Don't you want to know how your brother died, Peter?"

He said nothing. His fingers worked around the brim of his hat. The heels of his boots dug impatiently into the soft blanket. The silence grew between us, as did my anxiety.

"No, Mother. I do not. Asa is gone. Isaac is gone. Dwelling on the details of how they died only makes it harder."

"But Asa was your brother. How can you not care how he

died? Will you not miss him? Did you not love your brother?"

"I might ask you the same question, Mother." He turned to me in anger, his face red, eyes flashing. "Am I not your son also? Do you not have other children? A baby, even? A husband? Yet, all you can think about is Asa and Isaac. You never speak of Oliver. He is fighting in this war too. Did you always love Asa and Isaac more than the rest of us?"

I recoiled as he pushed his face close to mine. His anger and resentment were palpable and I felt as if he had slapped me.

"Son. Son...please..." I pleaded. My head and heart were reeling from his outburst. A vein throbbed in my temple. "No. No. How can you think that? Of course, I love you. I love all my children."

He jumped to his feet. "Then why don't you act like it? You've been away from your home and children for almost three weeks. They are all grieving too and you have not once mentioned them, or Father. What kind of woman does that?"

I had no answer. Tears filled my eyes and I turned away and looked into the distance. The silence was louder than ever words had been. My heart felt as if it might explode. I had never felt such anger directed at me from a child of mine. I struggled to gain control of my emotions, my chest heaving with the effort. I was overwhelmed at the response of my son and I knew not how to react. I stood on wobbly legs and faced him.

"Leave me, Peter. I wish to be alone."

"Is that what you want then, Mother? To be alone? You needn't have gone to such measures as dragging off into the mountains if all you needed was to be alone."

"Peter, you can't understand. One day when you have children, perhaps you will. It is not in God's plan that a child should die before his parents. Especially fully grown, strong young men. Your brothers will never know their children, their grandchildren. They are...."

"Dead, Mother! They are dead. But I am alive, here in front of you. And my brothers and sisters are alive and in need of you. I am done with this. I'm going home, I miss my brothers and sisters even if you do not."

My hand seemed not to be attached to my body. I slapped him with a strength I didn't know I had. It happened without my knowing. He stared at me in disbelief, his hand raised.

"This is your choice, Mother. I'm leaving. Are you coming with me or not?"

"No, Peter, I am not. Tell your sisters and brothers I love them. And your father."

Before I could recover he was on his horse and riding off into the woods.

I whispered the words to myself.

"I love you, Peter. Don't leave. I love you."

CHAPTER SIXTEEN

ABIGAIL

June, 1863
Southwestern Virginia

MY EYES FOLLOWED Peter until he was no longer visible, my heart begging him to turn around. He was swallowed by the deep woods, then silence surrounded me, and I was alone. The stillness calmed me. I lay back on the blanket and watched sunlight flickering in the leaves above me. It did feel as if that was what I wanted all along, to be alone with the pain and sadness that any mother would know when a child died before her. I closed my eyes and summoned the spirit of Isaac and Asa. I could almost imagine them sitting on either side of me. Sobs racked my body as I gave into the full realization they were gone. Gone forever. Alone, I gave way to the anguish I had held back until then.

Perhaps I did love Isaac and Asa more than my other children. They were the first and second born. Isaac, born of such pain I did not think I could bear it. In the midst of a long labor I screamed at Andrew as he waited outside the bedroom door. "You will never touch me again, Andrew. Do you hear me! Never!"

My mother wiped my brow and said, "Stop now, Abigail.

You are not the first woman to bear this pain. Are you not the woman I thought you were...that Andrew thought you were?" Her comment made me grit my teeth and endure the rest of labor in near silence. When I held Isaac in my arms, his eyes intently searched my face and my heart melted. Then there was Andrew bursting into the room with a smile so wide that I could only laugh.

"My boy..." he bellowed. "...I knew it. We have a son! I am so proud of you Abigail."

I was so in love with Andrew. His joy made my heart swell with pride. And Isaac was such an easy baby. His every move and word became a celebration to us.

After Oliver, there was a blank. I remembered the births, but few other details of their infancy and early childhood. I was overwhelmed with sadness at the realization. I loved all my children equally, but Peter was right. How would they know it?

How could I have left them with so little explanation? What must they have thought as they watched their mother ride away from them? I was short tempered and callous in my treatment of them in the weeks before I left. I could still picture Jane holding baby Sara in her arms, the baby reaching out for me. I recalled the look of confusion and apprehension on their faces. I felt ashamed to have left them so. I hoped they would forgive me. In that moment I knew I would not continue to search for Isaac. I had failed in my duty to my other children, and Andrew. I had to return home the next day. My heart felt lighter at the thought.

There were now long shadows in the woods where Peter had disappeared. It was fast becoming dark. The horse had wandered a good distance from me, munching on lush green grass. He raised his head when he saw my movement and followed me as I gathered wood for a fire.

It was perfectly quiet and I felt a familiar sense of peace settle over me. I heard only the soft sound of leaves moving in the breeze. It lifted the tendrils of hair that had fallen from my bun. I startled when I heard a sound in the woods...the snap of a twig. My eyes narrowed and my heart raced. I reached for my pistol. I leaned into the horse, grateful he was between me and the woods. Spirit wasn't spooked, and after a few minutes my heart calmed and I smiled at my alarm. It was most likely nothing but a small animal, perhaps a deer or fox. My heart slowed and I moved to the edge of the woods to make camp for the night. It was warm and I didn't really need a fire, but I made it for comfort. The nearly full moon outlined the trees and leaves in silver.

I prayed for my family. I prayed for Peter, that he would make it home safely, and that if he must join the war, that he survived. I prayed for Oliver, alone in the midst of battle, grieving for his brothers. I wished I could put my arms around his slight frame and console him.

Now that I had decided to return home, my heart was at ease. My eyes closed and finally I slept.

I was awakened by the sound of the horse blowing. I could make out a low masculine voice murmuring. "Shush, quiet now." My hand was already on my gun as I waited for my eyes to adjust to the dark. Slowly I crawled to the tent opening and peered out. In the moonlight I could see the outline of a man. I wasn't fully awake, but it was obvious he was attempting to untie my horse. Spirit resisted and tossed his head. The man didn't look toward the tent, so intent was he on taking my horse.

I raised up on my elbows and aimed my gun at his leg. I had no way of knowing who the man was. He might have been a Confederate soldier, a deserter, and I wouldn't wish to kill one of our own. If I maimed him, I could stop him. Carefully I aimed for his calf and shot. He doubled over, screaming in pain, grabbing his calf, exactly where I aimed.

I stood swiftly and left the tent, approaching the man slowly, my pistol aimed at the head of the intruder. "What are you doing? Trying to steal my horse?"

He moaned, writhing in pain.

I stood over him and waited. He was young, and wore the remnants of a blue uniform. A Yankee!

"I said, what were you doing?" Now that I knew he was a Union soldier I had no concern for his pain, or his feelings.

"Help me, please. You put a bullet in my leg!"

"Help you? You were stealing my horse! Are you armed?"

He shook his head. "No, Ma'am. No. Please help me."

"You would have taken my horse and left a woman alone in the mountains? And now you want my help? Why should I help you? You're a Union soldier!"

"I'm only trying to get home, Ma'am. I thought to borrow your horse to get there faster. My mother is very ill and alone. I'm her only child." There was enough moonlight that I could see care worn creases around his young eyes. "I'm sorry, Lady. I would never have hurt you." He had a soft lilt to his speech, unlike the clipped manner I was accustomed to. "My mother needs me. I wish only to go home to see her and make certain she is cared for."

Against my will something softened in my heart. There was a sincerity in his voice that touched me. He was perhaps only a year older than Peter. "Where is your home?"

"New York. I'm with the Sixty-ninth Regiment. I mean...I was. It's called the Irish Brigade. I'm not deserting, and I am not a coward! I fought at Fredericksburg and Chancellorsville. I'll rejoin my regiment after I see to my mother. Please, Lady. I am sorry. I just wanted your horse." He grimaced and touched his leg. "I'm in pain. Can you help me?"

"Just my horse?" I almost laughed. "That would be akin to taking my weapon." I'd heard the Northern soldiers knew little of horses or of their value to a Southerner.

"I would never think a lady had a gun, Ma'am, and I didn't know who owned the horse. I just wanted..." He let out a groan. "Ma'am, please, will you help me?"

"Well, stop howling. Let me take a look." I kneeled down to examine his leg. He scuttled away when I took out my knife. "You'll have to let me cut your trousers if I am to help you." He leaned back against a tree and extended his leg. The bullet was not lodged in his leg. I had grazed the outside of his calf. It was bleeding, but otherwise the wound was not life-threatening.

"What is your name?" I asked, gathering what I needed from my saddlebag.

"Daniel. Daniel Murphy." He looked longingly at the whiskey flask. "What have you got there, Ma'am?"

"Whiskey to pour over that wound. My name is Abigail Quesinberry. Mrs. Quesinberry. I live here, in Virginia. I meant only to stop you from stealing my horse and prevent you from attacking me. I had no intention of killing you." I caught hold of his eyes with mine. "I could have, if I wanted to."

"I would never attack a woman. Do you think all Northerners are savages? Please, let me have a drink of that. I am so thirsty." He recoiled as I examined his leg again. "My leg is bleeding. Is it is ruined, my leg?"

"No, it is not ruined. I'm a good shot. The bullet only grazed your calf. Your leg will heal. It's a bad wound, but you will not be crippled." His face contorted as I poured whiskey on his wound. I handed the flask to him and he eagerly drank the rest. I tore a long strip of cloth from my petticoat to bind his leg.

"Thank you." He handed the flask back to me. "I've had neither food nor drink for two days."

We sat in silence, taking the measure of one another. He looked young and frightened. His eyes roamed from my face to the woods, as if he was thinking to run away. I watched as he carefully extended his leg and flexed his foot.

"I guess my leg is not so bad after all. I expect I could make it to New York in a couple of weeks." He tried to stand but couldn't do so on his own, and fell back against the tree.

"I don't think you'll be able to get far with that leg, Son." The word was out of my mouth before I knew it. Gone was the fear or hatred I might have felt for this young man. A man who might have killed my own sons. He was simply a boy to me, no longer an enemy. He shivered, a reaction to the wound and lack of food and sleep. I had no idea why or how I would help him, but I knew I would.

"Here, eat this." I gave him a slice of the dried beef. He lifted his eyes to mine and we exchanged a look of understanding and bewilderment.

"Thank you, Ma'am. I never expected a Southerner to help me."

"Did you think all Southerners were savages?" He focused on the ground when I repeated the word he used. "Three of my sons are—were—fighting in this war. I left my family in search of two of them. I thought I might find them alive or find their bodies. But they're gone. They are dead and I will never know where they are buried." When I said this aloud, to a stranger, tears streamed down my face. "You see, I know the pain and worry your mother suffers. I know how she must fear for your life. It is the same for all mothers of sons in this war. We are helpless. I pray another mother would help my boys."

"I am sorry you have lost your sons, Ma'am. I lost a number of friends at Chancellorsville. It was a terrible thing to watch them die. I could do nothing to help them. Somehow, I was spared."

His eyes gazed at me with compassion. I tried to resist the sympathy I felt growing in my heart. He was not my enemy, nor was I his.

Dear God, I prayed, let this end. Let us have peace again and be free of this heartache.

"I have an extra blanket. It was my son's. He left without it. You rest. We'll talk in the morning."

I lay down and stared up at the sky, sleepless. What was I doing? I prayed he would be gone when I awoke.

The old Quesinberry farmhouse. Built in 1858

Fields surrounding the farmhouse

All that remains of the cottage by the creek.

Creek in front of cottage

on the death of my dear Brothers who died May
in May 1863

My life is like a drooping flower
that once was fresh and gay
now smote by grief's heart crushing power
is fading fast away
my brothers now since thou art gone
oh what is life to me
my aching heart now sad and lone
must constant weep for thee
led by their patriotic hearts
while in their twenty-fourth and sixth year
from kindred home and friends to part
a soldiers fate to share
Tis for my country's weal said they
that we obey her call
dear Sisters do not grieve for us
if in her cause we fall
but when the trying hour drew nigh
to bid them quickly go
They heaved a sad lugubrious sigh
and tears began to flow
with quivering lips and tearful eye
and grief never felt before

Oliver's original poem. Folded and found in his father Andrews wallet at the end of his life

us for my country's weal said the
That we obey her call
Dear sisters do not grieve for us
if in her cause we fall
but when the trying hour drew nigh
To bid them quickly go
They heaved a sad lugubrious sigh
and tears began to flow
With quivering lips and tearful eye
and grief never felt before

Close up of Oliver's poem

Andrew and Abigail Quesinberry. In the latter years of their lives

Abigail's sidesaddle
(Photograph taken at the Carroll County Historical Society and
Museum in Hillsville, Virginia.)

CHAPTER SEVENTEEN

PETER

June, 1863
Southwestern Virginia

I DARED NOT look back to where I had left my mother. I felt her eyes on my back as I rode away. If I had turned around I knew I would have gone back to her. Although I was shocked at the blow she struck to my face, and my pride, I feared for her safety. She was so stubborn and independent. I wondered at times if Father still loved her spirited nature which drew him to her when first they met and married. We, her children, learned early to respect and fear her temper. Even so, I do think that I was the first of her children she had physically harmed. In my heart I knew I deserved it. Mother had been the solid heart of our family—always. I knew she loved her family more than her own life.

She and my father had often said I was most like her. I paid little attention to the comparison, but now, after the tense weeks spent together, I realized we were very much alike. We grated on each other's nerves when under such stressful circumstances.

It might be that I too, as Mother did, needed time to be alone with my thoughts and fears. I was not prepared for the harsh realities our search had shown me. Never would I have imagined our brave, courageous soldiers would be in such a destitute state as we found them. We saw so many defeated and wounded men, both in body and spirit. Did Isaac and Asa suffer so, and Oliver even now? The thought of my brothers in such wretched conditions created a deep ache inside me. Surely all our soldiers were not in such pitiful shape, even though, most men we encountered spoke of the lack of food, clothing and basic supplies. I had thought to lie about my age and join the battle before I turned eighteen, but no longer. I would turn eighteen soon enough and then I would have no choice.

I would never have known this side of war had I not accompanied Mother. How hotheaded I was, to be in such a rush to join the war. I felt as if I had aged ten years in the last three weeks. I no longer felt certain of the validity of this war, and I was no longer certain that Virginia would survive...at least not as I knew it.

It was my family's long and fierce love of Virginia that weighed on me now. How could our life ever be the same? Our farms and families were impoverished, fathers and sons gone. It would all seem a bad dream had I not seen the reality of the condition of our soldiers for myself. I had imagined them a strong army of brave soldiers. But it was not a bad dream. This war would leave not only Virginia divided, rich from poor, east from west, but our whole country. It had already divided my family. Had I not just left my own mother alone and grieving?

I stopped my horse and called the dog to my side. The angry exchange with Mother had taken a toll on my emotions and I felt an urgent need to rest. I spread my pallet and looked up at the sky. It was too early yet to sleep. The sun brushed the tops of mountains in gold before it would set in a few hours. There was such a weight on my heart. What little hope I had held that my brothers might be alive was gone. It was then, alone, that I wept. They were my heroes...my older brothers, Isaac, Asa and Oliver, already tall and strong when I was but a boy. They taught me to handle a gun, to fish and to hunt.

I was like my mother in my grief. I could not let her know how devastated I was when I knew Asa was truly dead. I needed to be alone. As night fell, I stared up at the stars and moon. I knew Isaac and Asa would never again feel the glory of an early summer evening. The softness of the cool night air that soothed and made all dreams seem possible, they would never know again. My heart was broken. Yet, no one would ever know how much I loved my brothers, except Mother.

I fell asleep knowing that with the first light of morning, I would go back to her.

I awoke with a start before first light. Sam was tugging on my jacket. He seemed to know I had decided to go back to my mother and was in a hurry to be on our way.

"What, Sam! What is it?" He stared at me as he crouched down on his front legs, then sprang up again. It had turned cooler and my clothes were damp. I never thought to ask my mother for my blanket. I was so angry when I left her, I only thought to get away from her. But I was glad she had the tent and blankets. At least she would have that comfort as she grieved alone for my brothers. Perhaps that was all she needed to help heal the loss of Isaac and Asa, to be alone for a while. My own heart had softened overnight. I missed my mother and hoped her thoughts were now on our home and how she was needed there.

Father must have struggled to plant the crops, with only my younger sisters to help, who were now also responsible for the cooking, cleaning and care of the younger children.

I pulled my jacket tight around my neck and my hat down over my face. Sam nudged me again, more insistently.

"Stop it, Sam! Down! Just give me a few minutes of peace!" I pulled him down beside me. Still, he would not settle. "What is it, Sam? What do you want?" He lowered his head and turned away from me, looking back the way we came yesterday.

I knew he sensed something that only a dog might know. I searched the sky. There was a slight cloud cover, but the moon was nearly full and gave off a shadowy light. It was early, perhaps four? A sudden fear gripped my stomach. Was Mother in danger? Was that what Sam was trying to tell me?

My stomach grumbled as I roused myself and prepared to go back to find her. Mother would have had a fire going and water boiling for hot coffee. Not real coffee. We'd all forgotten what that tasted like. We had just a mash of chicory. But it was hot, and somehow Mother made it taste comforting, adding just a precious pinch of sugar. Father would be furious if he knew I had left her alone. With the dawning of a new day I felt ashamed. Shame that I could not control my temper, and for leaving Mother.

I saddled my horse and urged him to a gallop. I knew Mother wasn't one to waste time and I felt an urgent need to get to her as quickly as possible. If she had decided to return to the farm overnight, she wouldn't linger. I estimated I traveled about three hours last evening before stopping for the night. Dear God, I prayed, let her be safe.

I understood now why she was so adamant that I not join the Army. I wanted to tell her I wouldn't volunteer. That would make her happy. I could not avoid conscription, but I no longer wanted to join the battle for the glory of it. I would do my duty when the time came, but my eyes were now open. My illusion of the honor of battle was gone and my thoughts of camaraderie and brotherhood shattered.

Sam ran ahead of me. Dashing in front and running back, trying to hurry me. He sprinted ahead and I pushed my horse to a run. In the pit of my stomach I sensed something was wrong. Then I reminded myself that Mother knew the mountains better than I did. She was probably a better shot than I as well. I breathed easier. I hoped to find her by the fire having a cup of coffee, ready to return home with me.

In a little over two hours, I reached the place where I had left Mother. Sam led the way without hesitation, running as fast as possible.

I stared in disbelief. She was gone. My heart raced and my stomach twisted. Sam ran from one spot to another, sniffing and pawing the ground. There were the remnants of a fire, but my mother was gone.

I eased from my saddle and stood on trembling legs. Sam was barking and shaking what appeared to be a dirty white cloth. Sam brought the cloth to me. I recognized it as part of Mother's petticoat, stained with what looked like blood. There were several pieces half burned in the fire-pit.

Oh God, what had happened here? What had happened to Mother?

"Mother! Mother!" I turned around and round, searching in every direction and shouting louder, hoping she might hear me and respond.

"Mother! Mother!

There was only silence

CHAPTER EIGHTEEN

ABIGAIL

July 1, 1863
Quesinberry Farmhouse
Dugspur, Virginia

LOOKING DOWN ON my home from the wooded knoll above, everything appeared normal, as if there was no war, and we had not lost sons and brothers and knew not where to find their bodies. It was late morning. Laundry hung from the line and smoke drifted from the chimney to the overcast sky. I could see Andrew at work in the field with Jane and Polly. The other children were chasing and playing around the house. I swallowed the lump in my throat as I watched Mary settle on the tree swing with Sara in her arms, gently pushing back and forth.

I imagined Oliver there, in the barn where he often went to read and write, and Isaac and Asa, off with the wagon, in town for supplies. I envisioned Peter, begrudgingly helping Andrew weed a row of beans. I wanted my home to be as it had been before the war. Life had not been perfect, but we were a close and loving family, despite the headstrong temperaments that often made for heated exchanges.

Was Peter down there, or had he gone off to join the army

after our angry parting?

My eyes filled with tears. The love I felt for my family was so great I was overcome with its power. It took all my strength to wait before I rushed to them and begged forgiveness for leaving them in a time of mourning.

I jumped when I heard Daniel ask, "Is that your family? You have so many children."

I was abruptly brought back to reality as I turned to look at the young man with me. He was the enemy and he was with me. I had brought him to my home. He leaned on a crutch we had fashioned from a branch. I turned away quickly and tied the horse to a tree. Spirit sensed home and would have galloped away toward the barn and hay in an instant.

"Yes, it is my family. Although I don't have as many children as I once had." My words sounded bitter, meant to sting. I couldn't believe I had left my home in search of two sons and returned with a man who might have killed them. I covered my face with my hands and breathed deeply. It was hard to think what I should do next. I knew that before I faced my family, I had to understand what I was doing. How could I ever explain it? I spread a blanket and asked Daniel to sit with me.

"Please, Daniel, we have to talk."

Hobbling over, he lowered cautiously to the ground. He took a handful of soil and let it sift through his fingers. "This is rich soil here. Good farmland."

"Yes, it is. Our families, mine and my husband's, have lived here for over a hundred years. We are farmers, as you can see. That is the reason our ancestors settled here, the farmland."

He was quiet and slowly shook his head in amazement. "A hundred years? I have only been in this country for ten. My mother came from Ireland when I was eight years old. There was an awful famine there. She came to America alone after my father died. She's a maid now and takes in laundry and sewing, that is before she became ill. She said in her letters that her illness is nothing, but I fear for her. I know she doesn't want to worry me, but there is no one to help her. I...." He looked away and reached inside the breast pocket of his jacket. "This is a picture of my mother." He held out a wrinkled photograph.

We had spoken little as we made our way to the farm. My mind was busy trying to think what I should do about Daniel. One moment, I was certain I should tell Andrew about Daniel and let him decide what must be done. The next, I wanted to be finished with Daniel and let him make his own way home. I wanted to be done with the responsibility for him.

"I had it taken in New York before I joined the army."

I refused to look at the photograph. I had already endangered myself and my family with my sympathy for Daniel. I didn't want to look at his mother's face.

"Did you volunteer for the army? Did your mother approve?"

He shook his head, "No, I did not volunteer."

"You didn't volunteer? Then why are you fighting?"

"I might have eventually volunteered. I was working as a street paver. I wasn't making a lot of money, but it helped. There was fierce competition for every available job in New York. I wanted to stay with my mother as long as I could. Then one day I was approached by a man who offered to pay me four hundred dollars to fight for his son. That was a fortune to me! He was a wealthy man, a shipper. He owned a large building where he stored cotton he shipped to England."

I looked at him quizzically. "You were paid to fight?"

"Yes. Wealthy men are allowed to pay someone to serve for them. The government calls it the Enrollment Act. Many German and Irish immigrants were approached as soon as they got off their boats. They were eager to take that money. I was eager to take the money. It was more than we could expect to make in a year. I thought with that money Mother could stop working as a maid. Perhaps we might be able to leave the city, buy a small farm in the country. I didn't know how long this war would last. We all thought just a short time. I hope I will live until I can take my mother from the hovel we live in."

I stared into the woods, my mind and heart filled with sorrow at how many young men were lost to this war.

Daniel still held the photograph in his hand. My instinct was not to look at it. Now I was home, I had a strong desire to be rid of Daniel altogether. I wanted only to be with my husband and children. I didn't need this young man to further complicate my life. But his voice was so soft and loving I could not help but do one last kindness before I left him.

I took the photograph and gazed at the image of a woman who looked very much like me. Her hair was in a bun. Large expressive eyes stared directly at the camera. She looked lovingly at the camera, as though she was looking at her son. I could see the resemblance to Daniel. I was overcome with pity for her. She probably knew as little as I did of why our sons had to fight a war.

I cleared my throat and willed away my tears. "This is what we must do, Daniel. First, you must promise to stay hidden. No one can know you are here. Do you understand? I'll find a way to bring clothes and whatever food we can spare. I'll leave the tent. Use it only if you must. When you are able you will have to leave, on your own. There is nothing more I can do for you. I shouldn't help you at all. I am putting both of us in danger by doing so."

"Yes, Ma'am, I understand. You have helped me more than I would have expected. I thank you." He reached for my hand, but I pulled it away. "I am so sorry for your loss, Ma'am. Truly I am."

"I'll be back tomorrow, if I can. If not tomorrow, the next day. I'll leave what little food I have with you now and bring a change of clothes as soon as possible. Do you understand that you must stay here? If you show yourself in that blue uniform, I needn't tell you what might happen. My own husband would shoot you."

"Yes, I understand. I'll be here. Thank you. Thank you, Ma'am."

I patted his hand as it seemed I had no choice. I could not bring myself to hate him.

I led Spirit slowly down the hill to the farm. I needed the time to gather my thoughts. I wanted to go slowly and give the children and Andrew time to know it was their wife and mother returning. The dogs ran toward me barking, alerting Andrew and the children. Andrew raised his head and stood erect from his work, as did Polly and Jane. No one ran to greet me. It was as if they saw a stranger or a ghost. When I got closer the little ones ran to meet me yelling, "Mama, Mama!" I kneeled and scooped Mary and Sara into my arms, closing my eyes and breathing in the scent of childhood, a fresh out-door scent that brought sudden tears to my eyes. I reveled in the strength of their firm young limbs. Preston and William ran toward the field shouting, "It's Mama! She's back! Look, Daddy, it's Mama!"

Here was my family, but for Isaac, Asa and Oliver—and Peter? I did not see him.

Andrew wiped his hands on his pants and rushed toward me. Suddenly, I was in his arms. I melted into him, feeling his solid embrace, smelling the good soil that clung to his clothes. I told myself to be strong. I couldn't fall to weeping as they watched. This was my family and I had to keep them strong. Jane and Polly eyed me with suspicion. I could see the resent-ment in their eyes. Why should I be surprised? I left them with the responsibilities of a grown woman, care of the little ones, the cooking, cleaning and farm work. I knew it would take time to regain their trust.

First, I thought, when we were all settled and calm, I would tell my family the truth of what I had learned in the mountains. I would tell them of the death of Asa and how I learned of it. I would tell them I had accepted the death of their brothers and that we would never know how Isaac died, or where either of them was buried.

If Peter was not here, I would tell them how and why we separated.

I would ask for their forgiveness.

Then I would lie.

I would not tell them the truth of how we found our soldiers and of the horrible condition in which they lived. I would say we found the soldiers strong and brave.

I would not tell them that I had brought to our doorstep the enemy. No. I would not let them know that.

CHAPTER NINETEEN

OLIVER

Mid-June-July 2, 1863
Virginia to Gettysburg

WITH EVERY FOOTSTEP, as we marched north, I yearned to be with the soldiers in my regiment who were sent back to Richmond under the command of General Corse—most likely looking forward to a furlough. I felt nothing but distress at being part of Pickett's Brigade marching north on orders of General Lee. Had I not been a drummer I would have been in Richmond. I wondered if Eli was somewhere in the group going north, or if he had been lucky enough to have remained with our regiment. If drummers were needed, I thought it likely a fife-player would be as well. It would be good to know a friend from childhood was still with me.

The wagons were loaded haphazardly, and horses and men seemed strangely filled with primal energy. It never ceased to amaze me how men renewed their will to carry on. I myself was so very weary and despondent. But as I joined my fellow soldiers, I forced an air of optimism. Most likely it was what we all did in order to carry on.

We marched for weeks. It was impossible to know how long. The endless days merged into weeks of trudging through rain and suffocating heat. We broke camp at first light, which meant I awakened before sunrise to sound reveille. I was near starvation and those who stumbled from shabby tents and lean-tos were thin as rails. I choked back bitter tears when I saw my friends in such condition, but I knew I was no better off.

July 2, 1863

Today I fell in with Will Barton. He grinned at me and shouldered his new Enfield rifle. Several hours into the march the silence of the morning gave way to the sound of artillery and gunfire.

"Sounds like this is it, don't it, Oliver?" He spat to the side and moved his rifle to his other shoulder. "We're gonna be killing us some Yankees today, by God. I can't hardly wait to use this new rifle."

"I reckon so." I yelled at him over the noise of the horses and wagons.

"Gettin' real loud now. You hear all that there noise ahead? Sounds like the end of the world, don't it?" He caught my eye and I nodded in agreement.

The noise grew louder as we drew closer. There had been a lull earlier in the day as we approached, but now the sound of cannons and gunfire was constant. Above it all we heard something else, the roar of men yelling and screaming. I could just make out the ragged sound of a band and I wondered if Eli was there playing his fife. It felt and sounded as though we were headed for the gates of hell.

"You scared at all, Will? It's our first time fighting on Yankee soil. Those men might fight as fiercely for their land as we did for ours in Virginia."

"Nah. I ain't afraid. We'll show them bastards what we're made of. We'll have 'em running for the hills. You wait and see. I ain't afraid." But his eyes darted all around, his pupils dilated. Perhaps the worst thing a soldier could admit was fear. Yet, I could smell it.

Nothing could have prepared us for what lay ahead.

As we emerged from the woods on a hill, we saw below us a scene of carnage. The field before us was covered with men and horses in what appeared to be a life or death struggle. I was commanded to sound the 'long roll' sending the infantry immediately into battle. Without hesitation, Will yelled and rushed onto the field along with the rest of the infantry. I stood perfectly still, after sounding the 'long roll' and took in what was unfolding before me. Having no weapon, I was hard pressed to know which way to turn. My drum would be useless in the midst of the slaughter unfolding before me. Who could hear a drum above the deafening roar? It hung like a lead weight around my neck. I felt paralyzed and my arms hung limp at my sides. There was such dense smoke from guns and cannon, that it hung like a shroud over everything. The blue sky above me was the only way I knew it was still daytime. I found it difficult to focus, unable to tell my fellow soldiers from Union soldiers as they converged on the wheat field below. Men who no longer had use of their rifles used sticks, rocks and their bodies to do battle against each other. Even from the ridge I stood on I was engulfed by the horror I saw before me. My nostrils filled with the smell of blood, smoke and death. I willed myself to move toward the battle, but I was unable to do so. The vision of men who tore at each other as brutally as would wild animals so unnerved me that my vision blurred. I backed away slowly, still facing forward. Then, I turned and walked away.

I was drawn to the stillness of the woods and I gratefully let it enfold me. With my back against an oak tree I slid to the ground and looked up at the branches. The limbs spread like a soft emerald fan above me. My chest rose and fell with a pulse that emanated from the slaughter behind me. As I listened there was a cadence that sounded like a hymn. A steady rise, a peak...a crescendo, and then a slow descent. I was able to forget for a while that it was the sound of men in agony, in the throes of death. The Rebel Yell of my own Virginia brethren was a loud burst of energy and then a cacophony of shouting and cries which brought me back to reality.

I lowered my head to my knees and breathed deeply of the clean scent of wood and soil. I wanted to be home. I could leave and who would notice? I could walk away from all the madness and wait for the end of the war in a safe place. For surely, we were near the end of this massacre.

I bowed my head and prayed for guidance and strength from God. I thought of my brothers, Isaac and Asa. Did they die in such hell as I had just witnessed? I focused on my hands. My head throbbed. I stood on trembling legs and walked farther away from the battle.

The cries of dying men began to recede. Then, like a stab at my heart I was sure I heard the scream of Will. I stopped, telling myself it could be anyone, but my knees buckled. The pain I felt was more than I could bear.

I was not the man my brothers were. My father was right. I was never meant to be a soldier.

CHAPTER TWENTY

OLIVER

July 2-3, 1863
Gettysburg, Pennsylvania

AT LAST DARKNESS fell and there was quiet in the Pennsylvania woods that surrounded me. The battle had raged until a late hour, never ceasing. Now, all I heard were the muted cries of men wounded or dying. I looked up at the dark sky and estimated the time to be around ten.I inhaled deeply, hoping to erase the images and sounds of the day from my brain, the frenzied noise of both men and horses, cannons and rifles. I had been in the woods at least four hours, unable to face the hell in the field behind me. A wheat field, like our own in Virginia, was now a bloody, unholy graveyard.

No, I thought again, I was not meant to be a soldier. After the battles I had witnessed, I thought I would not have had such a visceral reaction to the slaughter of men. I thought nothing could be worse than what I had already been a part of, but this battle was different. We had fought on our own soil at Chancellorsville and most of the battles in which I had been a part. Here, on this foreign soil, there was a sense of desperation on the part of both Union and Confederate soldiers, as if they knew the battle they were now waging would determine the outcome of the war. They fought as animals would, flinging themselves headlong into a certain and brutal death.

I felt I was a coward, alone, weary, frightened and numb. I prayed to God for guidance. I listened to the sound of small animals scurrying through the leaves and brush. With the sound of an owl, I was reminded of home. If I should walk away, back to Virginia, what would I do? I couldn't go home. In spite of the love my parents had for me I knew they were proud of their sons. Proud of the strength and courage they had instilled in all their children. It mattered not to me who won the war now. I only wished for peace again, for food and shelter. I curled on my side and fell into tortured sleep.

Some hours later I awoke with a start, sweating, my heart pounding, unsure of where I was. I felt weak as I sat up and looked around. It was perhaps three in the morning and still dark. There was no sound, only silence. I shook my head and tried to get my bearings. Searching my pack for food, I found a bit of hardtack and a small piece of dried beef. I ate the last of my rations. Feeling stronger, I still could not rouse myself. I stretched my legs and feet. The blisters formed from hard marching hurt and bled.

After an hour or so, the silence was broken when I heard the faint sound of music drifting across the field from a nearby ridge. It was Sunday and as I listened, I thought I heard a hymn. It was not a hymn, but I recognized the tune. I was unable to hear the words if they were being sung. I stood and walked toward the music, humming softly to myself. It felt as though I was being called back to my own countrymen. I could have been delirious, perhaps from a lack of food and sleep. I had a strange feeling that my brothers, Isaac and Asa walked beside me, singing along. I had ceased to care whether I lived or died. A mysterious spirit had possessed me and I felt I needed to be with my regiment. I began to sing the words I knew well.

I'll place my knapsack on my back,
My rifle on my shoulder,
I'll march away to the firing line,
And kill that Yankee soldier,
And kill that Yankee soldier,
I'll march away to the firing line,
And kill that Yankee soldier.
I'll bid farewell to my wife and child
Farewell to my aged mother,
And go and join in the bloody strife,
Till this cruel war is over,
Till this cruel war is over,
I'll go and join in the bloody strife,
Till this cruel war is over.
If I am shot on the battlefield,
And I should not recover,
Oh, who will protect my wife and child,
And care for my aged mother?
And care for my aged mother,
Oh, who will protect my wife and child,
And care for my aged mother?
And if our Southern cause is lost,
And Southern rights denied us,
We'll be ground beneath the tyrant's heel,
For our demands of justice,
For our demands of justice,
We'll be ground beneath the tyrant's heel,

For our demands of justice.
Before the South shall bow her head,
Before the tyrants harm us,
I'll give my all to the Southern cause,
And die in the Southern army,
And die in the Southern army,
I'll give my all to the Southern cause,
And die in the Southern army.
If I must die for my home and land,
My spirit will not falter,
Oh, here's my heart and here's my hand,
Upon my country's altar,
Upon my country's altar,
Oh, here's my heart and here's my hand,
Upon my country's altar.
Then Heaven be with us in the strife,
Be with the Southern soldier,
We'll drive the mercenary horde,
Beyond our Southern border,
Beyond our Southern border,
We'll drive the mercenary horde,
Beyond our Southern border.
I'll place my knapsack on my back,
My rifle on my shoulder,
I'll march away to the firing line,
And kill that Yankee soldier,
And kill that Yankee soldier,

I'll march away to the firing line,
And kill that Yankee soldier!!!

The words seemed sadly innocent to me as I stumbled over things I could not see, things I did not wish to see. I didn't look down, but I knew I was walking among the bodies of dead men and horses. Yesterday had been unbearably hot and the stench of death was all around me. I kept my eyes straight ahead as I approached the camp.

I made my way in near darkness, settling quietly among the exhausted men, as those still asleep awoke from a troubled slumber. Their eyes were glazed, clothes and bodies caked with dirt and blood. They rubbed filthy faces with hands covered in the wounds of battle. Those already awake sat slumped in stunned silence, heads hanging low.

I thought I must look out of place, but when I glanced down, my clothes looked the same as every other man's. Some men knelt in prayer asking God for victory. I wondered if this third day of July would be their last on earth. Would it be my last? I joined those in prayer, praying that on this day the war would end. I prayed for victory and I prayed we would all survive the day ahead.

I spoke quietly to a man around my age as we settled back after prayer. His vacant eyes stared straight ahead.

"How bad was it yesterday? Do you know how many men we lost?"

He shook his head mournfully. "No. Ain't got no idea. We tried to take that hill the Yanks have, call it Little Round Top. Anyone crossin' that rock wall was a dead man." His eyes narrowed. "You wasn't here?"

"No. I was...I was held back." I knew I had to lie, or he might kill me or call me out to the officers. I swallowed hard, unable to look away from him.

"Well, these damn officers have us goin' ever which way,

that's for sure. Tryin' to take that high ground them Yanks hold. Them bastards mow us down like we was sheep. I pray to God Lee knows what in hell he's doin', cause we musta lost over half our regiment yesterday. I seen at least ten of my buddies shot dead. They're still out there on that field, rotting, like they was nothin.'' He turned his face away and briskly wiped tears from his face.

Shame spread through me as I realized what men had gone through while I sat paralyzed in the woods. I silently swore to God, and to Isaac and Asa, that I would do my duty. I would stand beside this man, or another like him, and beat my drum as if I could save my life and theirs. I felt a surge of determination to make up for my lack of courage, to be worthy of the men around me.

I stood and looked out over the field where men lay where they died. The sun was coming up and I saw beyond the fields and orchards the high ground the Yankee's held.

"God help us." I said to the man who stood beside me. "I hope to be alive at the end of this day."

He shook his head slowly. "It'll take God and ever man in this army to survive this day. Good luck to you, drummer."

"And to you." I said, as I lifted my drum to go in search of my regiment.

CHAPTER
TWENTY-ONE

OLIVER

July 3, 1863
Gettysburg, Pennsylvania

WHEN I FOUND my regiment, I was overcome with sorrow and breathed deeply to control my emotions. A man standing beside me muttered in an angry voice, "They're wantin' us to take that high ground over there." He gestured with his chin *toward a* distant hill. "Cemetery Ridge they call it." He shook his head. "God help us."

We could hear already cannon being fired by the Union trying to drive our men from Culps Hill on our left. Above the sound of artillery, we heard the Rebel Yell, over and over as our men charged the enemy.

There was quiet just before noon, and we knew our men had been driven from Culps Hill. We could not look at each other, for we knew the silence signaled a defeat for us. More of our fellow soldiers lay dead or dying.

I took what time was allowed before we received our next orders to examine my drum and drumsticks. How would my drum be of use? When the battle started, artillery and gunfire were a deafening roar. I thought again that I would be useless. No one could hear the orders my drum was meant to convey. Men around me prepared for battle in their own way. Some in prayer and others in silent brooding. Many had friends or relatives who lay dead or dying on the field before us. It was unbearable to think of a loved one in such agony, and yet not be able to help them. Who around me would survive the day? I wondered if I would survive.

By mid-afternoon officers relayed the orders of General Lee to prepare for battle. It was hot and humid. Sweat ran down my back and arms, making my drumsticks hard to hold. I moved into a drummer's place at the rear of my regiment, as we moved into position. The wheat field stretched nearly a mile in front of us. Flies buzzed angrily around our heads. Smoke from our own artillery obscured our vision as we began to march across the field.

Half way across the field, I was given the order to sound the 'long drum roll' signaling the men to commence to charge. Cannon balls exploded and tore apart everything in our path. Men fell all around me. Their screams were excruciating and I knew not whether to help them or leave them to suffer. My instinct was to stop and attend to them, but the wounds were so severe I knew I could be of no help. I was hypnotized by the chaos, and as happened before, I seemed to leave my body and float above the field. As I continued to drum, I marveled that I was not shot dead. I was an easy target for our enemy.

When I thought we could endure no more, General Lee ordered a full charge towards Cemetery Ridge. Men who arrived with Pickett and Longstreet, of whom I was one, were the most rested, and we were ordered to form the center of the charge. In a straight line we marched directly ahead, as would toy soldiers pushed from behind by an invisible force.

It seemed we had fallen even further into hell.

Yankees fired upon us and opened gaps in our line. With blood curdling screams, men ahead of me breached the stone wall, with or without rifles. It was suddenly man against man, and I could not make out which side was which. My hands bled and my drum was covered in blood. I was unsure if it was only my blood that covered it. There was blood everywhere. The cries of those wounded were deafening. Bile rose in my throat and I retched, unable to stop it. A man beside me was shot and grabbed my hand as he fell to the ground. I leaned over him. His eyes, a clear blue, found mine and held me captive. He clutched his stomach but spoke no words. I leaned closer to him as his lips moved, feeling his hot breath on my face. He seemed to want me to hear his words. It was of no use, I could not hear over the roar. I put aside my drum and knelt beside him.

"What do you say? I can't hear you. Speak louder."

His lips continued to move, but his eyes no longer focused on mine. He stared at the sky. Still his lips moved. I wanted to scream at him, to scream at the mass of humanity around me "STOP! I cannot hear this man. I need to hear this man!"

His lips stopped moving. Slowly his eyelids closed. He shivered and took a last labored breath as I felt the full weight of his body sink into my arms. I wanted to pray for him, but God seemed a cruel joke amidst such carnage. I brushed tears from my eyes as the frenzied movement around me came back into focus. It was as if I had just arrived in the midst of hell. There were men dying all around me. I stayed where I was with the unknown man in my arms. In some strange way he was an anchor in a sea of dying men. I looked around me, squinting to focus amidst the smoke and chaos. I took up the man's rifle, along with my drum. I thought I had not the heart nor strength to stand and fight another man. Yet, when the order came, I stood and took my place at the back of Pickett's men. We charged the Yankees with bayonets lowered, screaming a blood curdling Rebel Yell as we ran and staggered toward Cemetery Ridge. I wondered again how it was I survived as men were shot and dying all around me. I expected at any moment to feel a bullet tear into my body. I sunk to my knees and sat among the dead and dying. Laying aside the rifle, I beat my drum as if the beats alone could push the men over the rock wall and up Cemetery Ridge.

Then it was as if the tide was receding. Men around me, and closer to the front line, began to fall back...down the slope. I was stunned by the realization that our army was retreating.

As I stumbled from the field a hand grasped my leg. My first thought was to kick it away. I wanted only to run with the other men and leave the unholy field behind me. But I could not stop myself. I looked down on the face of a man who wore the blue of a Union soldier. I shouldn't have stopped. I should have left that bloody field forever. But he looked like my brother Peter, and I hesitated. His eyes implored me to help him. I was held hostage by his fierce gaze. There was a gaping wound in his chest. He groaned as I slowly turned him over to find there was no exit wound. He would surely die.

"My...my mother...my wife...tell them..." His speech had an Irish lilt and his voice was so soft I could barely hear his words. But his grip tightened on my leg, "...tell them...love them...."

"Yes, yes I will soldier. I will."

I wrenched my leg from the man's grasp, turned my back on him and staggered back across the field, almost entirely covered now by the bodies of horses and men.

God had forsaken us. We were defeated.

CHAPTER
TWENTY-TWO

OLIVER

July 3-4, 1863
Gettysburg, Pennsylvania

WHY HAD GENERAL Lee left soldiers on the battlefield with the dead and dying? I could not imagine what those men must have endured remaining there. I thanked God that I was not among those men. I was not sure I could have endured being forced to stay on a field with men in agony or dead all around me. It seemed to me, we were defeated at Gettysburg. Why did the General order some of our men to remain on that ghastly field?

Did Lee think we could repulse another attack with the condition of our men? Did he leave men on the field to raise an alarm if the Union should attack? Was it an attempt on his part to convince the Yankees that we were not defeated? Did he do it to allow time to remove as many wounded and dead as possible before we retreated to Virginia? I could not fathom what must possess the General to think that we were still capable of fighting after the gut-wrenching failure of Pickett's charge yesterday. Surely our dead and wounded must number in the thousands.

I heard that General Lee rode among the troops late into the night. Surely the death of so many of his men must weigh heavily on his spirit.

In camp I helped attend to the wounded, which were too numerous to count. Field hospitals were hastily set up and the heartbreaking task of caring for the injured and dying began. Make shift surgeon tables were simply planks of wood laid upon barrels. I prayed there was enough opium, morphine and whatever else was used to ease the pain of those who suffered. It was beyond heartbreaking to be among them.

I tied around my mouth and nose the last of the handkerchiefs my mother gave to me when I joined the army. Had it been nearly three years now? I ran my fingers over my initials embroidered there, and choked back tears. I wished I could stop the cries of men with wounds so dreadful it was difficult to look upon them. I had at times pressed my lips together to keep from retching. The smell of festering wounds and death was sickening. Surely, I thought, until the day I died I would never forget the smell of death, but after a while the stench of sweat, blood, urine and rot no longer reached me. It was a shock to realize I carried the same odors on me. My clothes were covered in blood and who knows what else. We loaded men unable to walk on wagons so closely packed there wasn't room to move a limb even if a man was able. Men who could still manage to walk were given as much support as possible, and the mangled mass of humanity huddled and waited for whatever Lee commanded of us next. I had deliberately not focused on individual men as I helped the doctors and surgeons. I went where I was called or needed and did as I was told by the officers in charge. Thankfully I recognized no one, but I wondered what had happened to Eli Lambert. I hadn't seen my friend for some time and I hoped he still lived.

Near the end of the day a hush fell over the men as the wounded had either died or been tended to as well as surgeons could do. Men still moaned in agony, but it was no longer as constant as it had been earlier in the day. There was near silence on the battlefield. The fighting had ended and still we awaited final orders from Lee.

Having been on my feet for almost twenty-four hours I could barely remain upright. I had done all that I could do to help, and now I could only pray that God would care for all the poor wretched souls still in agony. I'd not had time to wonder how once again I had survived. I did not know God's plan for me or why he let me live while so many died.

Walking toward the setting sun I removed my handkerchief from my face. Inhaling deeply, I turned to look behind me and sunk to the ground exhausted. There were no words to describe what pain and suffering was amassed there. I turned my back and covered my face with my hands.

A hand fell softly on my shoulder and I jumped to my feet. "Oliver, that you?"

It was Jacob! "Jacob! How good it is to see you!" I grabbed his free hand in both of mine. I focused then on his face. There was such sadness written there. He looked older, worn out. "Are you well, Jacob?"

"Yes, I be fine. But, Massa, he been hurt bad. I ain't sure he gonna make it. His Mama and Daddy...they gonna die of grief if he don't. He's the only son they got. I done all I know to do for him. He shot in the head, he in terrible pain." He bowed his head and when he lifted it tears ran down the grime that coated his face.

"I'm so sorry Jacob. But maybe..."

"I know better, Oliver. I been helpin' with the wounded too. The surgeons got him now. I almost sure he ain't gonna make it. I don't know how I gonna tell that family."

"Then you are going back, Jacob, to his family? After all this? You're in Pennsylvania. You could be a free man. All you have to do is walk away."

"Like I say before, there ain't nothin' up here for me. I be goin' back to Richmond. They's my family too. I ain't got none else. An I got my own cabin. Cook my own food. I'm too old ta be pickin' tabbaca out them fields." He got a faraway look in his eyes. "I never done that work, pickin' tabbaca. That hard work, out in the hot sun all day." He shook his head as if trying to dispel an image. "I work in the big house. I wonder if it still there?"

I realized more than ever that I knew little of the life of a slave, or a slave owner. Farmers in the western part of Virginia were far removed from the wealthy tobacco growers in the eastern part of the state, and their way of life was foreign to me.

I put a hand on his shoulder and waited for his eyes to find mine. "You've done all you can for your mas...master." I still found the word hard to say. It sounded demeaning to Jacob. "We should rest while we can, Jacob. If Lee gives the command to leave, there will be no time to waste, and you look as exhausted as I feel. I'm sorry about your master, but I am so glad to see you, Jacob. I was afraid..."

"Yes, it good to see you, Oliver." He turned to leave, and then turned back. "If I don't see you agin', I pray for you, Oliver. This war gonna change ever thing I know. But you're young. You got time to make a life after this war over."

"Thank you, Jacob. I will pray for you too. I hope you are right. I hope I live to see my family again. I don't know how I've survived this long. It's in God's hands. Goodbye, Jacob." I extended my hand, but he pulled me into a quick embrace.

"Goodbye, Oliver."

Within hours we were directed by Lee to move out across South Mountain towards Hagerstown. Rain was torrential, but we were not allowed to halt. The wounded were moved out first, in springless wagons, which added to their suffering and they groaned constantly. I marched among a few thousand able-bodied men who were so exhausted, I believed we marched while asleep.

I feared the Union would pursue us as we struggled into Maryland. I prayed not, for in our condition, we would not have survived another assault.

CHAPTER TWENTY-THREE

ABIGAIL

July 1863
Dugspur, Virginia
Quesinberry Farmhouse

I'D TAKEN FOOD and water to Daniel for the last three weeks. He had gained strength and his wound was almost healed. He now walked with only a slight limp. I prepared to make one last trip to see him and take as much food as I could spare. I would insist he leave within the week. I made a rough map for him, which would take him through the mountains and into Maryland. He seemed oddly reluctant to leave, but I had to make him understand that he was in danger of being discovered by one of our neighbors. I feared my own family might learn of his presence. It was true I'd become very fond of him in spite of my effort not to do so. It was easy to forget that he had fought against all I held dear. He was simply a human being, in need of help and kindness. When I returned home after being with him, the reality of what I was doing terrified me. I knew I would be branded a traitor not only by our neighbors, but my own family as well, if they knew what I was doing.

It had been a slow process, but finally my family had for-given me for leaving them at such a time of sorrow for every-one. Andrew smiled tenderly as I served the biscuits that were most like his mother's. At night he again embraced me and I breathed deeply of his scent I knew so well. I was at peace with him.

Even Peter seemed to have let go of his anger toward me. We spoke privately in the barn and settled our differences. Although I pleaded with him, he would not promise me that he would not join the army when he was of age. That heartache was yet to come. I had hoped to convince him to wait as long as possible to see if the war might end before he was forced to join. But, like all my children, it seemed he had inherited my stubbornness and would do what he thought he must.

It was Jane who baffled me. She followed me everywhere. Her attitude had changed from one of anger and resentment to constant watchfulness, as if trying to predict my actions. I knew she had grown weary of the isolation of the farm and missed interaction with young people her age. Many of her friends had already married. When I first made packages for Daniel, and she thought they were for our soldiers, she had pleaded with me to let her accompany me to town. She no lon-ger did so, but would often add some item to the supplies.

I added more food to the last package I prepared for Daniel so that he would not starve on his way home to New York. Isaac and Asa's clothes fit him well, even the work boots. He would be well prepared to make his way North on his own. If he followed the map I gave him, and was careful, he should be able to avoid the known Home Guard encampments. Still, he must remain vigilant. Fortunately, the weather was warm and there would be no need for campfires which might have alert-ed others. He was grateful for all I had done for him and was always polite and kind. In that way he reminded me of Oliver.

We heard General Lee had moved most, if not all, of his army north, and I feared for Oliver. I was ashamed of how my grief over the death of my oldest sons made me forget my other children. I could only attribute it to the intense loss I felt. I wondered if I would react the same way if I learned of Oliver's death. Would I be better prepared for another son's death? I prayed fervently to God that I would not have to endure such pain again.

Jane surprised me when she quietly entered the kitchen as I worked. "Mother, isn't that enough? Will you leave some for us?"

When I turned to her I was delighted to see a smile on her face. But there was something in her demeanor that confounded me.

"Oh. Well, maybe so. I find it hard to forget the way we found our soldiers, thin and starving." I hesitated, remembering I had chosen not to tell my family of the sad condition our soldiers were in when Peter and I found them. "We can spare this much. We'll have vegetables coming in soon. You know I will not let our family starve." I smiled at her. I would have liked to hug her, but I was still reluctant to take that liberty with her. It pleased me when it was she who threw her arms around my neck and kissed my cheek.

"I know you won't let us starve, Mother. I'm teasing you. We are indeed lucky to have more than our family needs. In fact, I just picked the first of the string beans." She pointed to a basket. "They'll be delicious with a bit of salt pork. If you have nothing for me to help you with, I think I'll go in search of more blackberries. The pie you baked was very tasty, even though we had no sugar. Honey is just as sweet." Her smile was a gift and her good humor welcome to my heart. It was good to see the Jane I remembered.

"Of course, if you can find enough berries, we'll have another pie, or perhaps a cobbler. I'll add some of last year's apple butter to sweeten it."

At the door she turned to me. "Are there no supplies at all in town, Mother? No sugar? You take food in almost every week and yet you never bring anything home in return. Is there nothing available? No way to barter for sugar?"

I was caught in confusion for a moment, trying to find an answer to her question. Jane was a smart girl and would know if I was untruthful.

"Jane, we are fortunate to have more than enough food for our family. Many families who live in town don't have the advantage we have. They have no way of growing food and have nothing preserved from other years as we do. Your father was wise to save the seeds from year to year. We have a good crop of vegetables coming in. It is even hard to come by seed to plant crops. We are blessed in many ways."

"I know, Mother. Of course, we are. I'll be back before supper, in time to help you make that pie or cobbler." She flashed a smile and my heart lifted.

It was my habit to dismount and walk quietly when I approached Daniel. I usually found him working at some bit of carving. I had given him Isaac's good pocket knife and he was quite a skillful whittler. He had proudly shown me a beautiful bird he carved for his mother. He was at work on a rather large piece of wood as he rested under a tree. I stopped for a moment and watched him before he knew I was there. A very fastidious man, he bathed in the creek daily and his dark hair shone in the sun. I had to admit, he was a handsome young man.

The sun had also brought color to his face and his deep blue eyes sparkled in contrast. I cleared my throat to alert him to my presence. He smiled and leapt to his feet, which meant his leg was well healed.

"Abigail! It's you!"

"Yes, of course. Were you expecting someone else?"

He shuffled his feet and put down his carving and knife.

"No. No. Who...who else would I expect." He sputtered and his cheeks flushed.

"Let's hope there is no one else, Daniel." I spread a blanket and patted a spot beside me.

He sat opposite me and we were quiet for a while before I spoke. "Daniel, you have to leave within the week. I'm afraid my family may be getting suspicious of all my trips to town." I gave him a lopsided grin. "Andrew, Peter and Jane have all wanted to accompany me. I can't put them off much longer. I've brought enough food for a few weeks. If you are prudent and follow the map you should be in Maryland by that time."

"You have been most kind to me, Abigail. I wouldn't want to put you in danger or create trouble for you or your family. I feel strong. I promise you I will leave in the next few days. It is time and I know my mother needs me."

I nodded. "I never thought I could help someone who fought against my own family, let alone bring them almost into my home, Daniel. Sometimes I'm not sure why do it. I will pray for you, and your mother."

I handed him the bundle and prepared to leave.

"Wait, Abigail." He walked to the tree and returned with an object in his hands. It was wrapped in paper I had previously wrapped food in. "Here, this is for you." He smiled shyly as he watched me unwrap his gift.

"Why, Daniel! This is beautiful." It was a carving of a girl. Her arms lifted to the sky in an exuberant gesture. Her skirt swirled around her legs. "It could be one of my daughters. I...I will treasure it."

"You have told me so much about them, Abigail. I feel I know them."

I wanted to take him in my arms as I would my own sons, I had come to know him so well.

"After this war is over, write to me, Daniel. Let me know how you are doing, how your mother is faring. Goodbye, Daniel. God Bless you and good luck."

I quickly turned away and mounted Spirit. I dared not look back. Tears were streaming down my face.

"Thank you, Abigail. And God Bless you and yours."

When I left Daniel, I rode slowly. I would no longer have to sneak food to him and lie to my family. Even though I would always be glad that I helped him, his departure would be a great burden lifted from my shoulders.

I was surprised to see Jane ahead of me, and then remembered she was picking blackberries. There were few blackberry bushes in the open field and she swung her empty basket casually. She looked startled as I approached her.

"Jane, you're looking for berries here? Have you found any?"

Her face flushed.

"Not yet. I'm still looking. I think the birds are getting to them before me."

"You should look along the fence line and the edge of the woods. That's where they grow best. You know that."

"I know. I was distracted by this beautiful day. It has been a long while since I've had time alone." She lifted an eyebrow and gave me a grin, as if to remind me of my long absence.

"I know, take your time. You deserve it. I'll be home. Polly and Mary will help with supper."

She nodded and then noticed the package I carried. "You brought something from town? Sugar, I hope."

"Oh. No. It's...it's, this." I unwrapped the carving with care. "It was given to me by a grateful man who needed food for his family." Another lie. How was it I lied so easily these days?

She stared at the carving, turning scarlet. I was alarmed for a moment. "Are you alright, Jane? Maybe you've been in the sun too long. Do you want to ride home with me? Climb up."

"No. I'm fine. I'll find the berries and be home before sup-per." She turned away quickly and then turned back. "It is beautiful, though, the carving. Isn't it, Mother?"

"Yes. It is. It reminds me of you or Mary. Don't stay out too long, Jane. You look flushed." I prodded Spirit into a walk. When I turned in my saddle to glance back at her, she was following the trail I had just left. Surely, she wouldn't go so deep into the woods that she might find Daniel? Fear twisted my stomach and I called out to her.

"Jane, come home with me now, you can look for black-berries another day. You really don't look well."

She hastily waved a hand. "I won't be long. Besides, I enjoy the walk and being alone. Sara hangs on me constantly these days."

It was true. In my absence baby Sara became extremely attached to Jane. I did not have a good reason to insist she come with me. "Alright, don't be too late, and do remember the blackberry canes grow thicker along the fences. No need to look in the woods."

"I know Mother. If I can't find any, I'll be home shortly." She lifted her free hand and waved me off.

"Don't be long."

I felt on edge and jumpy. I told myself I was being silly. There was no reason to believe that she would come upon Daniel.

That night I wondered if Daniel had left and was on his way north. I prayed for him when I prayed for Oliver and the rest of my family.

I was unable to sleep and I thought of how life was before this war began. How simple it was, and how sweet. How much I cherished Andrew and each child. How very proud I was of the health and beauty of my children. Each one was beautiful to me. To my delight, Andrew's ardor had returned, but I feared bringing another child into the world. I didn't want more children. I knew not where we would be in the months and years to come. I prayed we would keep our land. It was all we had, that and our family. I snuggled deeper into Andrew's arms. It was a warm night and we had thrown off our covers and slept with as little as possible to cover our bodies.

"What keeps you up tonight, Abigail?" He murmured in my ear as his arms pulled me closer.

"Did I wake you? I'm sorry, Andrew. I was thinking of how our life was before this war. This war is senseless. Men are starving and dying on both sides. I worry Oliver might be killed and that Peter will join when he is eighteen. Will we lose all our sons and our land?" I sat up in bed and wrapped my arms around my knees, rocking back and forth. I was finally beginning to feel myself with my husband. Andrew no longer looked at me as though I might fall apart before his eyes. I wanted to stay strong for him and for my family, but a nameless fear haunted me day and night and disturbed my sleep.

I curled my body against Andrew and rested my head on his arm. "I can accept the loss of our land, but not our boys, Andrew. I try not to think about it, but I still worry. Surely this war will be over before William and Preston are eighteen. It couldn't possibly last so long, could it?"

He gently ran his fingers through my hair. "No, no, Abbie. It can't last much longer. The Revolutionary War lasted eight years, but we were fighting the British. This is one country and the war has divided families. I don't think the people will stand for it much longer. I hear that folks in the North are growing as weary of this war as we are. Try not to let fear make you ill, my love. We have each other and I will not lose this land. That, I promise you. My father and his father fought too hard for it. Go to sleep, Abigail. It will soon be over."

"You wouldn't go to war, would you, Andrew? You wouldn't leave us alone?" This fear hit me suddenly, like a hammer. One thing I knew well was that Andrew would fight anyone for our land. He didn't answer right away. In the light that filtered through the window I could see his jaw tighten. He shifted and rolled onto his back.

"Only if I must, Abigail." His voice was low and rough. "Only if I must." He rolled on his side, his back to me.

"Andrew, tell me you will not leave me alone on this farm with our children. Tell me, Andrew!" I pushed roughly at his shoulder to make him answer me.

"I told you, Abigail. I will only fight if I must. I cannot give you any more assurance than that. I do promise, I will not leave you to run this farm on your own. Go to sleep, please. It's almost morning." I knew we would speak no more it. I knew too, that if my husband decided he must fight to keep our land, he would.

I was still awake when Andrew quietly slipped from bed to start the morning chores. I pretended to sleep. When I heard him softly close the back door, I went to the bureau and removed from a drawer the carving Daniel gave me. I enjoyed looking at it. It reminded me of a younger me, and a time when I would have flung my arms skyward and embraced the whole of life with abandon. It reminded me of falling in love with Andrew, of the happiness I felt and how few cares I had. I let my fingers caress the face and arms of the figure, the folds of her skirt. It was carved with love. That much was obvious. Who was Daniel thinking of when he carved such a beautiful thing? Perhaps he had a sweetheart at home. He never spoke of one, only his Mother. Perhaps it was she he tried to capture. I sleepily closed my eyes as my fingers explored the carving. The wood was polished and smooth and I wondered how Daniel had managed that. As I moved my fingers along the carving I felt something on the bottom. At the window I examined it. It was an initial, the letter J. I studied the figure. Why a letter J? Perhaps Daniel did have a girlfriend with that initial. Could it mean something else in his Irish tradition? I decided for me, it would stand for joy, for that is what I felt when I looked at the carving, pure joy, something lost to all of us during the war.

I would always treasure it. It could have been me or one of my daughters. Andrew said Jane looked more like me every day. I held the figure close to my heart. It was all I would ever have to remind me of Daniel. It still amazed me that I could love and care for him. I knew that I would have to go one last time to make sure he had left. I crept back into bed for what I knew would be just a few minutes rest before the children awoke and clamored for breakfast.

"Mama. Mama." Sara was calling from the children's room. I slipped on a dress and pulled my hair into a bun. It was always a delight to see my baby's face in the morning. Her cheeks flushed from sleep, her blonde curls a halo, her arms reaching out for me.

When I opened the door to the children's bedroom, Jane was already there. She lifted Sara into the air and whirled her around the room, her skirt and hair flying. My heart skipped a beat. I stared in silence.

A new and bewildering emotion overcame me. My daughter was an enigma.

There before me was the carving made real. I was almost certain it was of Jane.

CHAPTER
TWENTY-FOUR

JANE

July, 1863
Dugspur, Virginia

AS SOON AS Mother was out of sight I ran to Daniel. Why had she taken so much food to him? Was it possible she knew that I had discovered him and had demanded he leave? She had been attentive to my every mood lately, as if she sensed something had changed in me. In my heart, I feared I knew the answer, that Mother suspected I'd discovered Daniel and she had given him an ultimatum—to leave or be turned over to the authorities. Daniel said she had been so very kind to him. He cared deeply for her, even though it was she who shot him. Surely, she wouldn't betray him after all she had done for him. Tears dried on my face as I ran across the field toward the woods where he waited. I knew he was expecting me.

What would I do if he told me he was leaving? I knew he must leave, but not so soon. Please God, not so soon. Would it be impossible for him to stay? Would Father accept him and help him as Mother had done? Father was a good man, a man who believed in God and the goodness of his fellow man.

Wouldn't he help Daniel too?

I quite simply love Daniel. How does one fall in love in only two weeks? My parents would say that I was too young, but I am of marriageable age, and many of my friends from church were already married. My parents would say I was drawn to Daniel because all the young men we knew were off fighting. Even I am mystified at how quickly I fell in love with him. I would never have imagined it, ever. I remember Mother telling me that she knew the minute she laid eyes on Father in church, that he would be the love of her life. Father said the same. I smirked at the time, but now I understood. That is how I felt when I first saw Daniel.

When I first saw him, wearing my brother's clothes', I thought surely, he was a Confederate deserter my mother was helping.

I was spying on Mother, suspicious that in spite of all her trips to town delivering food, she never returned with supplies of any kind. She never returned with anything. I wasn't sure what she was doing with the clothes and food, and I admit I was angry that she wouldn't allow me go to town with her. I was desperate to get away from the dullness of the farm. Except for church on Sunday, I rarely saw anyone my own age. Why couldn't she understand a girl of sixteen would long to leave the farm, even to deliver supplies to the depot for our soldiers?

I followed her, knowing well the route she took.

Waiting at the halfway point I watched as she left the road to town and disappeared into the woods. It was not difficult to follow the trail her horse made. The grass and small seedlings were crushed. I had no idea what I would find. If she was helping a deserter she would have to keep that a secret from Father. He wouldn't have allowed it and surely would have returned a traitor to the army.

There was still a part of me angry with Mother for leaving us the way she did. I don't think she knew how difficult it was to watch her leave, and not understand why she felt compelled to go in search of Isaac and Asa when we were all heartbroken. My younger brothers and sisters were especially confused and cried after her for days.

I told myself, as I followed her path into the woods that first time, that I would let my father know of the presence of a deserter and let Mother suffer the consequence of her actions.

Mother and Daniel sat on a blanket in deep conversation when I came upon them. As I crouched behind a tree, I couldn't hear their words, but I could tell their discussion was serious. I waited until Mother left, and then I confronted the man, certain he was a deserter.

I stepped out boldly, though my heart was in my throat. "Who are you? What are you doing here? And why is my mother bringing you food? Did you fight with my brothers? Are you a deserter?"

His soft laughter caught me off guard. "Ah. Indeed, you are one of Abigail's daughters!" He lifted deep blue eyes to my face and looked directly into my own, a smile crinkling the corners of his eyes.

"Yes, I am. I'm Jane. How would you know my mother has daughters?" I narrowed my eyes, but could not ignore his unwavering gaze.

"Yes. You're the oldest. Then, there is Polly, Mary and baby Sara. Oliver, Peter, and the younger boys, Preston and William. I feel as if I know all of you."

His smile was dazzling and I felt myself blush. "How do you know all about our family? Who are you?"

"Will you sit a moment, Jane? I would like to explain who I am, and why I am here. Your Mother saved my life. That is after she shot me." His eyes danced with mischief. The way Father's did when he teased Mother. "She is a very brave, kind woman. You are lucky to have such a mother."

"That blanket belonged to my brother. As do your clothes. Why is my mother helping you? And why is she hiding you?

You are a deserter, aren't you?"

"Yes, I am. I'm a deserter from the Union army. At least I would be branded as such."

I could do nothing but stare in disbelief, astounded that my mother would help a Union soldier. I turned to leave, not knowing what else to do, but he gently grasped my wrist. "Please, Jane, let me explain how I came to be here. You needn't be frightened. I won't hurt you."

There was something in his voice and his gaze that stilled the fear I felt, and I lowered myself beside him.

"Jane, I know this might be difficult to understand. But if you will allow me, I'll do my best to explain how I came to be here. Believe me, I know that I am at your mercy, as I was at your mother's."

His eyes held mine. I nodded indicating he should continue.

"Before I joined the Union army, I worked as a paver in New York City. My mother brought me there when I was eight years old. We fled the famine in Ireland. My father made her promise just before he died that she would take what money they had and come to America. It was his dream that we could all escape the famine together and make a new life in America. He died before he could fulfill that dream."

"Ireland? You and your mother came to America alone? You had no family here?"

"No. We had no one. We came on a ship, in steerage class, which was so crowded with Irish immigrants we could barely move. Even though I was just eight, I don't think I will ever forget the weeks spent on that ship. Many died from the crowded conditions. There was no air and very little food. I think it was there my mother caught a disease that still plagued her when we reached New York. I think that is what is now causing her serious illness."

"I don't understand. Why did you leave Ireland? Had you no family there?"

"They all died. My father, grandparents and two of my

younger siblings. We all lived together in a small cottage. Only my mother and I survived."

A deep look of sadness crossed Daniels face as he spoke. I thought of how very painful it was to learn of Isaac and Asa's deaths and the profound sorrow their deaths had brought my family, and how very much more I cherished my family as a result.

"How difficult that must have been for you and your mother. I cannot imagine losing all my family."

He nodded. "My mother is the only family I have, and I am all that she has."

I listened as he spoke tenderly of his mother and my heart melted. There was nothing harsh or deceitful about him. He spoke from his heart, and with every word he overcame my defenses. I could easily understand how Mother forgot he was a Union soldier and only think to help him. I felt the same way as I listened to his story.

Now I rushed into his arms and burst into tears. He needn't tell me he was leaving. I knew.

"Daniel, please don't go. Please. We can figure something out. We can go to West Virginia, or Kentucky. We'll be safe and it will take only days to get there. You can't leave now. I...I..."

"Jane. My dear one."

I nestled my head under his chin and rested my cheek against his chest, listening to his heart beat strong and steady. I tightened my grip as he lowered his face to the top of my head and drew me closer.

We clung together until I caught my breath and looked up at him. "Daniel? Will you stay with me? Please tell me you won't leave. My Mother will understand. She will help us. I know her, she cares for you."

"I can't stay. I've told you, I have to go to my Mother. I am all she has, Jane. There is no one else to help her. It is not like your family. There are so many of you. She has only me."

I could not stop the sobs that racked my body. "But I need you! I love you. I never thought to do so, but I cannot imagine life without you now." I drew away from him and cleared my throat. "Then I'll go with you. I'll go to New York with you. We will travel as husband and wife. I can be ready tomorrow. I needn't tell anyone. I'll leave a note where Mother can find it. She will understand."

"I couldn't put you in danger. You have no idea what this war is like, or how far away New York is. I couldn't...."

"I am as strong as my mother, Daniel. I know this area and the people. I can help you." I placed my hands on my hips and backed away from him, in a stance I recognized as one my mother often took.

A sad smile spread across his face. "I can see that, Jane. How strong you are. That is one of the reasons I love you so. I would be honored to have such a wife as you. My mother would adore you, as I do, but I cannot put you in danger. How could I live with myself if you were harmed?" He took my hands in his and I lifted my face to his.

"There are so many dangers, Jane, desperate men who would kill me and abuse you. I won't take that chance."

"Daniel, I will take that chance. I will not let you leave without me. Do you hear me? I'm going with you."

"Listen to me." He held my face with a steady, warm hand. "I'll come back for you. I promise. I will come back. Do you think I could forget you? I am not only in love with you, I am in love with your family. To be part of such a family would be a gift. I love this land, too, the mountains, the valleys and rich farmland. I can think of no better place to marry and raise a family. Perhaps I can bring my mother. She misses the country and longs for a quiet life. She never really wanted to stay in the city. Nor do I. I promise you, I will come back for you."

I backed away from him, my hands still on my hips. "I'm going with you Daniel. Who knows what will be left of this farm or of Virginia when this war is over. I love you and I want to be with you. If you don't let me go with you, well, I'll...I'll tell Father." My words sounded like a childish threat and I felt a blush creep up my neck to my face.

"My God, did Abigail raise nothing but stubborn, reckless children? Surely this war will not last much longer. When it is over I'll come back for you, you, you daft girl."

"Daft? What does that mean, Daniel?"

"It means you are...you are...impossible. You're.... "

"Never mind. It means I love you and I will be your wife. I'm going with you."

He rushed to me and lifted me in the air, his hands around my waist. "Yes. That I know, Jane Quesinberry. Why do I bother to try and dissuade you? I want you with me always."

Clinging together we both knew that our bodies were starved for each other. Breathlessly Daniel pulled away and whispered in a husky voice, "We must marry as soon as possible. I won't take you as a man would a wife until we are joined in God's eyes as husband and wife."

Although, at the moment, I hardly cared if we were man and wife, my respect for Daniel grew even more. "Yes, my love. We'll marry as soon as it is safe to do so. I would like to meet your mother and have her bless our marriage."

He kissed the top of my head and said. "Well now, my future wife, we must make a plan."

CHAPTER TWENTY-FIVE

ABIGAIL

July 1863
Quesinberry Farmhouse
Dugspur, Virginia

BENEATH THE IRON skillet I used every morning to pre-pare breakfast, Jane had left a note that only I would find. I slipped it into the pocket of my apron before Andrew could see it.

When he went to the barn I opened the envelope. I knew before I read it that it would be bad news. Jane was gone.

Dear Mother,
I'm sorry to leave you this way. I discovered Daniel weeks ago and we have fallen in love. Do not be angry with him. I insisted on going with him to New York. We'll be mar-ried there. I know this will be hard for you and I know it will be even harder to explain to Father.

I love you and I will miss you all terribly.

I never thought I would leave my home. I never thought I

would fall so desperately in love as I have. I know Father would never accept Daniel, at least, not now. You know Daniel and in time you would accept our decision. Father would never do so.

I know you cannot tell Father the truth of what I have done. He would never forgive you, or me.

Many of my friends from church have left home to nurse the wounded in hospitals. Wagons leave every week for Lynchburg and Richmond. Tell Father that is what I have done. When this war is over I will come home. I promise you.

Daniel wants to be a farmer. He wants to take his mother away from the city and come back to Virginia when the war ends. I'll write to you Mother, when we get to New York.

Please don't worry. We will be careful and avoid the Home Guard camps. Please give us your blessing, Mother. I know you love Daniel as much as I do.

Your loving daughter,

Jane

I buried my face in my hands and cried silently.
Oh, my daughter, what have you done?
I wasn't sure how much more I could withstand. My life had spun completely out of my control, two children dead, Oliver might yet die in battle and Peter would join the army as soon as he was of age. Now Jane had gone north, into enemy territory, with a Union soldier that I brought almost to our doorstep.

I understood now the haunted and desperate appearance of women who lost sons and husbands in this war. I felt as helpless as they looked. I thought I was different, that I was stronger, that I could find my sons in the middle of a war. I was so sure I could hold my family together no matter what happened around us.

How foolish I was. I was nearly brought to my knees with grief and sadness. I dragged myself through the days and wondered how I would get out of bed in the morning and face another day.

I scoffed at other women who gave up their farms when all the men had gone off to war, certain that I could always take care of my own.

I knew not what to do or where to turn.

What should I tell Andrew about Jane? Should I tell him that Jane had gone to volunteer as a nurse? More lies. What would he do if I told him the truth? Would he forgive me? Would he ever forgive Jane? How could I tell Andrew that our daughter had left us and was on her way to New York with a Union soldier, a man that I brought to our land? How could he understand? Why should he? I left our family to search for our sons and returned with the enemy.

Every day there was word of another family devastated by the death of a husband, father or son. The Home Guard had become as much a place for mercenaries as those whose purpose it was to help innocent farmers. Everyone was vigilant, keeping a close eye on livestock and wood. Hardship and grief were breaking the strongest of families apart.

My eyes welled up with tears and longing. A part of me wished to be with Jane and Daniel. Young and in love. To know once again that euphoric feeling which diffused every worry and concern in the world. Children and brothers might die, wars rage, people fall ill, yet, the love of youth was so eternally hopeful, ever looking ahead to happier times.

Sara was calling. She called for Jane, not me. I heard Polly talking softy to her.

I tried to steady my heart and the panic I felt. How would I tell my family of Jane's disappearance? I told myself I still had a family, six children to care for. I had to be strong. Women were leaving farms which had been in their family for more than a hundred years, unable to keep up with farm work after husbands and sons had all joined the war. Many had left for cities where they found work in order to feed their children. Would I become one of them?

I gazed out the window on the fields of my home. Andrew was leaving the barn to check the corn and vegetables. His back was straight as always, but his limp seemed worse to me.

For a moment I remembered him as he was when I sat in this chair with Isaac asleep in my arms. So many years ago, in our first home, now Oliver's and Mahala's home. It was nestled in lowland below this house, with hills surrounding it. A creek ran a stone's throw from the front porch. I placed Isaac in his crib and went to the field to help Andrew. It was late October. We still had root vegetables to gather. The day sparkled with a different sort of light, as if trying to wring the last bit of summer from the cloudless azure sky. Trees still held leaves in mellow hues of gold and pale orange. We were so young and fearless. In the field, under the warm sun, I believe we conceived Asa, born nine months later. We splashed into the creek afterwards. Laughing and filled with happiness. Andrew brought Isaac from the house and the two of them sat at the edge of the creek throwing stones into the water. Isaac's sweet laughter carried into the kitchen where I prepared supper.

Would we ever have days such as those again? Would we ever know happiness as we did then?

I shook my head trying to dispel the memories. I seemed to dwell in the past more and more these days.

Polly entered the kitchen giggling with Sara. "Where is Jane? She's usually up before me."

I knew not what to say.

"I'm not sure, Polly. Let's make breakfast. We'll talk at supper time."

She looked at me quizzically, but thankfully did not press me for an answer. I knew I had but a few hours to decide what to tell my family about Jane's absence.

If not for my children I thought I would simply fall apart.

I felt completely alone.

CHAPTER TWENTY-SIX

OLIVER

July-October, 1863
Petersburg, Virginia

NEAR THE END of July, we met up with fellow soldiers of the 29th Virginia regiment who were sent to Richmond around June 9 on orders of President Davis. How fortunate they were to have missed the battle of Gettysburg. Those of us who fought in that battle felt disheartened and feared we might have lost the war. More men had deserted each day as the sense of defeat grew.

We marched as a full regiment to Culpepper, where we camped until the end of summer.

On September 14, we boarded a train at Petersburg, heading for the town of Bristol, on the border of Tennessee, where Federals threatened General Jones. Men covered the flat cars, cattle cars and even the tops of cars. I squeezed into a flat car with men who had wounds still unhealed. It was stifling and I was almost overcome by the smell of sweat and the stink of unwashed bodies. I knew I smelled the same. I found my handkerchief and covered my nose.

We arrived in Sullivan County on September 16, but by the time we had reached the border town, the fighting was over. At the end of the month we were back on the train to Petersburg.

In Petersburg, given we were so close to our homes, Colonel Giles gave the regiment a short furlough. Perhaps he felt there would be fewer deserters if we were given time to visit our families. It is a fact, a great number of our men deserted when the Union forces pressed us with greater numbers and better supplies and equipment. We had until mid-October to return for duty and we were all in a happy state of anticipation. I had not seen my family for almost three years and I was overjoyed at the thought of seeing them again.

It took two days of solid walking to get to Hillsville. I only stopped when my feet started to bleed. As I tended my feet I watched an eagle soar overhead. Oh, how I wished I could fly.

I thought I would run to my family the moment the farm came into view. But now, as I looked down on my family home, I had to stop and watch for a while. I was unable to control my racing heart and I felt a strange reluctance to approach my family. It was a beautiful fall evening. Smoke drifted lazily from the chimney. All looked peaceful and calm, as if there were no war.

I glanced down at my blood-stained clothes and rubbed a hand across my face. What did I look like? I didn't want my family to pity me. I continued to watch. When I saw my father walk from the field to the barn, I could wait no longer. My feet barely touched the ground as I ran toward home. The dogs, barking, charged toward me, and when they knew me, jumped on me and bounced around my legs. My father looked up and slowly walked toward me. Then, when he recognized me, he broke into a run. I nearly knocked him off his feet as I fell into his embrace. Embarrassed at such a display of emotion, we separated and stared at one another. I knew there were tears in my eyes and Father hastily wiped his away.

"Well, praise the Lord, Oliver! Is it really you?" He stood back and studied me. I saw the concern on his face. "Are you wounded, Son? Have you been discharged?"

"No, Father. We were given a short furlough. I've been walking for two days. I'm sure I look like I'm wounded." I managed a laugh.

"You look...fine, Son. Just fine. But, you have changed. You look older...and...well, you look like you could use a good meal." He tenderly put an arm around my shoulder. I felt his strength even though I could see how much the last three years had aged him.

At that moment the rest of my family burst from the kitchen door. Mother ran to me with arms outstretched.

"Oliver?" She stopped quickly and gasped, covering her mouth with her hand.

"Oliver?"

Before I could answer I was in her arms, my younger brothers and sisters encircled my legs and waist. I winked at little Sara, who wrinkled her nose and hid in Mother's skirts. Peter stood back, reticent, but a grin was on his face.

I felt a peace I had not known in years. To be surrounded by so many who loved me was overwhelming. Trembling in Mother's arms, I feared I might break down.

She instinctively understood I was struggling to control myself and nudged my siblings away.

"Look at you, Son! We need to get you out of those filthy clothes. Polly, Mary, William, Preston, heat some water. Your brother needs a bath." She turned to Peter, "Peter, give them a hand, please."

When my brothers and sisters left, she whispered, "Are you all right, Son? Are you wounded or ill?"

"Mother, I am fine. My regiment was given a furlough. I've walked for two days with little to eat or drink. I'm close to starving, that's for sure." I laughed and changed the subject to distract her from my appearance. "Is Mahala at the cottage?"

"Yes, she is. But let's get you cleaned up and fed before you see her and your son. Lawson is a big boy now. He's walking and talking." She stopped suddenly and looked at me, tears brimming in her eyes. "Oliver, are you really, all right?" Are you well?"

Wrinkles and lines scored her face where there were none three years ago. My heart broke as I saw what the war had done to my mother and father.

"Mother, I am here and alive. I am grateful God has spared me so I might see all my family again. But Jane? Where is she?"

"We'll speak of Jane another day, Son. Let's get that bath and some food into you, before you go to your wife and son."

I was thankful to be allowed some time before I saw Mahala and Lawson. I needed to gather my thoughts. I would be a stranger to my son. What would Mahala think of her husband now? She sent a healthy, strong young man of eighteen off to war. I knew I was very much changed in appearance and in spirit.

After a bath, I found clean clothes in the room I had shared with Isaac and Asa. Reminders of my brothers were all around me. A collection of stones, turned up as we plowed the fields, remained in a basket on the dresser. Asa was certain they were arrowheads. A jacket, belonging to Isaac, still hung from a hook. The reality of their deaths overcame me in the bedroom.

There was a soft knock on the door. "Oliver? May I come in?"

"Yes. Come in. I'm decent."

There was a wide smile on Mother's face as she handed me a bouquet of flowers. "For Mahala, Son. You need to go to her."

I brought the flowers to my nose and inhaled the clean fragrance. "Are these the roses Asa planted?"

A sad smile crossed her face as she nodded. "Yes. The bushes have reached their peak, it's almost the end of their season."

I returned her smile knowing we both felt the presence and absence of Asa and Isaac.

She turned to leave the room and then turned back to me. "Are you worried about seeing your wife and son, Oliver?"

How did she read my mind?

"No, not worried. It's just been so long. How do I look? Have I changed, Mother?"

"You look like a man. Any woman would be proud to call you husband." She flashed a smile and the years seemed to fade from her face.

I took my time walking across the fields and down the hill through the woods to the cottage. I heard the soft sound of the creek gurgling over stones before I saw it. The path which ran alongside the creek was covered in the saffron colored leaves of fall.

I stopped and stared. Ahead was the cottage. It was all as I had left it.

And there was Mahala, in the garden, bending over some patch of vegetables. She stood clapping her hands and called, "Lawson, Lawson." A little boy ran to her. It was my son. No longer an infant. Mahala lifted him and whirled him around, both of them laughing.

My heart stopped. It was as if I was an observer, watching two strangers. Mahala's hair hung loose as it had when we married. She looked exactly as she did at our wedding four years ago. Something caught in my throat. How could she still look the same, while I felt like a completely different person?

She had always possessed a sixth sense which I attributed to her Indian grandmother. She looked toward me. I felt her intense gaze and then her quiet recognition.

Mahala had never been overly emotional and she walked calmly toward me, whispering in Lawson's ear. He too, had the same gaze as his mother. I matched their pace and we met halfway. I was breathless, but at the same time felt a tremendous sense of peace.

There was no hesitation in Mahala's voice. "Oliver. You are home." She said softly, taking the bouquet I offered and bringing the roses to her nose, inhaling the fragrance.

I nodded. "Yes, for a few weeks. I have a furlough."

She whispered in Lawson's ear.

"Dada," he exclaimed, reaching for me, a smile on his face, pleased with himself. "Dada."

I took Lawson in one arm and encircled Mahala's waist with the other. Together we walked to the cottage.

It was as though I had never left. Mahala's head rested on my shoulder and my tears fell on her hair. She ran her arm around my waist and I felt the warmth of her hand.

We had no need for words.

Mother and Mahala prepared a meal that evening that made me ache with anticipation, roasted chicken, kale prepared with salt pork, canned tomatoes, and an apple cobbler. The scent alone made me feel faint. I tried to eat slowly, but it was impossible. I sensed the family held back as I had my fill.

After dinner I helped Mother put my younger brothers to bed. Their questions tumbled over each other.

"How many Yanks did you shoot, Oliver? Did you get that new rifle we been hearing about? Where's your drum?" William and Preston looked at me with eyes filled with admiration, the way I once looked at Isaac and Asa.

"I'll tell you all about it tomorrow. I'm mighty tired tonight." I rubbed the top of their heads with my knuckles. "Goodnight, Billy and Pres. Sleep well." They grinned at my nicknames for them.

As I passed the room where my sisters slept, I blew kisses

at Polly and Mary. I was rewarded by their sweet smiles. I didn't see Jane and was puzzled again by her absence.

In the front room Father sat in his chair near the fireplace. He had placed another for me between his chair and Mother's rocker. Mahala and Lawson sat on the floor stacking blocks.

"Are those the blocks you carved for me, Father?"

"Yes, they are. He doesn't knock them down nearly as often as you did, Son." He chuckled, with a twinkle in his eye. Peter sat by Lawson, one of the dogs curled beside him.

While we waited for Mother to put Sara to bed, my eyes wandered from one familiar object to another. The chairs, table, bureau, every piece of furniture in the room was made by the hands of my father or grandfather. It was all familiar, yet seemed strangely foreign to me. The fire crackled. We all waited for Mother to join us.

When Mother entered the room, she took her pipe from the hearth stone, lighting it with a twig from the fire. She settled with a sigh in her rocker.

It was I who broke the silence.

"Thank you, Mother, and Mahala, I've dreamed of your chicken dinners every night."

"We hope to fatten you up before you go back to battle, don't we, Mahala?" Mother smiled and patted my hand. "How go the battles, Oliver? How are our troops?"

I stared at the fire, not knowing where to begin to tell my family what I had experienced. How can one explain what hell on earth is, describe the sound and smell of death? My mother's admonition to always speak plainly came back to me. I began with Gettysburg, the most recent and bloody of all the battles I'd witnessed.

"Our march into Pennsylvania and the battle at Gettysburg was a defeat. I cannot guess the number of men who died, and the wounded...were...are...beyond my...." I swallowed hard. "I cannot begin to describe it." Taking a deep breath, I continued. "We finally retreated and marched back toward Virginia.

It took ten days for the Potomac River to drop enough for us to cross. All the while the wounded men were in pain and suffered dreadfully. Thankfully the Union forces did not pursue us from Gettysburg. I don't believe we could have repulsed another attack if they had. You can't imagine the number of soldiers who were gravely wounded, missing arms and legs, so many died...." I cleared my throat and leaned forward in my chair, my arms resting on my legs. Mahala put a steady hand on my knee. "Earlier battles. Thousands died on both sides. From wounds and disease." I stood and faced the fire, pretending to warm my hands. "I don't know why I was spared. I don't know...while so many died."

"Tell us no more, Son." Mother's voice was soft and comforting. "I know you are suffering at the telling of it. Come, sit down. You'll be with us such a short time."

When I sat, her hand covered mine. "There's been too much grief and sadness in the time we have been apart. Let's talk of other things."

I silently thanked Mother, for I could speak no more of the horror of war.

The flickering of the fire seemed to cast a spell over me. I felt sleepy and warm and my eyelids started to close. I recalled how hard it had been to find firewood the previous winters, how cold and miserable the nights in camp were and how I longed to be home with my family. I was home with my family. Yet, I did not feel as though I was home. Home seemed like a make-believe place, a place I wondered if I would ever find again. I couldn't understand why I felt so alone. I searched the faces of my family. They were all with me, but for Isaac, Asa and Jane. I forced myself to acknowledge my family and join in the conversation. I remarked on the absence of Jane. I was troubled by her absence and wondered if my family was keeping something from me. I missed Jane, we were the closest in age, and I had always felt protective of her. I wasn't sure what to think of her absence. I was almost afraid to ask where she was.

"Where is Jane? Has something happened to her?"

Mahala squeezed my knee. "I should get Lawson home before it gets too dark to see the path. Will you follow soon, Oliver?"

I walked her to the door. We embraced and our kiss was so urgent it left me breathless and longing to go with her.

"Yes, Mahala. I'm desperate to lie with you in our bed again."

Her smile was a promise that she would be waiting for me after I said goodnight to my family.

When I returned to my chair by the fire, Father was sitting next to Mother. He reached for her hand and started to speak, "Son, Jane has...."

Mother interrupted him. "She has gone north with Daniel. A Union soldier."

I looked at her in disbelief. "What do you mean? A Union soldier? How could that happen?"

"Oliver, I have always told you to speak plainly and truthfully, and I will do the same. After we received your letter I was unable to accept your brothers' deaths, that they were gone. I had an overwhelming need to know where they were, or where their bodies were. I persuaded Peter to help me look for them among the Home Guard. One of the wounded soldiers told me of Asa's death. He gave me his handkerchief."

"You searched for Isaac and Asa, among the Home Guard?" I was amazed at the boldness of my mother. I had always known her to be strong and willful, but never foolhardy. "What were you thinking, Mother? Did you know there are thieves and mercenaries camped with the Guard?"

"My grief consumed me, Son. I was not myself. I can't explain it." Her eyes closed and she shook her head.

"Do you know then how Asa died? The man who gave you Asa's handkerchief knew him?"

"Yes, he was in the Asa's regiment, and on the same train

transporting the wounded to the hospital in Petersburg. Asa gave him the handkerchief to bind his wound. Your brother died of fever at the hospital."

Tears brimmed in Mother's eyes and slid down her cheeks. I nodded. I knew all too well the toll the fever had taken, but Asa, my brother? He was strong and healthy.

"Fever…'the fever?'" I shook my head in bewilderment. We were all quiet as I absorbed this news. In the few letters I received from my family no one ever mentioned how my brothers died. I thought they would both have died in battle.

"Did it bring you some comfort to know how Asa died?" I searched my parents' faces.

"It did, Oliver. But still, I couldn't forget Isaac. I couldn't give up hope that…that he might still be alive. I wanted to keep searching. They were together in the Tennessee regiment. I thought if Asa died of fever, perhaps Isaac might be alive and recovering with the Guard." Brushing away tears, she glanced at Peter.

"Peter felt I was neglecting my duty at home. He said I was forgetting about you, your brothers and sisters and thinking only of Isaac and Asa. Perhaps he was right. I know I wasn't thinking clearly."

Peter lifted his head, but quickly looked away.

Mother continued, "Peter and I argued, I think we were both overcome with grief and guilt."

I glanced at Peter. His mouth was set in a firm line as he stared at the fire. My brother had changed. He was no longer a boy, but a young man. No doubt he would join the army as soon as he was eighteen.

"Peter left and I stayed alone in the woods. It was where I wanted to be. Alone. My heart was broken. I wasn't sure I could carry on. Two sons gone. I just needed time. But thank God we still have you, Son."

"Thank God you are safe, Mother. You might have been killed for your horse alone."

"Yes, I know. But Spirit wasn't taken. Instead I shot a man."

"What happened? What do you mean you shot a man?"

"I was awakened by a man trying to take my horse. It was dark and I could only see the outline of a man. I couldn't tell if it was one of our own men, or a Yankee. It was Daniel. I shot him in the calf. I wounded him, which was my intention." Mother stopped talking and stared into the distance, her eyes soft, as if trying to recall something important. "He was a Union soldier, from New York. He said he was with an Irish brigade. He was so young and pleaded with me to help him and I...I couldn't help it...I felt sorry for him. I tended to his wound. He told me he was trying to get home to care for his mother, who was ill. He said he was her only child. His story touched me. I thought of how I hoped a stranger would help you, or Isaac and Asa, if you were wounded. I brought Daniel home with me. He hid in the woods until he was well enough to travel. Jane followed me one day and discovered him, and... and...."

I watched Mother's face as she spoke. She may have thought I would be angry that she would dare help a Northern soldier. An invader. There was no need to explain my own feelings of ambivalence toward our enemy. I had seen the best and worst of men on both sides of the war. My heart went out to her. I too had felt the desire to help a wounded Union soldier, many times. It made me feel sad to think that even we questioned the compassion we both thought God would want us to show our fellow man. I wanted to embrace her and let her know I understood and cherished her kindness.

"And, they fell in love." It was hard to believe my own sister had married a Northerner. Yet, somehow it gladdened my heart to know that war could not destroy all feelings of sympathy, even for our enemy.

"Is this Daniel a good man, Mother?" I smiled at her. She nodded, looking down at her hands.

"Yes, he's a good and honest man. It seems they fell in love, almost at first sight."

Mother smiled shyly at Father. "They are married and in New York, but promise to come home when the war is over. Jane is caring for his mother and Daniel is back with his regiment. I pray God, he survives."

We were all quiet. Each waiting for the other to speak.

"I hope Jane is happy. I know she's not a frivolous girl. She must love him deeply."

I watched as they exchanged tender smiles, relieved the story was told.

"It's getting late. I think it's time for me go to my family." My parents stood and together they embraced me.

"Goodnight, Son." They said in unison.

It was dark when I left my parents' home. I borrowed Father's lantern and made my way through the field and down the hill to the cottage. It was a clear night and the stars above seemed to hang so low I felt I could reach out and touch them. I wished I could gather them and take them to Mahala, to light her life, and Lawson's, if I should not survive the war. I heard only the call of an owl and the sound of animals scurrying as I made my way over newly mown fields. I was awed by the silence and peace, the fresh smell of hay and soil. There were no cries of men in agony, no sound of cannons and muskets, no smell of death. I seemed to be always close to tears these days and I knew not why.

As I neared the cottage I saw Mahala had left a lamp on in the front room. The cruelty of war had so eroded my expectation of human kindness, I was overcome at the beauty of that simple gesture, to know I was missed and welcomed home. How many men had deserted the war to find this solace again? After three years of constant battle, I felt as though I was living in a dream. At this moment I fully understood why men deserted the army.

I realized with profound sadness that I saw before me all I ever wanted. How would I ever find the strength to leave it all in two weeks?

"Mahala, what would you think of me if I deserted? If I stayed here and we moved to Kentucky or West Virginia?" We lay spooned together, my face buried in her hair. My hand moving over the soft curves of her body beneath her thin cotton nightgown.

She said nothing and turned onto her back. I studied her profile in the soft light of a flickering candle.

"Mahala?"

"Of course, I would love you, Oliver, no matter what you do. You think I don't want you here with me and Lawson? I have missed you so very much." She twined her fingers through mine as she spoke.

"I could stay here for a couple of months. The army won't count you as a deserter until you miss two pay cycles. Of course, we aren't paid. That's just how they keep track. But I could go back after Christmas and not be listed as a deserter. The war might even be over by then."

I waited for Mahala to respond. I could hear her steady breathing. Her thumb caressed the callouses on my hand made by my drumsticks, but her silence made me feel anxious.

"Mahala," I turned her face toward me and searched her eyes, "what are you thinking?"

"I am thinking Oliver, that it is your choice. I cannot make such a decision for you. There is nothing I want more than to have you here. I have wanted so much to share with you Lawson's first steps, his first words. I have prayed for you, and for an end to this war every day." She turned to face me. She placed a warm hand on my cheek. "It is all I want. But Oliver,

I'm not certain you would be the same man I married if you deserted. Your brothers died fighting. Knowing this, can you reconcile deserting in your own heart?"

I knew of course the answer. I could not desert. I would feel a traitor, not only to myself, but to my brothers. But the thought of returning to my regiment was agonizing. Three years of the bloodbath of war made me feel as though I was an actor in a play. I had no fight left in me. I just followed orders like a trained animal. Men on both sides ached daily for an end to the fighting. I had seen the look of relief, and at times, almost rapture on the faces of Union soldiers we took as prisoners. The faces of men at last free from the perpetual fear and torment of not knowing if they would live another day.

I pulled Mahala closer and she clung to me. "No, I cannot desert now, as much as I might wish to. If only out of respect for my brothers, I must see this to the end."

"I love you, Oliver. You will survive this war."

Two weeks later I left my family. I forced myself to walk away with my head up and my shoulders straight. My brothers and sisters ran alongside me. But once they turned back toward home, my shoulders slumped and I lowered my head, overcome with sadness. I never looked back. I couldn't. Had I looked back I would have been unable to walk away.

CHAPTER TWENTY-SEVEN

ABIGAIL

The Quesinberry Farmhouse
Dugspur, Virginia
October 1863-May 1864

THE JOY OLIVER'S furlough brought our family in October was short-lived. Peter turned eighteen that month and solemnly announced he would join the army. A sharp pain twisted my stomach as I watched him pack his belongings. I wanted to beg Peter to wait for another month or two, but I knew I couldn't change his mind. In town I had heard of many battles lost by our army since the defeat at Gettysburg. It made me think surely the war could not last much longer. It mattered little to me if our army won or lost the war. I had little fear now that the Northerners would find our remote farm and take it from us. I only cared that Oliver and Peter return home safely.

There wasn't the fanfare that accompanied the departure of Isaac, Asa, and Oliver. The family, which now included Mahala and Lawson, gathered and waved goodbye as Peter and Andrew took the wagon to the recruitment center in

Hillsville. My heart ached as I watched him leave. I'm not sure he heard me when I cried out to him, "Be careful, Peter. I love you, Son."

Dear God, I prayed, please do not take another son from us.

I rejected the war, and I'd become disdainful of those who continued to support it, even at times, my own husband. I did not speak of my feelings with Andrew, for I knew he, as other men, would not admit the futility, loss of life and deprivation it had caused Virginia and our families. Men continued to insist, with a false sense of pride, that the war was not all but lost. It infuriated me, but I swallowed my anger and said nothing. With winter bearing down, my concern grew beyond normal proportions. I was filled with anxiety that our boys would have neither food nor clothing. At times I felt such despair I had to force myself to care for the needs of my family. All I wished for was an end to the war so we might live in peace.

Added to my prayers were Jane, Daniel and his mother, Bridget. We'd had just three letters from Jane, in which she said Daniel's mother's health had improved, and she was able to take in laundry and sewing again. Jane helped supplement their meager income with her skill in sewing. Daniel and his Mother, and now Jane, live in a dark cellar beneath a milliner's shop, a shop selling fancy hats for women. I was mystified that such a shop existed at all. What sort of women looked for hats in the midst of a war causing such loss of life and destruction? She wrote that shortly before she and Daniel arrived in New York, there were violent protests against the draft, mainly involving the Irish. Daniel told her of the anger felt by the poor against the rich, who were allowed to pay three hundred dollars and avoid conscription, while newly arrived Irish and German immigrants were thrown immediately into the draft. It surprised me to hear that the Irish and German workers of New York had turned against the Negroes, who competed with them for lower-paying wages. It seemed they resented the fact that Negroes were exempt from the draft because they were not American citizens. I was confused by it all, but it seemed to me the people of New York were as tired of the war as we were in Virginia.

Mahala lived with Lawson in the cottage by the creek and obviously enjoyed the peacefulness I had always felt there. She helped me with the last of the canning and we filled the root cellar with apples, potatoes and root vegetables. She hung thin apple slices from her cottage ceiling to dry, adding herbs gathered from the fields and her family's farm. I helped her slice the apples as thin as possible and we strung them from the ceiling above the woodstove. The cottage was fragrant with the combination of the scent of the apples and herbs. Mahala's name meant "Indian woman" in these parts. We had not spoken of how she got her name, but Oliver mentioned an Indian grandmother. She learned a great deal from her father in the use of herbs to maintain health and heal the sick, and she was diligent in keeping a supply of tonics prepared for use if needed for ailments.

She walked up the steep hillside to our house a few times a week. Such a beautiful young woman, almost as tall as Oliver. Her amber colored eyes were striking, with a ring of black around the iris. It was easy to see why Oliver fell in love at first sight. There was about her an air of both mystery and serenity.

She asked me to teach her the complicated blanket patterns I made on the loom. I was pleased to have her help and her company. The work usually led to easy conversation between women, since we were together for long stretches of time. Mahala was by nature quiet and thoughtful, one to keep her most private feelings to herself. But she was beginning to share her thoughts with me.

"Is everything well at the cottage, Mahala?" She smiled, her eyes crinkling at the corners.

"Oh, it is fine, Mother Quesinberry. It's peaceful, and very cozy for Lawson and me." She passed the shuttle back to me with ease. "Is that where Oliver was born?"

"Yes, it is. Isaac, Asa, and Oliver were all born in that house. I loved living there, so near the creek. It was easy to get water for the vegetable garden and fruit trees. The boys loved playing in the creek on hot summer days. I could sit on the porch and watch as I did other work. I miss that house."

"I'm happy there too. As you know the apple trees still produce a good crop." A delighted grin spread across her face. "And the sound of the creek puts me to sleep at night. What made you move? It seems an enchanted place to me."

I passed her the shuttle, which she quickly sent back to me. "We moved because the house was too small for our growing family. The creek would often flood in the spring thaws, making it difficult to get to town. We had this land here, on higher ground. When it came time to make that house larger or build elsewhere, we chose this spot. I'm very fond of the cottage, though. I'm happy that you and Oliver will be living there. And please, Mahala, call me Abigail, we're family now."

"Yes, I will call you Abigail. Mother...I mean...." We laughed together at her hesitation. "When Oliver comes home, we will raise a large family there." She spoke as though certain Oliver would return unharmed from the war. I wished I shared her faith.

"Abigail?"

Mahala brought my attention back to the loom. She held the shuttle between us.

"Oh, I'm sorry. I was thinking of Oliver. I wish so much he could be here to watch his son grow."

"Yes, I know, I do as well. He adores Lawson. But we'll have many more children. We will have a daughter next."

Mahala frequently surprised me with her predictions. She was often right, and it was a bit unnerving. Whatever would I do if she should foresee the death of Oliver or Peter?

"A daughter? Well, Oliver would love a little girl. That I know." I quickly changed the subject, uncomfortable with her foreseeing of the future. "We'll get more wood down to you soon. Once the snow starts it will be harder to climb up here. You might be stranded there alone at times."

"That's very kind. I know it's hard for Father Andrew to do all the work alone. I could help chop the wood. I always helped my grandfather put up wood for the winter. Please don't worry, I have a good supply that I chopped myself."

I admired her self-sufficient nature. Perhaps because it reminded me of myself at her age. As a newly married young woman, I worked alongside Andrew in all the work of the farm and making a home. Even after the birth of my first three babies, I still wanted to help with the hard-outdoor work. But after the birth of Jane, I found I did not have time to work with Andrew. I missed that bond with him.

Our work at the loom passed quickly, as Mahala learned everything with ease, even the complicated blanket patterns. I was even more impressed with my son's choice of a wife.

November, 1863

It was late November and getting colder. I suggested Mahala come live with us, but she would have none of it.

As Christmas approached I had no heart to celebrate, but I made the effort for the little ones. In spite of my mood, and with the help of Mahala, we had a Christmas celebration. She gave each child a pair of knitted mittens. Where she found so much yarn I could not fathom. She knitted for me, a lacy shawl, not overly large, but a welcome gift to wrap around my shoulders. For Andrew, she knitted a hat with yarn left over from all the other gifts she knitted. It looked quite handsome on him. We had little to give her, but Andrew carved a small rifle from pine wood for Lawson, and I gave Mahala a blanket she admired when we worked it on the loom.

We had heard nothing from Oliver or Peter and I prayed fervently for them every night. Andrew began to hint in early December that after the spring crops were planted he would enlist in the army in whatever capacity he could serve. I reminded him regularly of his age and his crippled leg, as well as his promise not to leave me alone to run the farm. As spring approached, he spoke more often of his determination to join the war effort. We had heard such bad news of our poor boys, that nearly every man who could stand upright had either joined or was planning to do so. I could not look at Andrew without feeling anger that he would think of breaking his promise to me. I looked around the house and saw two women who would have total responsibility for a farm and six children, all under the age of thirteen. How could he leave me when he vowed he would not do so? I lay awake at night, staring at the ceiling and wondered how I could manage when Andrew left.

It had turned bitterly cold. I would not have flinched a few years ago at the prospect of caring for the children and farm and animals, regardless of the weather. But I was no longer as confident as I once was.

I was unable to hide my worry when alone with Andrew. At night I turned away from him and moved to the far edge of the bed. I never thought I would feel such resentment toward my husband. I could only pray that my anger would help me rise to the challenge ahead when I would be without his help.

He was ever more attentive to me as the cold winter months progressed. When the weather began to warm he told me of his plans each night.

"Abbie, please listen to me." He gathered me in his arms when we were in bed, but I was filled with apprehension and turned my face away from him.

"Abbie?" He released me and turned on his back, an arm thrown above his head. "I'll get the crops in before I leave. My position in the army won't require me to do battle. Why can't you understand? We've lost two sons to this war, and two more are fighting. What would you have me do? Let every able-bodied man fight, and I stay here and do nothing?"

"Yes, Andrew. That is what I'd have you do. You are fifty-two years old. You are crippled. We have six children to care for. What of your responsibility to us?"

"Have you forgotten how you yearned to search for Isaac and Asa? The need you felt to do something to ease your torment? Now I understand how you felt. This helplessness I feel in the face of the suffering of our soldiers eats away at me every day and every night. It is not even the Southern Cause I would fight for now. It is about our boys, and how much blood and treasure Virginia has given to win this battle. I fear we might have lost, but I will never be able to live with myself if I don't at least do something to help. Can't you understand that?"

I said nothing, but his words had found a soft spot, and I understood more his need to do something to help our boys.

Yet, I asked myself if I would be able to save the farm with my husband and grown sons gone to fight? Was I strong enough to survive when so many other women had failed? I had seen the families fleeing the farms, wagons filled with their most cherished possessions. The faces of the women and children were sad and defeated. Tears ran down their faces as they waved goodbye to friends and neighbors. It broke my heart to watch.

May, 1864

When Andrew was ready to join the army, I was over-whelmed with longing. Oh, how I would miss him. I watched him limp from the barn toward the house and my eyes filled with tears of sadness and regret. Regret that my good husband felt such a strong duty to join the army, that he felt compelled to leave all he loved and enter a war that many now thought might end in defeat. And what was to be gained? Four sons and now my husband would be gone to fight a wretched war. How much longer could I endure? How much longer could Virginia endure?

On the day he left us, the children encircled him, grasping him around the knees and pulling on his trousers. Little Sara took to crying and calling, "Papa, Papa, don't go."

Mahala gathered the children to her, promising a treat in the kitchen. With Sara in her arms, she turned back to us at the kitchen door. "Be safe, Father Andrew. Do you have the herbs I prepared for you?"

Andrew smiled and held up a small bag. "Indeed, I do, Mahala. Thank you."

"If you brew them, they will help you ward off illness." She nodded and coaxed the children into the kitchen.

Now I had to say goodbye to my husband. It was so very hard to do. Every fiber of my being was longing to drop to my knees and beg him to stay.

"Here, Andrew. These are your handkerchiefs. Bring them back to me. Do you hear me?" I was determined to hold back my tears, as Andrew pulled me into his arms.

"Abbie, I am in the reserves. I won't be in battle. I'll probably drive the supply wagons. And surely, I'll be allowed furloughs. Where's my bold, spirited, Abigail?" He gave me a sad smile, and his eyes glistened as he gazed at me, as if trying to memorize my face.

"Andrew, how will I ever manage without you? So many women have been unable to keep their farms going. I'm afraid I won't...I'm...."

"You're my wife, Abigail Banks Quesinberry. You are the most capable woman I know." Reaching into his pocket he withdrew an envelope. "I made you a promise, Abbie. Open this after I leave." His eyes were locked on mine. "I always keep my promises. You know that."

His embrace grew stronger as we clung together. His voice was soft and raspy as he whispered in my ear, "I love you, dear Abigail."

Then he was walking away. I watched his back and swallowed hard. His limp seemed worse than ever and I wanted to run after him, to make him stay with me.

"I love you too, Andrew. I love you! Come back to me! Do you hear!"

I had not the heart to open the letter Andrew gave me until the following morning. When I read it, I sat down on the edge of the bed to steady myself. I knew not what to think. It was dated December 24. A Christmas gift? My good husband had bought a slave to help on the farm. I stared at the receipt. It was for the purchase of a man named Charlie. A man my husband bought for $4000 confederate dollars! A man who according to Andrew's letter should already be in Hillsville. I had only to go and pick him up. I was dumbfounded, stunned that Andrew would do such a thing.

I didn't recognize the name of the man who was to convey such a purchase. The purchase of a human being! Charlie was purchased in Richmond and brought to Hillsville by a slave trader!

I could not contain my fury at the thought that Andrew would do such a thing. I knew what I had to do.

As I readied the horse, I called out to Mahala, who was working with the children in the garden. "Will you please watch the children today. I have to go to Hillsville on business that Andrew left unfinished. Will you mind? I might be all day."

"Of course, Abigail. Do what you must. Take care."

"Thank you, Mahala."

I had no doubt Andrew thought I would be grateful to have the help of a slave. But I could not imagine using another person in such a way. I knew he made the decision out of love, but

I would have none of it!

I would soon free a man named Charlie. I had no desire to ever see his face. A part of me was in pain that Andrew would think to do such a thing. I was eager to release this man Charlie and myself from this burden.

I might not be able to do all the work of the farm, nor have the strength or fortitude that I had always taken for granted, but I would always have my pride and dignity, and never willingly take it away from someone else.

I coaxed Spirit into a gallop, letting the wind blow my hair from my bun, and for a brief time allowed myself to remember who I was before the war.

Finding the slave trader was not as difficult as I thought it would be. Everyone seemed to know where he was, perhaps because it was unusual for a man like him to be in Hillsville at all. People looked at me suspiciously, but did not ask the question I knew was on their minds. "Why are you looking for such a person?"

Farmers in our area didn't own slaves. At least I knew of none. My face turned scarlet as I muttered a response. "I have, well, business. I just have a question for him." Their eyes followed me as I walked toward the tavern. A deep bitterness had built up toward wealthy slave owners among people in our area during the four years of relentless fighting and destruction. People were fully aware now that the war was not about saving their farms from northern aggressors.

The slave trader was a hard-looking man. Sitting alone in a corner of the tavern, he hunched over what appeared to be several glasses of whiskey. I approached him slowly, all the while looking for a Negro man. I lowered my voice and looked around for neighbors who might know me. I was embarrassed to be in the tavern and seen with the man. I cleared my throat and he looked up. I had never seen such a stony look on a person's face. "Excuse me, I am Abigail Quesinberry. I understand my husband purchased a…" I found it difficult to say the word slave, "…a man."

"A slave. Named Charlie." His voice was rough and filled with scorn. "Well, I don't have him. Goddamned son of a bitch ran away. Escaped, right outside Richmond. Union troops are all over the place around there. We've lost a damn fortune in slaves lately. All they have to do is run a few miles to the Yanks and they're gone."

I wasn't sure what to do. It was my thought to set Charlie free. I forced a smile. "Well, sir, I expect you will return the four thousand dollars my husband paid for the man, and I'll be on my way."

He raised his head slowly, a cruel smirk on his face. "I don't have your money. That slave was paid for in Richmond. I's just paid a few dollars to bring him here. I didn't have to come here at all after he ran away. Reckon I's just curious. First time I ever been to these parts. Not too many folks lookin' for slaves around here."

I had no reason to doubt him. I had never heard nor seen slaves being traded in Hillsville. I was puzzled again at what must have driven Andrew to spend such a large sum of money, and it angered me. I had no idea we had such a fortune! I nodded and left with a great sense of relief.

On the ride home, I thought about what would drive my husband to purchase a slave to help me on the farm. Did he think me incapable of surviving without his help? The thought renewed my sense of purpose and I felt a new strength and resolve form in my heart.

My family would survive this war. We would carry on. With or without my husband, I would see this struggle to the end and care for my children and their future.

I urged Spirit into a gallop and I felt once again the freedom I thought forever lost.

CHAPTER
TWENTY-EIGHT

OLIVER

May 1864 - January 1865
Battle of Cold Harbor and Siege of Petersburg

I WONDERED AT times where I would have been if I had taken the oath of allegiance to the Union offered by Lincoln five months ago.

On December 8, of 1863, Lincoln issued a proclamation which would pardon Confederate soldiers if we took an oath to the Union. We all knew it was a way to encourage those of us who were doubtful about the outcome of the war to give up the Confederate cause. We knew we were nearly defeated as the war progressed into the new year. Rations were scarce and what clothes we had hung from our bodies like rags. I don't know of anyone who took the oath, but I admit I thought long and hard about it. It set my mind to dreaming of freedom. I imagined returning home and taking Mahala and Lawson to Pennsylvania. I thought of going to New York to find Jane. Surely, I could find work there.

Each time my regiment left Virginia, I feared it would be the last time I saw it. I worried that I might be killed in the north and never see my wife and son again. All soldiers, on both sides must dread such an end to their lives.

My regiment had been marched like cattle, in and out of Virginia numerous times since the new year started. It seemed aimless to me, but the officers never explained their orders to us and we did as we were commanded.

We broke camp on May 9, near Kinston, North Carolina, and boarded a train for Petersburg. The rail line was broken by the Union in several places, forcing us to march at night along the tracks to Swift Creek. There we boarded another train which finally took us to Petersburg.

Alongside Pickney Howlett, I marched north from Petersburg to Richmond in the pouring rain.

Pickney's voice was seething with frustration when he leaned close to me and growled, "What the hell are they doin' to us, Oliver. We've been knocked around all over Tennessee for the last three months. Then Corse sent us to North Carolina, marched us twenty-five miles through them Goddamn swamps. After that hell I thought we was goin' back to Virginia, to Richmond. Then they turned the damned train around to send us back down to North Carolina. Now, praise God, we're heading back to Virginia! What's it been? Four months of marching back and forth? That damn train is slower than fog off shit!" He shook his head angrily. "I swear when I get back to Virginia, I might just up and disappear."

"Well, I reckon Lee wants us up around Richmond. At least we'll be back in Virginia." I shifted my drum from my right to my left shoulder. I had finally received my new one, which I ordered back in October. It seemed heavier than my old one. That could have been because I was tired of carrying a drum. I was tired of drumming reveille, breakfast call, drills, attacks and the long roll. As most men I was simply tired of war.

Our march was slow at first because we thought the Union army was ahead of us and no one felt the need to hurry. As the day wore on, we learned the Federals were not in front of us and we made better time.

Hungry and weary, I shared the last of three-days rations, issued on May 9 in Kinston, with Pickney. We were worn out from two nights of marching through a constant downpour. As we made camp that night we were still unsure how much further we had to go. We had become used to the mud we marched and slept in and we prepared as best we could for another night in leaking tents.

Pickney asked if I knew where we were headed when we settled for the night. "Do ya know the name of this here fort we're headin' to? Where the hell are we now?"

"I think I heard General Hokes call it Drewry's Bluff. It's close to Richmond, but I don't know for sure. Either way I think we better get some sleep. Who knows when we'll be up tomorrow and marching out."

We pulled our wet blankets over our heads and hoped for sleep. The rain continued all night. Sleep was at best fitful.

I was awakened within a couple of hours to rouse the men. The rain had become heavier overnight and my drum was as wet as I was.

Pickney staggered to his feet, pulling his blanket around him.

"God almighty, Oliver. What time is it? It's still pitch black."

"Maybe three, four. It doesn't matter, the order has been given and we have to march."

By daylight we reached Halfway House and were thrown immediately into skirmishes. In early darkness we finally took our place in the earthworks already established by our fellow Confederate soldiers. We were packed together in trenches of mud and tried to settle in for the night. The rain seemed endless, becoming heavier as the night progressed. Our thin wet blankets were of little use. Not even the healing blend of herbs Mahala had given me could mask the scent of filthy men and the acrid smell of smoke from guns and cannons.

May 14

General Corse gave us a day of rest yesterday. But few could rest knowing we would be sent out again.

We had been thirty-six hours in the trenches. A sudden chill overcame me as we were sent out to skirmish again, to engage the Union and slow their advance. After many hours of bloody battle and holding the Union advance on our right flank, Pickney Howlett and six others of my regiment were dead and a number missing. When we were back in the trenches I learned that Pickney's brother James was shot in the leg and taken to hospital in Richmond. I said a prayer for him as I leaned against the muddy wall of the trench and stared up at the sky, the rain washing the grime from my face. Around me a tangled mass of exhausted men sprawled in the mud. No one spoke. Surely this had been one of the bloodiest days for my regiment, and the loss of our friends weighed heavily on all of us. I thought I would never be able to reconcile the sudden death of men who one day shared a meagre meal with me and then were gone from the earth the next. I wondered when my time would come, for surely, I thought, I could not escape the war unscathed.

May 15

Fog was so thick when we awoke we could barely see one another, let alone the enemy. Other regiments had advanced as early as five. Although we were unable to see more than fifteen yards ahead, we heard the fierce fighting and gunfire. I reckoned the time to be around ten when we were given the order to attack. We charged, screaming the Rebel Yell, at the Union's left flank, through smoke, broken ground, tree limbs and deafening noise. Perhaps we stumbled over bodies as well and I dared not look down. I drummed an unrelenting beat as I lurched forward. Slowly the Yankees retreated to Bermuda

Hundred, leaving behind their dead and wounded. Quickly men went through the belongings of the Yanks, and I admit I joined them. There was equipment, clothing and rations to be had. After days of starvation it mattered little that it belonged to a man now dead or dying in front of us. Among those terribly wounded, we heard language we couldn't understand, most likely German. I looked into the eyes of one such man. His anguished voice was piteous and I knew he was mortally wounded. I lifted his water to his mouth and encouraged him to drink. His last word was 'Mutter'. There was an enormous weight on my heart, but still, when his eyes closed and he took his last breath, I hurriedly grabbed rations from his pack. In doing so I found the photograph of a young woman. A lovely young woman, her chin lowered as she gazed with clear eyes at the camera. On the back were written words I could not decipher. I could not bring myself to discard the photo. I put it in my pocket and quickly moved on to other wounded men. If there were food or supplies to be had, we would take what we could to survive.

Although the battle was considered a victory, the cost had been great. As the Yankees retreated back toward the town of Bermuda Hundred, we discovered that in only an hour's time, seventeen of our regiment had been killed, perhaps another fifty wounded.

May 16

We lost four more men in another day of fierce fighting. They were shot dead trying to take the bluff overlooking the James River. Joel Webb from Carroll County was among them. I considered searching for his body, to retrieve some personal item to take to his family, but I knew that would have been a fool's task. I could never have found his body among all the dead.

As beaten as we were, we were told that General Lee

desperately needed reinforcements to repulse Grant northeast of Richmond. Pickett's division would be sent north in the next few days and on the night of May 19th we marched out, fifteen miles into Richmond.

May 21

We boarded a train which carried us forty miles north to Penola Station. In the next two days we marched seventeen miles and united with Lee's Army of Northern Virginia near North Anna River. We were there only four days and then moved on to a place called Cold Harbor on June 1.

With the sun beating down mercilessly, it was a pitiful group of men we joined in the trenches at Cold Harbor. Given the number of Union troops assembled to the East we were thankful for the protection of the trenches as we took our place in the line. Overnight the rain started and by the next day it was pouring. Through it all we continued digging the trenches.

The day dawned cool and foggy on June 3. We were lined up shoulder to shoulder. I stood next to a man who looked familiar, but I could not recall his name. Although wet and hungry, we were well protected as we waited orders in the trenches.

It came suddenly, a frontal assault by thousands of Union men. I watched in disbelieve as we mowed them down in windrows. When the soldier next to me was shot, I put aside my drum and shouldered his rifle. I didn't need to look at him long to know he was dead. The men I shot that day were so close I could make out their features and the looks on their faces. I had seen that look in the eyes of a deer I killed for food, a look of terror, then a slackening of facial features and a widening of the eyes. Then blankness as they fell before me. I knew I would carry the image of the men I killed with me the rest of my life.

By day's end the field in front of us was littered with the bodies of thousands of Union soldiers. Around us were hundreds of our own wounded or dead. A familiar sense of numbness came over me, as though I was there and yet not. I felt bile in my throat and forced it down. The day had turned very warm and the smell of death was already pervasive. The flies were relentless and a torture to all of us as we tried to attend to our fallen.

The killing continued for ten more days, though not as intense as before. I was not an officer, and knew not the art of warfare, but I wondered at the slaughter of so many men. What could the Union officers be thinking to command men to a certain death? The days had become a blur to me, marked only by the knowledge that I had survived another day.

On June 13, my regiment was removed from the lines and marched to Malvern Hill near the James River. We had no idea why or where we were to go next. The question was answered on June 16, when we marched to the James river and were loaded onto a pontoon bridge near Drewry's Bluff. We were sent back to Bermuda Hundred which the Union had now taken from us. After a hard and fierce battle, we managed to retake part of the Bermuda Hundred line, claiming only a portion of the ground that only a month before we had fought so hard to hold.

How could we have known we would spend the next nine months in trenches on the Howlett line in front of Bermuda Hundred. As winter set in we constructed rough log huts, some better than others, depending on the willpower of those doing the construction. It had rained so hard the water stood around our huts and our wet blankets froze on our bodies.

We scavenged wood from nearby farms, but by the end of November we were carrying wood a mile back to our huts. As the siege continued the Federals had overrun the rail lines and food was scarce. There was some plundering of the nearby farms until General Corse set up patrols behind the lines to end the pillaging. By winter our rations had been reduced to a pint of corn and an ounce or two of bacon a day. Some days there was no meat at all. For a time, we subsisted only on frozen turnip tops. With a lack of food, we became increasingly weak and there was a steady stream of men taken to hospital in Chester Station.

There was little shooting as we waited for our orders, but picket duty was constant. I took my turn every third or fourth day. As if I was without a will of my own, like every other man, I did what I could to survive.

Each day I awoke and wondered if it would be the day I died. It shocked me to realize that on many days it made no difference to me one way or the other.

CHAPTER
TWENTY-NINE

OLIVER

January 1865 -
April 1865

IT WAS FREEZING cold on January 4 and a blanket of
snow covered the ground as we were sent from the Howlett
line to Fort Chaffin, north of the James River. A brilliant sun
glistened off the snow and my eyes watered and burned from
the glare. Although it was very cold indeed, it was good to be
out of the frigid wet trenches, moving about and marching toward the fort.

Only weeks after we reached the fort, we were turned
around and marched back to the Howlett Line to take our
places again in the trenches. I wondered at times what the
reasoning was behind some of the orders we were given by
our officers. With the weak physical condition of men, those
marches drained our endurance even further.

Back in the trenches, it was all we could do to keep from
freezing. There was scarce action between the Yankees and
our line. The mud was so deep between us there was little either side could do.

We hadn't much to talk about as we awaited orders. The bone-chilling rain seemed to envelop our very senses and discourage conversation. Often it was mere nods and grunts that became our way of communicating. Time was spent huddling around fires, and if we talked at all, it was of how little we knew about how the war was proceeding. We didn't know if the Yanks were defeating us or not. We did know they had to be better fed and equipped than we were. It had been some time since we had even a scrap of meat.

In the trenches, a fellow who was hunched beside me nudged my elbow and pulled his blanket around skeletal shoulders. "Do ya have any idear what day this is? Is it still December?"

"I reckon it must be early February now. I was with Pickett's division when we were moved out in early January. We were up around Fort Chaffin about four, five weeks. I guess it's February now."

"I'll be damned. My birthday done come and gone, and I been in these goddamned trenches for I don't know how many months."

When I turned to look at the man, I nearly gasped. Few of us knew what we really looked like, but the man was more emaciated than most. All but a few of his teeth were missing and his cheeks were so sunken his cheekbones were sharp as knife blades. I saw lice in his beard and turned away, wondering if I looked the same, and if I had grown accustomed to lice on my own body. I answered staring straight ahead. "I've been here about the same amount of time, but for that march up to Fort Chaffin. Not sure why we went there. We turned right back around in just a few weeks and came back here. I wonder if the officers even know what's going on. We've been hunkered down across from those Yanks for nearly eight months. We can't fight for all the mud. For the life of me I can't figure what we're doing. I hope Lee knows."

He shook his head and growled. "I don't think they's

nobody knows what's goin' on anymore. We ain't been fed or paid. God knows we's freezing to death here. I think we done lost this war. I'm just praying I get home to my family now."

Sleet began to fall and we were silent. I felt him shudder, then curse under his breath. I had never felt such intense cold or a harsher wind. We huddled closer, in an attempt to get warm and our breath mingled in the frigid air.

It seemed to me we had lost the war, and yet on March 5, my regiment under Pickett's division again marched out of the Howlett Line trenches. The weather was so foul that we marched only about two miles. We made camp near Chester Station in driving cold rain that lasted for two days. As odd as it seemed to me, after the storm passed, Pickett ordered a review of the troops. We were sodden, and surely a pitiful looking sight, but we shouldered our weapons and I took up my drum for the review.

We rested that day and at night crossed the James River into Manchester and on to the fieldworks north of the city, taking a position on the Brook Turnpike. We then marched or countermarched for several days. It seemed we were following the Yankee troopers, but no one knew for sure. We skirmished on March 15 and thanked God that no men from the 29th were lost since there were so few of us left. We heard the Federals were trying to break the South Side Railway in Dinwiddie, one of only two rail lines that supplied goods to our army and to Richmond and Petersburg. If the Federals took the railway, it would be disastrous, both for the cities and the troops. On March 29 we crossed the Appomattox River on pontoons above Petersburg to reach the South Side Railway, where we boarded trains to Sutherland's Station. It was only a trip of about ten miles, but it took hours to load, move and detrain all the troops. We marched at night to Five Forks, a crossroads only three miles below the South Side Railway.

On the 31st we headed out to Dinwiddie Court House. In the early afternoon we encountered Federals holding a ford, and after a second assault we were able to clear the way across to the country road leading to Dinwiddie Court House. Half an hour later we met more Federals, a stronger and more persistent group. Thankfully our cavalry unit was there to help rout the Yanks and together we gained access to the court house road. I don't know where the courage and strength came from, but with patience we drove the Yanks down the road toward the village. Still, we could not break the Federal line, and at sunset, in darkness, General Pickett ended the offensive.

At daylight on April 1, we left Dinwiddie Courthouse for Five Forks, taking our wounded with us over roads that mud had turned into a quagmire. When we arrived, we took our place along White Oak Road. The time passed so peacefully General Pickett went to the rear with other officers to eat shad just caught from the Nottaway River.

I left the line during the respite from skirmishing to move around, keeping low and close to the ground. I felt anxious with so little activity, and with the low spirits of my fellow soldiers. The fact that I was a drummer and had no rifle made it easier to leave the line.

The officers, including Pickett, were gathered at the rear for a meal. I could smell the fish the officers were having for their supper and I found myself drawn to the scent. I admit I felt great resentment at the sight of the officers feasting, and by the looks of it having a fine time, while we men in the trenches starved. I turned away from the sight in anger, when a soft voice called my name.

"Oliver?"

"Jacob! I should have known it was your cooking I smelled." I resisted the urge to embrace him. "What are you doing here? I thought you would be back in Richmond by now."

"I almost went back after Massa died. But one the officers ask me to stay on. Cook the meals for him. I weren't sure what I want to do, but here I am. Praise the Lord, Oliver. We's still alive! So many dead and gone. It a miracle ain't it? We's both still alive!"

We stared at each other for a long while. Each taking in the changes evident in the other. I was no longer a youth, or at least I no longer felt young. My beard had grown long, and my once sturdy body was thin, almost frail. Jacob still retained his dignity, but there was a sadness about him that wasn't there when I first knew him three years ago. His back was not quite as straight. His eyes no longer twinkled in good humor.

"Yes, I reckon it is a miracle. I don't understand how I still live. So many battles...that one at Cold Harbor." I shook my head, remembering the terrible slaughter. "I'm not sure how much more we can endure, but then I've felt that way for months now. Still, we carry on."

We fell silent. Both looking off toward the line of men facing the Federals.

Jacob nodded. When he lifted his eyes, they were filled with despair. "This been a long hard time. I been wishin' I had a wife and childern. I got no place callin' me home now. I heard them officers say Richmond and Petersburg soon be taken. I don't see no reason to go back there, but I have no place else to go." He sighed and turned to me with a sad smile on his face.

"But how your family, Oliver? They still on the farm? You get any news?"

"I had a furlough last year in October. I saw my wife and son and the rest of my family. My boy, Lawson, he's gotten so big. He didn't know me. I...I hope he will remember me if I should not return." I swallowed hard and cleared my throat. "With all the men gone, the women and children are leaving the farms, moving to the cities to try and find work." I glanced at him and smiled. "But I don't think my family would leave that farm. I can't imagine any force strong enough to make my mother leave."

"Well, from what I member you told me of your mama, I wouldn't bet against you on that." He grinned.

We were startled by the sound of heavy gunfire. "I best get back to the line, Jacob. I left my drum there."

He turned toward the officers feasting behind us. "Yes, I reckon so. And I best get back there." He gestured with a hand toward the officers. "I hope this battle be short. We got lots a wounded to take care of."

"Yes, God knows how we can manage to care for more wounded. There are so many. So many."

Jacob nodded. "I knows, Lord I knows."

"Well, be careful, Jacob. God keep you."

"You be careful too. That boy of yours be wantin' his daddy come home." His smile warmed my heart before I turned and ran back to my regiment.

We were being attacked from all sides. By the time General Pickett reached the field, the Union was at our rear fighting fiercely to take the White Oak Road. Mayo's Brigade was taken from our line to try to hold the road.

Then we were isolated. Under attack from all sides. Men were falling all around me. I put aside my drum and took up the rifle of the man next to me. Some of the cavalry dismounted and joined in the battle. We were outnumbered and overwhelmed.

There wasn't a command to retreat. It was if a rolling thunderous storm was all around me. I ran, my drum banging against my leg. We had no choice. We all ran, scattering like chickens in every direction, leaving our fallen behind. We ran north into the woods and fields. Splashing through creeks and stumbling over rocks and fallen trees. My brain was screaming "It is over. It's over." Yet, I still looked desperately for Pickett, Corse or some other officer to give us direction. I found myself alone, not another man in sight. Where was our army? Were we still a regiment? Was every soldier, as was I, running, shocked and in fear toward the South Side Railway, hoping that Lee or Pickett would be there to restore order? Tears of fury and exhaustion streamed down my face, but I could do nothing but run toward the railway and hope to find my regiment.

I reached the South Side Railroad in darkness. Officers were there and sorted out what was left of the regiments. I looked around for men from the 29th. I saw but a few. What was left of the 29th were ordered west to join Pickett. I, along with those remaining of my regiment, staggered west toward Sailor's Creek. Most of us were little more than skeletons, hardly able to shoulder weapons. We were starving, bone tired and weary. The group became smaller as we marched, many falling behind from fatigue or simply giving up. Had I known we were to fight again at Sailor's Creek, I too might have fallen behind.

Something inside drove me on. Perhaps it was the thought of my brothers, Isaac and Asa. I recognized in myself my mother's stubborn bull headedness, to persevere and finish what you start, to see it to its end, even if the end should mean defeat.

CHAPTER THIRTY

ABIGAIL

Quesinberry Farmhouse
Dugspur, Virginia
1864-1865

WE HAD RECEIVED no news of Andrew, Oliver, or Peter. Every day Mahala and I watched anxiously for the mail carrier. I prayed for just a word from one of them to let me know they were still alive. I doubted they could find a scrap of paper to write to us at this point. Still, I hoped for news—but it seemed we had been forgotten in our little corner of Virginia.

Along with the constant worry about my husband and sons, I found the work of the farm and care of the children exhausting. I had to talk myself into getting out of bed some mornings, only to repeat the never-ending tasks. We were running short of the vegetables Mahala and I canned last fall and the root cellar was nearly bare. All that was left were a few potatoes, carrots and turnips. In desperation I'd hunted squirrels, from which I made stew. I didn't tell the children what it was they were eating. Perhaps they knew, for they never asked. In the past when Andrew would bring home a squirrel from winter hunting, the children would refuse to eat it, instead having only cornbread and vegetables. I was grateful that spring would be coming soon and bring the wild greens we found to supplement what little else we had. We slaughtered our last hog this past October and frugal as we had been, there was little left but a few scraps of salt pork. I thanked God for the cow and the laying hens. If things continued as they were, we would have to eat the chickens. But for now, the eggs were like gold.

Mahala was a great source of comfort to me. She was strong and always cheerful. I must once have had as hopeful a temperament as she, but it seemed very long ago. I felt the burden of the farm and responsibility weighing me down as time passed. My sleep was disturbed by fearful dreams, and I lay awake much of the night, my pistol at ready. We hadn't heard of families being assaulted by marauders or thieves, but as each day passed, men fighting on both sides of the war must feel desperate for it to end and more apt to pillage and take what they needed to survive.

Though often months old, I treasured the letters I received from Jane. She reported that riots against the draft were growing more violent in New York. Could it be the relentless fatigue felt by both the North and South could end this war?

Jane sent news of Daniel, who had rejoined his regiment. She received letters from Daniel often, and said he was doing as well as could be expected. I knew the Union soldiers were far better equipped and fed than our poor boys. It shocked me at times to realize I had a husband and sons fighting against a son-in-law. I prayed for all of them. Jane wrote there was a great deal of domestic work available to her and Bridget, Daniel's mother, and they had saved enough money doing laundry and sewing to build a home on our land when the war ended. Her letters lifted my spirit.

It was almost impossible to ignore the devastation the war had wrought on our farming area. I could not count the number of proud families who continued to give up on maintaining their life in Virginia. Their fields lay fallow and their homes, lonely and haunted, were falling into disrepair. Some of the families who left had received word their husbands or sons had perished. I understood the desperation of those families. But I found it difficult to understand those who had yet to learn the fate of their men, and chose to leave anyway. Many of those who left had gone to Richmond or Petersburg. Perhaps a few of them kept going West, or North. I hoped some would return home.

March, 1865

No one knew exactly how our army fared. There was more bad news than good. In town I heard that our boys were holed up in trenches near Petersburg all winter long, a bitterly cold winter. I couldn't imagine what that must have been like. How could they survive without proper food and clothing under such conditions? I tried hard not to let myself sink into despair. I made the effort for the children and Mahala. I sat by the fire late into the night, my mind never at rest. I busied myself with mending or remaking clothes and smoking my pipe more than I used to. There was little other than Lawson and the children that brought me pleasure anymore, but I looked at them and agonized over what would happen to them if Andrew, Oliver and Peter did not survive the war.

Early April 1865

From the kitchen window, I watched my children work in the field, William, Preston, Polly and Mary. Mahala patiently instructed them on how to sow the seeds. They used shovels and hoes to turn the soil and plant early crops from seed saved from last year. Andrew would have used the plow horses, but they had been sold. I received little money for them, but there was no choice. We still had the laying hens and the cow, the other animals had been sold.

What would become of us if we did not win the war? Would we be forced, as many of our neighbors had been, to give up and leave Carroll County. Tears welled in my eyes as I remembered how hard our ancestors fought to gain our land so many years ago.

I looked out on the field again. Even little Lawson tagged along with his mother, a stick in his hand, which he poked into the soil with abandon. Forcing a smile on my face, I took a few deep breaths and left the kitchen to join them. They all turned to me and smiled, as if I had given them a gift. I was the person the whole family looked to amidst the turmoil.

Picking up Lawson, I gave him a swift kiss. "Here we go, Lawson. Let's plant these bean seeds. Your father and grandfather would want you to know how to do it. Your daddy will be home soon, along with Grandpa and Peter. Oh, and won't it be a wonderful celebration. We'll all be together." He clung to my neck and planted a wet kiss on my cheek. "Dada home, Granma? Dada home soon?"

Mahala nodded in her knowing way and murmured. "Yes, Lawson. They'll all be home soon."

Late-April 1865

Preston burst into the house, breathless and jumping with excitement. "Mama! Mama! Come look! Is it Daddy?" From the doorway he pointed to the road and rushed to me, taking my hand and pulling me to the door.

A man walked slowly down the road to the farm. I would only have known it was Andrew by his limp, otherwise my husband was unrecognizable.

"I believe it is, Preston. I believe it is."

He rushed from the house shouting, "It's Daddy! He's come home!"

The children all ran up the road toward their father.

My heart leapt into my throat and I exchanged an anxious look with Mahala. My legs were trembling. I prayed that Andrew was not so different from when last I saw him, that he had not been released from duty with illness or missing a limb. I could not tell from a distance if he was whole or not. It had been almost a year since he left. I was uncertain how we would react to each other after such a time apart. We had parted in anger with doubts about our commitment to each other and to the Southern Cause. Neither of us was the same person we were when the war started over four years ago. And Andrew's absence this past year had been especially punishing. Each day we heard that the battle was surely lost. Families nervously, yet eagerly, watched the roads leading to their farms, hoping to see a loved one walking toward home, and here was my husband—come home.

I quickly glanced in the mirror and tucked loose tendrils of hair into my bun. I saw the face of an old woman, a bitter old woman. I buried my face in my hands and breathed deeply. Pinching my cheeks to bring a bit of color to the sallowness of my skin, I prepared to face my husband.

CHAPTER
THIRTY-ONE

OLIVER

April 2- April 9, 1865

LEE COMMANDED WE retreat from the Union forces that were advancing on Richmond and Petersburg. As we tried to move south, our route was blocked by the fast-moving Union cavalry. Even though our regiment suffered a great many casualties, we tried to battle the Union at our hospitals in Richmond and Petersburg on April 3. At least ten of our men were taken prisoner from the Richmond Hospital and we lost another group at the hospital in Petersburg.

We made our way west from the South Side Railway to Sailor's Creek. The heavy bombardment from the Union artillery broke our defenses, cutting through our right flank. Our losses were many, but we knew not how many.

I watched from a distance, with a small group of men, as General Corse surrendered. We were overcome with deep sadness. Eli Lambert and I found each other among the group of men from the 29th who had escaped capture by the Union at White Oak Road.

"What day is this, Ollie? I believe this is the day we lost this war." The look on my friend's face was one I would never forget. There was nothing left of the adventurous, young soldier I had signed up with four years ago. His shoulders slumped and deep lines of misery creased his face. He now had the appearance of a tired old man.

"I'm not sure. I reckon it must be April 5th or 6th. I can't rightly make sense of it. Do you really think this day we have lost the war, Eli? What's happened to General Lee? His son Custis surrendered with Ewell, but where's the general?" I knew Eli hadn't an answer, I was talking to myself. I asked the question anyway.

"How the hell should I know?" Eli shrugged his shoulders, a grim look on his face. "Not many of us left. How many do you think we lost at Dinwiddie and Five Forks these last battles?"

"I don't know, I haven't seen George Phelps or Jebez Johnson. Last I saw them was on the White Oak Turnpike before the Union cavalry attacked. For the sake of their families, I pray they're wounded, not dead."

"I reckon we won't know if they're dead or alive until this war is over. I can't believe we've made it this far, can you, Ollie, what with so many of the regiment dead or missing. And now our officers are surrendering?"

"But Lee has not yet surrendered!" I held onto that bit of hope, although in my heart, I truly feared we had been broken. "We have to search for General Lee, Eli. He hasn't given up. I don't know what God's plan is for us. I don't see how we are going to win this war—but we have to try to find General Lee."

"Win? I don't know what that means anymore. We've already lost so many. It looks to me like the Yankees have us beat." His voice was quiet and sorrowful.

I couldn't dispute what Eli said. I felt the same. Our pride was a false front, but it was all we had left, and together we set out in search of the rest of our army and General Lee.

Near Farmville, we met up with General Lee, and what remained of his Army of Northern Virginia. We skirmished there, but the Union broke our retreating column and took what seemed thousands of prisoners. Eli and I were lucky to escape with Pickett's Brigade and marched to the west with Lee's column to a place called Appomattox.

We were among perhaps thirty who were with General Lee as he prepared to surrender.

I stood with Eli, he with his fife and I with my drum, as those who had weapons gave them up at Appomattox Courthouse. Inside a farmhouse nearby we were told General Lee would surrender to General Grant.

Tears streamed down gaunt and rugged faces. There were no words to describe the sense of despair that was felt all around as we realized that General Lee was surrendering.

We looked at one another as if to find an answer to what we should do next. There was no one of rank to direct or give us orders. We were like flotsam adrift on an unknown and indifferent sea. No one, not one officer told us we were relieved of duty. We were soldiers no longer, just men, not sure what we believed or where we belonged.

I searched for Jacob, hoping to see him one last time. He was nowhere in sight. I prayed that he was on his way to freedom in the north. How difficult it was to know I might never see him again.

We stood aimlessly—a group of humbled and defeated men as our flag was furled. The looks upon the faces of those around me, and I am sure upon my own, was one of utter sorrow. We wept openly as the ragged Confederate flag was folded for the last time. What a terrible tragedy, I thought, the last four years had been. My brothers, dead. Friends and neighbors perished without a family member knowing where they were buried. So many souls lost, their last words and breath a prayer only to be with their loved ones.

I wiped tears from my face as I felt a terrible anger rise within me. No officers were with us as we marked the last day of war—the end of four years of constant battle. I wondered where they were, and why they had no time to say goodbye and wish us Godspeed.

We were all beaten men, no longer soldiers. I studied the faces of the men around me. I knew only Eli. Some men quickly tore pieces of the flag as it was furled, as if to remind them of what it was they had given four years of their lives for. I wanted no part of it. To me it would only be a reminder of four years of death and destruction. Nearly four years of my life that surely, I would never forget, nor fully comprehend.

After the Union distributed rations, every man was on his own.

I turned to Eli and nodded.

Together we took our first steps toward home.

CHAPTER THIRTY-TWO

OLIVER

Mid-April 1865

AFTER THE UNION distribution of salted beef, hard bread and cubes of dried vegetables, Eli and I set off. Neither of us remained in Appomattox to hear General Lee's farewell speech or receive the Union parole pass which would have allowed us safe passage if confronted by Federals. I wasn't sure how Eli felt, but I had no allegiance to either the South or the North.

There were no trains or wagons to carry us home. A few men had use of a horse, but most men knew they would walk whatever distance it was to return home.

Eli and I knew the mountains and woods and that is where we headed.

We were constantly on the look-out, for we knew the countryside was filled with Confederate deserters from the Appomattox campaign, as well as thieves and law breakers. We made our way steadily homeward, staying away from farms and towns, where we might have been mistaken for thieves and shot on sight.

We walked in near silence for two days, as if we were

strangers. We bedded down at night using the blankets given us by the Union army. Sometimes I heard Eli cry out in his sleep. I am sure I disturbed his sleep with my own nightmarish screams. We spoke so little to each other that I felt more alone in his company than I would have had I walked alone.

We didn't agree to separate—it just happened.

"Eli, I'm going this way now." I gestured toward the distant mountains to the west. I extended my hand in goodbye.

"It's just as well, Ollie. I've been thinking of heading south. I hope to see you once we have reunited with our families. I'm...I reckon we need some time to be...well...."

He never finished his sentence. He didn't need to. Without words we understood we needed to be alone.

"Be careful, Eli. God be with you."

"And with you, Oliver." He took my hand and gave a firm squeeze.

I took notice of Eli calling me by my full name, not 'Ollie'. It was a somber parting—almost as though we were going into battle again.

In a way we were. What a man's mind is filled with after four years of constant battle is impossible to put into words. Even though I prayed to be rid of the memories, images and thoughts, they surfaced unwanted at any time. Then I had to stop and sit for a while. Closing my eyes, I breathed deeply and thought of Mahala and Lawson. I imagined a farm, our farm—and our family. I inhaled the scent of soil I scraped from around me. I concentrated on the way I felt in spring when I helped Father prepare the fields, and the hope that always came with spring and the sowing of crops that would feed the family. Those thoughts of home would sustain me for a while and then without warning, I would become fearful. I had to stop suddenly, my heart racing and my body trembling. I questioned my sanity, for I had expected to feel comforted knowing I was returning to my family.

Crouching behind a tree, I stared into the dark woods like

a wild animal. I was sure I saw men, ragged, some bleeding from bandaged wounds. I shouted, "Show yourselves! Are you Union or Confederate?" Even though I had no weapon I screamed, "I'm armed—do you hear me! I have a gun!" My voice sounded hollow and the ominous silence of the woods increased my panic. I waited, but there was nothing—no one was there.

Sometimes it would take an hour or more to calm myself and feel strong enough to stand and continue on.

When I thought of my family it was with both fear and longing. It had been over a year since I last wrote them. There was little time to write, even if there had been paper available to me. The fighting and skirmishing had been endless, especially in the last days before Appomattox. I couldn't recall every battle we fought. There were days we fought in three different places and I couldn't remember the names. Would my family believe I did not think of them—that I didn't care? It was possible they might think I hadn't survived.

I was so exhausted I considered discarding my drum to help ease my fatigue. But it was the only tangible thing I had left from the last four years of my life. I looked at it with new eyes. I could not recall what I had done with my first drum. After Gettysburg it was all but ruined. The drum I carried showed the scars of battle—all were deeply etched in its shell. The blue paint for the infantry was so worn that the maple wood was clearly visible, the painted eagle and eleven stars were hard to distinguish.

My mind was jumbled with thoughts that had no continuity. I seemed to lurch from thinking I was still in battle—the faces of those killed and wounded flashing in front of my eyes, and then suddenly I was on the farm, with my father planting crops, waving to Mahala as she brought water to ease our thirst. I thought I was losing my sanity and stopped when those feelings overwhelmed me, trying desperately to regain my composure.

I said aloud over and over, as though I had to convince myself who I was. "You are Oliver Quesinberry. You are the son of Andrew and Abigail. You are a farmer, as your fore-fathers were before you. You have fought a terrible war—but it is over. The South has lost the war, but you are alive. You have a wife and a little boy waiting for you to return to them. You have a mother, father, loving brothers and sisters waiting to welcome you home. You are strong. You have survived." I repeated those words over and over as I put one foot in front of the other.

When I came upon streams I soaked my feet to soothe them. I rarely wore my boots, they were thin and provided little protection for my bloody feet. Even though the water was cold from winter runoff I removed my filthy clothing and plunged into the deepest part of the streams to bathe. I scrubbed my clothes in the water and beat them against the rocks—but I could not remove the ground-in blood and dirt, nor the lice. I spread my clothing out to dry on nearby rocks. I could find only a few moments of peace as I closed my eyes and lay in the warm sun before I would bolt upright, startled by the slightest sounds around me.

How many days had I been walking? I thought surely it had to be nearly a week. I estimated it was around 130 miles from Appomattox to Dugspur. If I had been in good health I could easily have walked the distance in a week. But my weak-ened state slowed my pace. I knew I was trying to rid myself of my fears and nightmares before I faced my family. I wanted to be strong for them. But how could I be? I was skinny and walked barefoot, my hair and beard long and filled with grime and lice. I had only the rags on my back and a worn drum.

I never thought I would return in such a pitiful state. Even in the darkest hours of the war, I never quite believed our army would be so defeated and humbled. I thought I would return home victorious, regardless of my physical condition. But to return as I was, in such a state of mental anguish, I asked myself if I wished to return to my family at all.

As I neared the farm, I struggled to understand the ambivalence I felt about seeing my family and the sense of sadness and depression that slowed my footsteps. It felt as if Virginia was no longer my home, as if I were a stranger. I no longer saw fertile fields but battlefields. I saw enemies hiding behind trees. Everywhere I looked I was reminded of all the death and suffering I had witnessed and contributed to on the soil of a state I called home. I asked myself what men had died for? I was certain now, it was not to save our homes and land from northerners. I knew it was to preserve the wealth of men who owned slaves. I tried to find honor in the war I had been a part of. I needed a sane reason for the death of so many men on both sides of the battle, especially the northern soldiers I had killed and the southern men I had watched die. I could find no honor in it. There was no glory in it. I had been but a pawn in the hands of men who sought to maintain their wealth through slavery.

I knew in my heart I would never know peace if I remained in Virginia. I prayed Mahala would understand how I felt. My decision would break my parents' hearts. I understood that once I took my place as the eldest son, I would be forever bound to the farm and land of my forefathers. I wanted to be free and independent. I longed to start a new life with Mahala. The desire burned in me and I knew I would have to follow my heart.

I reached the farm just as the sun was setting and saw my family home from the shadow of the woods. Father and Peter walked slowly from the fields. Mother stood in the doorway of the house. I remembered her like that four years ago, before the war, as she waited for Father to come to supper. Father's limp appeared to be much worse, and Mother did not look quite as strong as she had four years ago. Yet, her stride was vigorous as she walked to meet them, taking Father's hand and lowering her head to his shoulder. That was as it should be. Andrew and Abigail Quesinberry together had made this land a home. They were the heart and soul of the farm.

I decided then I must go to Mahala and Lawson first. They were my family, and the source of the strength and courage that sustained me on the long walk home. I could only pray that Mahala would understand my need to start over and to leave a place that burdened my heart with such sadness and despair.

As night fell, I made my way across the fields, stopping to watch my parents and siblings at supper through the kitchen window. It was as if nothing had changed. As always, Father sat at the head of the table with Mother at the other end. Peter was waving his arms in the air as Preston and William clapped and nudged each other, their eyes bright with excitement. There were three empty chairs, those that belonged to Isaac, Asa and me.

Tearing my eyes away from the window, I looked around at all that was so familiar to me, and yet now was somehow foreign. The farm, fields, barn, even the sounds of the animals and birds were different. The sensation of being home and yet feeling disconnected from everything around me only made stronger my wish to strike out on my own.

Mahala and I would make our own way. If she would follow me.

CHAPTER THIRTY-THREE

MAHALA

Mahala and Oliver's Cottage
Dugspur, Virginia
1865

I COULD FEEL the promise of spring in the air. After putting Lawson to bed, I returned to the front porch of the cottage. Sighing deeply, I lowered myself into the rocker. It was a beautiful evening. The sweet scent of freshly turned soil lifted from the newly plowed field. A moist coolness wafted from the creek still swollen from spring runoff. I had always loved solitude, even as a child. I had only in the last few weeks begun to feel lonely in the cottage. Perhaps it was the homecoming of Father Andrew and Peter from the war that made me long for Oliver. I was missing Oliver terribly and I wondered if I would have the same nervous reaction to his return as Abigail had to the return of Andrew. I recalled reassuring Abigail that her appearance was not much changed when she asked my opinion. My mother-in-law's face was ashen and her hands trembled as I took them in mine. Her husband was finally home from the war he joined a year ago. We could hear the excited voices of the children greeting him outside.

She walked to the mirror and straightened her bun, staring intently, as if she didn't recognize the woman reflected there. She pinched her cheeks and turned to me. "Am I much changed, Mahala?"

I knew it was of no use to lie to her. "We are all changed. But not so much as you would think, Abigail. You are the one who has kept this family together. Many women have not been able to do that." With that she squared her shoulders and straightened her back.

"How do I look?"

"The only change I see are a few streaks of gray in your hair. Quite handsome really. And after ten children you still have the slender waist of a girl."

She placed her hands on her waist, a sparkle of mischief in her eyes. "Well, that is so now, isn't it?" Years melted away as a smile crinkled the corners of her eyes.

"I'd like to change my dress, but..." she ripped her apron off and smoothed her hair again, "this will do." I marveled at the resilience of my mother-in-law. I had watched as she had gone nearly mad with grief over the death of Isaac and Asa. I was amazed by her resolute determination to find them. I'd been stunned by her compassion for a Union soldier. Felt her guilt and fear when a daughter fell in love and ran away with that very man. I'd suffered her torment as Oliver, Andrew and Peter were in what seemed a never-ending war, one that might take all their lives. And, I'd watched as her anger, fear and loathing against the Southern Cause renewed her determination to keep her family together and unbroken until the war was over.

"Abigail, I admire you greatly. You are the strongest, most courageous woman I know."

She embraced me quickly, then was out the door, racing to Andrew, the children parted to encircle their parents.

Andrew was not the man who left for war a year ago. His

limp had let the children know it was their father, for otherwise he was almost unrecognizable. He had always been a fastidious man, keeping his beard and mustache neatly trimmed and washing up outside before coming indoors from his chores. Now his limp was far worse and his beard long and unkempt. His clothes appeared to be those he wore when he joined the army, now rags that hung from his body.

From the window I watched my in-laws a few moments. They gazed at each other almost shyly. There was such love between them. I only hoped I would feel the same when Oliver returned. They held hands as the children pulled them toward the fields, proudly pointing out the rows of newly-planted vegetables. Andrew grinned broadly and I knew not where he found the strength, but he lifted Abigail, swinging her around, her hair coming undone and flying wildly. He did the same with each child, planting a kiss on the tops of their heads and whirling them until the whole group was laughing uncontrollably. I wiped tears of joy from my eyes, gathered Lawson in my arms, and walked outside to welcome his grandfather home.

We were enveloped in a circle of loving arms. I felt the love the family had for one another strengthen as we held each other closer, until Andrew abruptly pushed away, yelling, "My God, I've got lice from head to toe!"

Then there was a frantic scramble as water was pumped from the well and heated for baths. We all laughed as we filled the old tub time after time for baths. Wrapped in sheets, our clothes were hastily thrown into a tub of boiling water and then laid in the sun to dry.

Lawson and I stayed at the cottage, allowing Abigail and Andrew time alone. I encouraged the children to visit often and stay overnight. Lawson delighted in having his young aunts and uncles to play with. It cheered me, and surely the children as well, to see that in spite of all the hurt and heartache that had passed between their parents, their bond was unbreakable. If hurts and offences were felt between them, they never spoke of it in front of me, or their children.

Peter arrived within days of Andrew. He was in much better condition physically, which his youth would account for. He was less cocky, and when before he had been reluctant to help with the farm chores, he willingly did so now. Preston and William never tired of hearing his stories of war and battle. Beneath all his bluster there was a new maturity about Peter.

I waited anxiously for Oliver's return. I had always held firmly to the belief that Oliver would survive the war. But as the days went by I began to lose some of my courage and resolve. What if he had been killed or wounded in one of the last skirmishes? There was no way to know for sure.

The children took turns watching the road to the farm, and promised to run to the cottage the moment they suspected Oliver's return. I found it odd that no solitary man ventured near the farm. Andrew spoke of the great number of desperate men who deserted after the last battles near Appomattox Courthouse and of the bands of thieves roaming the countryside. I was comforted knowing both Andrew and Abigail knew well how to use their guns.

The whole family anxiously awaited Oliver's return. They tried to hide it, but I knew they feared he might not have survived the last battles and skirmishes. Andrew told us of the destitute state of those men who deserted. Some men who fought to the end simply walked away rather than wait for General Lee's surrender. He said they left without a crumb of food or supplies of any kind. I know Oliver would never have deserted. It was more likely he left before the formal surrender of General Lee. When he had his furlough, I remembered his low regard for his officers and the course the war was taking.

For several days I had felt the presence of Oliver drawing ever closer. It was as if I could sense his movement. I wondered why he did not hurry.

The tap on the cottage door was soft, followed by a whispered, "Mahala."

Wrapping my shawl around my shoulders I took up the fireplace poker and stood at the closed door. It was almost dark and I felt uneasy. "Who is it?"

"Oliver." His voice was low and raspy.

I opened the door cautiously. In the waning light I barely recognized my husband. I stifled a gasp and reached to touch his cheek. He flung my hand away.

"Please, Mahala. Let me clean the...let me clean up and get out of these rags."

"I'll put water on to heat."

"No!" He barked.

I was startled by his outburst and stared at him, unsure how to react.

"I'm sorry, Mahala, I don't want to come in the house like this. I'll bathe in the creek. And I want to burn these rags. Have you a lantern and soap?"

I nodded and found the lantern, soap, and a cotton sheet.

"And scissors. Do you have scissors I might use to cut my hair and beard? I don't want to touch you, Mahala, until I have washed the dirt from my body. Do you understand?"

"Yes, I do. Of course, I do." I watched as he stripped. I handed him a piece of kindling from the fireplace, he placed it on the pile of rags which burst into flames. His ribs and collarbones stood out sharply in the light from the blaze.

"Shall I go with you, Oliver?"

"No. Stay here until I am clean, Mahala. I am sorry to arrive home in such a state. I want you and Lawson to see me when I am... when I'm...."

"Oliver. Stop. Please stop. I know you have filth on your clothes. And I know you have lice on your body. Your father and Peter did as well. I will heat water and bring it to you. God has granted my prayers. You are here, Husband. Alive. I love you as you are. You survived, Oliver. God has blessed us. Surely He has His reasons and His plans for us."

He nodded, but there was no happiness on his face and there was bitterness in his voice. "I'll bathe in the creek. I'm used to it. My father and brother did not have to live in the trenches for six months. Nor did the blood of hundreds of men soak into their skin and clothes."

Tears ran down my face when he walked alone to the creek. I wished he would let me go with him, to scrub his body. I wanted so much to take his face in my hands and kiss away the grief and sadness there. I knew he was proud, but I was hurt by his harsh manner.

It seemed hours passed before Oliver quietly opened the door to the cottage. "Do I have clothes here, in the bedroom?"

"Of course, you do. You are home, Oliver. This is your home."

He pressed his lips together and turned away. I could sense that his emotions were raw and he was striving to control them. When we married I knew he was sensitive, with tender feelings. He was not a callous man, but this was a different man. His sensitivity was still there, but underneath there was a new hardness, a determination in his voice and actions I dared not question.

I waited for him by the fireplace. He finally opened the door and eased into a chair I placed near the fire. I sensed it would be some time before my husband would willingly share his feelings about the war—if ever he did. I kept my eyes on the fire as I waited for him to speak. There was only silence. When I looked at him I saw his skin was rubbed nearly raw and he had trimmed his hair and beard as close to his skin and scalp as possible. I had no idea how he did so in near darkness—but I thought he must have been desperate to rid himself of the filth.

I waited—but after a half hour or more I could stand the silence no longer. "Oliver, let me get you some cornbread or milk. You must be starving."

"I'm not hungry, Mahala."

I knew not how to break the tension between us. I recalled Abigail's words to speak plainly and truthfully.

"Oliver. Talk to me. I am your wife. I love you. Your silence is hurting me more than I can say. Tell me what you are thinking?"

He cleared his throat and slowly pushed up from his chair. He stood in front of the fire, his back to me. His clothes hung from him.

"I don't want to speak of the war. I want to talk to you about leaving Virginia."

His words stunned me. "But why Oliver? You've just returned. This is our home—our land. I don't understand."

"Mahala, I want to live on land that is not—that I have not—" He choked on his words. "I want to live on land that is not desecrated by the souls of men, my brothers, my friends, who gave their lives for nothing. Nothing! It was all for nothing, Mahala!"

His voice was loud and hard. It frightened me. I didn't know this side of my husband, but I understood he did not need a challenge, but compassion from me.

"You've just come home, Oliver. Give yourself time to rest and be at peace. Lawson and I have missed you so. We need to learn to be a family again."

"I cannot do that here, Mahala. I realized that as I walked home through the mountains these past weeks. I heard and saw the souls of men and the destruction of this war everywhere I looked. I want to go to Kentucky. To start a new life there—with you and Lawson."

"Kentucky? This is so sudden, Oliver. Perhaps you just

need time to...." I took a deep breath.

"No, Mahala. I have made up my mind."

"But what of my feelings? Have I no say in the matter? Kentucky? Weren't there battles fought there, too?"

"Some were. Very few. But the state signed a declaration of neutrality before the war. It doesn't have the taint of the war as Virginia holds for me. Kentucky is beautiful and fertile, Mahala. We can make a good life there." He dropped to his knees in front of me, taking my hands and capturing my eyes with his. "Please, Mahala, do this with me. I promise I will make a home for you and Lawson and all our children to come. You will not regret it. I will make a home for us. A home that will make you proud, and those who come after us."

"What of your family? It will break your parents' hearts if we should leave. You are now the eldest son."

His hands tightened on mine. "Yes, I know. That is why I must leave. This might be hard for you to understand, Mahala. But if I stay—if I take on the responsibility of this farm and land, I will never know a day of peace again. I will always love and respect my parents, but Virginia is no longer where I want to live or die."

"But your grandfather and his before him—they all gave their lives for this land. Their spirits reside here, in these mountains, woods, valleys and streams. And mine do as well. How do we leave all that behind?"

"With courage and love, Mahala. That is how our forefathers did it. That is how my parents did it and that is how we will do it. If we are together, we will make a new life. It will be ours alone, and our children and grandchildren will see that we were brave and resourceful. They will know we were as fearless and courageous as our forefathers. We will leave them that legacy."

"You hate Virginia so much, Oliver? So much that you must leave to be happy?"

"Virginia is but a name. At one time Kentucky was part of

Virginia. The Iroquois called it 'ken-tah-ten' the land of to-morrow. I want that, Mahala. The land of tomorrow. I dream of a new life there for us. I want to escape the memory of this war. So many of my friends are gone—their farms abandoned. If I stay here I will feel anew this painful loss every day. It will haunt me forever. Will you help me, Mahala? Will you go with me?"

How good it was to slip into Oliver's arms. To feel them around me, still strong and comforting. I thanked God then, to hear him speak of tomorrow—to speak of our future, to hear his heart beat when so many of those we knew were dead and no longer had a future.

"I'm your wife, Oliver. You know I will follow you wherever you go."

My husband's eyes glistened with tears.

"I want to see my son. He won't know me, will he?"

"He's a big boy now. He looks like you Oliver."

We peeked in on our son. Oliver gazed at him and reached out as if to stroke his head, then pulled his hand back.

"I'll wait until tomorrow. I might frighten him if I wake him now. I'm a stranger to him."

"I have told him of you every day, and we pray for you every night. He will know you."

I brought his rough hand to my lips and kissed his palm. "Come outside with me, it's a beautiful night."

We sat together on the porch steps. The creek was silver in the moonlight. We were quiet and listened to the gentle sound of the creek and night birds. I rested my head on Oliver's shoulder and inhaled his scent, marveling at his presence, his body whole, and his heart full of love and dreams. "Oliver, I am so very happy you are here with me."

He kissed the top of my head, his warm hand squeezed mine. "I thought only of this every day and night I was away from you Mahala. To feel you next to me—to sit with you in peace. It kept me alive."

The lantern cast a shadowy light around us.

"What is that?" I pointed to something in the shadows on the side of the porch.

"It's my drum." He shrugged his shoulders in a dismissive gesture.

"We must bring it in the house, Oliver. Lawson will want that one day."

End

AUTHOR'S NOTE

The main characters in this book, Oliver, Abigail, Andrew, Mahala and the Quesinberry children other than Jane are all true characters. Jacob and Daniel are fictional.

Of course, I could not know how these people reacted on a daily basis to the events in their lives. However, I learned a great deal about their character and temperaments by reviewing extensive written family history.

Oliver, by all accounts in family history, was a self-educated man. His poem, in honor of his brothers, was written with sensitivity and beautiful penmanship. Perceiving his sensitive nature through his writing, I believe he not only grew to hate the war because of the unrelenting hardships, suffering and death it caused, but also because he came to reject the true cause for which the South was fighting. I also believe that Oliver suffered from what we now know as PTSD. Oliver was disowned by his father, Andrew, after the war, and moved his family to Kentucky, where he was a successful farmer who hybridized new strains of corn much sought after by local farmers. No one in the family knows why Oliver was disowned by his father. It could very well have been his disdain for the Southern Cause, which likely also contributed to his decision to move his family to Kentucky and leave Virginia altogether.

According to family stories, after moving to Kentucky,

THE LAST DRUMBEAT

Oliver stayed in close touch with his family in Virginia, sending them many letters, all of which Andrew kept even though he disowned Oliver.

I was unable to learn much about Oliver's life in Kentucky after he moved there. There are no photographs of Oliver or Mahala. According to family members still living in Kentucky, his home burned to the ground later in his life and destroyed family photographs and memorabilia of the Civil War.

Abigail was indeed a strong-willed, excellent horsewoman. She did manage to keep her family together on the family farm in Dugspur after her sons Isaac, Asa, Oliver, Peter and husband Andrew all joined the war effort, leaving her alone with Mahala to care for her six young children.

The character of Jacob is fictional. When I learned that wealthy officers could take a slave with them while in the army, I wondered what the soldiers assigned to the regiments with these officers would have thought about that practice. Confederate soldiers, mostly poor farm boys, must, I thought, have found this offensive, especially since many of these slaves were paid a higher salary than the ordinary infantry soldier. Soldiers were, especially as the war progressed, without sufficient food and supplies and were rarely paid their salary. The rate of desertion was high and grew higher as the war progressed. Knowing Oliver's sensitivity and his religious foundation, I wanted to portray how he might have viewed the servitude of another human being. Social and political inequities became painfully obvious to Oliver and his fellow soldiers soon after joining the Confederate army, including the fact that wealthy men (on both sides) could hire another man to fight for them, and wealthy slave owners who owned twenty or more slaves were actually exempt from conscription.

In my research I learned that 23.4% of Irish and German immigrants were drafted into the Union army, often directly after disembarking from their boats. I also learned of the opposition of the Irish to the draft law in New York City and the riots that ensued because of that.

The characters of Jane and Daniel are fictional. I wanted to show that in spite of the fierce conflict raging and dividing families, that common decency and the goodness of humanity need not have been lost.

I took many of the names of individual soldiers mentioned in the book from a history of the 29 Virginia Regiment, written by John Perry Alderman. Some names I mention in the book were actual soldiers listed as having died at the battles I referenced. Some I fabricated to carry the story.